KU-023-437

# Billionaire under
the Mistletoe

## CAROLE MORTIMER

*USA TODAY* bestselling author **Carole Mortimer** was born in England and currently makes her home on the Isle of Man. Happily married to Peter, they have six grown-up sons, so Christmas was always a fun-filled but busy time of year, she reports. Carole has written nearly two hundred books for Mills & Boon and divides her time between the Mills & Boon® Modern™ and Mills & Boon® Historical lines. Carole loves spending time with her family, travelling and reading. Visit her website at www.carole-mortimer.com for news on upcoming books and more.

# *PROLOGUE*

'IT'S A SIMPLE enough request to make, surely, Sally? After all, you are my PA and— Why are you laughing?'

'Wasn't I meant to laugh?'

'Hell, no!'

'Then you were actually serious when you asked me to have Christmas delivered to your apartment by Friday morning?'

'Does it look as if I'm joking, Sally?'

'Oh.'

Sophie had arrived slightly early at Hamilton Tower for her lunch date with her cousin, Sally; she certainly hadn't intended to find herself standing transfixed in the plush hallway outside her cousin's office, inadvertently eavesdropping on Sally's conversation with her boss, Max Hamilton, billionaire CEO of Hamilton Enterprises.

Although she understood Sally's humour and disbelief: who on earth had Christmas delivered?

The super-rich Max Hamilton, apparently.

As far as Sophie was concerned, Christmas had always been a time of traditions, built up over years and years of family holidays spent together, with decorations kept and treasured by generation after generation.

Obviously, Max Hamilton had missed that particular memo…

Sophie knew from what Sally had told her that her cousin's boss was something of a workaholic. Just as Sophie also knew, from reading about him in the tabloids, that the man appeared to play as hard as he worked, changing his women as often as he changed his no doubt designer label silk shirts— daily, if not twice a day.

Having seen photographs of him, Sophie wasn't in the least surprised. Tall, dark and handsome didn't even begin to describe the thirty-four-year-old owner and CEO of Hamilton Enterprises. With overlong and fashionably tousled dark hair, mesmerising green eyes, high cheekbones, sculptured lips above a strong jaw, he was sex on long, long legs.

He also had the most seductive voice Sophie had ever had the pleasure of listening to—a mixture of molasses and gravel, honey over satin, with just the right hint of husky.

Although the subject of his conversation still seemed slightly bizarre.

'I thought you were going skiing this Christmas, as usual?' Sally prompted uncertainly now, as she obviously realised her boss wasn't joking, after all.

'I was. Notice the past tense.' Max Hamilton sighed, showing his irritation. 'My sister and her husband are having marital problems, and she telephoned me last night to say she thinks it's a good idea for her to join me in England for Christmas this year, along with my five-year-old niece, Amy.'

Ah, that explained part of his dilemma.

But not all of it.

Having Christmas delivered just seemed... Well, it was just wrong.

Admittedly, Sophie was spending her own Christmas alone this year, while her cousin, aunt and uncle went to Canada for two weeks so that they could all meet Sally's in-laws-to-be. They had very kindly invited Sophie to accompany them, but she had preferred to stay in England and cat-sit for Henry, Sally's spoilt but adorable pet.

There were very legitimate reasons why Sophie's own Christmas was going to be so different this year, and it certainly wasn't through choice. Max Hamilton just sounded as if he was too busy—or perhaps considered himself too important?—to trouble himself bothering to organise Christmas for his sister and niece.

Though, to his credit, he was changing his plans to suit his sister and his niece's needs, and was no longer going skiing, as he apparently usually did, but he obviously had no idea how to go about providing the rest of Christmas for his small family.

'Which reminds me, I'm also going to need more presents than the ones I already sent to them in the States,' the man continued distractedly. 'Lots of

them. Under the tree, for Amy and my sister to un-
wrap on Christmas morning.'

Okay, now he had gone too far! I mean, really,
couldn't the man even be bothered to personally
pick out the necessary presents for his niece, at
least? A little girl who was no doubt already seriously emotionally distressed by her parents' problems.

Obviously not.

'And I'll need a cook,' Max Hamilton added.

'A cook?' Sally echoed slowly.

'Well, I have no idea how to cook a Christmas
lunch, and it doesn't seem fair to ask Janice to cook
for all of us when she's so upset about the separa-
tion.'

'You do remember that I'm flying to Canada the
day after tomorrow?' Sally reminded him softly.

'I also know you're the best damn PA in the
world.'

Oh, yes, let's try flattery when all else fails,
Sophie noted disgustedly.

He might be 'tall, dark and handsome', and have
a seductively sexy voice to go with it, but, from
what Sophie had overheard, Max Hamilton was also
manipulative. Clearly a man who believed, when
all else failed, that he could charm his way out of
a problem.

'I know that and you know that,' Sally answered
him drily.

'But…?'

'But I have to admit, best PA in the world or not, that I have no idea how to even begin ordering Christmas to be delivered, let alone find someone to cook for you over Christmas at such short notice.'

'Aren't there party organisers, agencies, who provide this type of thing?' Max Hamilton muttered irritably. 'I don't care what it costs, Sally, as long as it's all in place by Christmas Eve, when Janice and Amy fly in to Heathrow.'

'I'm not sure any amount of money can provide all of Christmas, and a cook, in just five days!'

Neither was Sophie. And it really was just all wrong, anyway.

Her own childhood Christmases had been a time of family and warmth, of those traditions so integral to the season. Her father had died in a car accident when she was nine, but that hadn't stopped her mother from continuing with all the Christmas traditions that had been such a part of their lives prior to that; if anything, it had seemed even more important that she do so.

Even since her mother had become terminally ill four years ago the two of them had always made the best of the situation, putting up the decorations as usual and exchanging presents. Sophie had been the one to cook the traditional roast turkey dinner and Christmas pudding, alternate years with her aunt and uncle and Sally as their guests, and spending Christmas Day at their home with them on the intervening years.

Not so this year, as her mother had finally suc-
cumbed to her illness six months ago, which was
why Sophie had been only too happy to distract
herself this Christmas by house-sitting and taking
care of Sally's cat. But her aloneness was down to
circumstances, rather than choice.

Max Hamilton obviously usually preferred to go
skiing over the holidays, rather than spending time
with his family. No doubt having his entertainment,
food—and women!—provided for him, with as little inconvenience to himself as possible.

A modern-day Ebenezer Scrooge came to mind.
The Scrooge who had yet to learn the true meaning of Christmas.

Did that mean that there might be some hope for
Max Hamilton too—if he was also shown the true
meaning of Christmas?

'It's been my experience that everything can be
bought for the right price, Sally,' he drawled cyn-
ically, almost as an answer to Sophie's unvoiced
question.

'I'll see what I can do.'

'I knew I could rely on you!'

'As no doubt I can rely on that huge bonus you're
going to put in my next pay cheque if I manage to
pull this off,' Sally came back drily.

'What was that for?' Sally sounded astonished
now.

'In honour of the season?'

'Okay...'

Sophie waited until she heard a door close, no doubt the connecting door between her cousin's office and Max Hamilton's, before finally entering Sally's office, easily noting the slightly dazed and flushed look on her cousin's face as she sat behind her desk.

'Did he just kiss you?'

'I— Yes...' Sally gave a rueful shake of her head as she touched her fingertips to her cheek.

Sophie instantly added *liberty-taker* to her list of Max Hamilton's faults. Unless he thought, as Sally was engaged, it was safe to kiss her? The revolving door through which the women came, and as instantly went, in Max Hamilton's life would seem to imply he had a problem with committing to one woman.

'Did you hear any of that?' Sally mused ruefully.

'Only the highlights,' Sophie answered drily. 'And I don't count that kiss as being amongst them!' she added disapprovingly as she perched her denim-clad bottom on the edge of her cousin's desk.

'It was only on the cheek, so no big deal.' Sally stood up to collect her coat and shoulder bag, ready for the two of them to head out to their lunch.

'I'm not sure Josh would see it that way.'

Sally smiled affectionately at the mention of her fiancé and her thoughts turned to their planned wedding for next summer. 'I'm more worried about how I'm supposed to have Christmas delivered to Max's apartment by Friday, as well as a cook, than

I am about Josh being in the least jealous of a grateful peck on the cheek from my boss.'

Sophie found herself thinking about her cousin's dilemma, and five-year-old Amy's Christmas too, as the two of them ate lunch together in the busy Italian bistro just down the road from Hamilton Tower. Max Hamilton obviously had absolutely no idea how to go about providing Christmas for his sister and the no doubt emotionally bewildered Amy.

'I'll do it,' Sophie announced decisively as they waited for their bill to be delivered to the table.

Sally frowned as she looked up from searching for her purse in her handbag. 'Do what?'

'Organise and have Christmas delivered to your boss's apartment.

'And I'll also cook for him and his family over the holidays.'

Her cousin stilled, her eyes wide. 'Are you being serious?'

'Why not?' Sophie shrugged. 'You obviously don't really have the time to organise it, and I have nothing but time at the moment,' she added gruffly. 'Besides, it might be fun to organise a Christmas that apparently has an unlimited budget. You don't look too sure about the idea?' she prompted uncertainly as she saw her cousin's frown.

'Not because I don't think you can do it, because I know you can,' Sally assured her quickly. 'It's just—Did I ever tell you what a disaster it was a couple of years ago, when I allowed my friend Cathy, who had just been made redundant and needed the money, to stand in for me at the office while I went away on holiday?'

Sophie frowned in thought for a moment and then her brow cleared as she began to laugh. 'As I recall, didn't you tell me Cathy made a play for Max Hamilton that he took exception to?'

Sally rolled her eyes. 'She didn't just make a play for him—she very quickly decided that she wanted to be Mrs Max Hamilton. To the extent that she used to lie in wait for him when he arrived at the office every morning, her clothes becoming more and more daring in an effort to attract his attention! I almost got fired over it.' She grimaced at the memory.

Sophie gave her cousin's hand a reassuring pat. 'Well, you can rest assured that I'm not in the least interested in attracting Max Hamilton's attention, romantically or otherwise. With any luck, he will barely even know I'm there. Besides, there's absolutely no reason why he needs to know the two of us are even related. We have different surnames, and he suggested you contact an agency, so why not let him just continue to think that's what you did? That way, if anything should go wrong there won't be any comeback on you.'

Sally chewed on her bottom lip, obviously tempted by the idea, but still feeling cautious after the disaster with her friend Cathy. 'What about Henry?'

Sophie grinned at the mention of her cousin's beloved cat. 'I'll be going back to your flat to sleep at night, and I can easily pop back during the day to feed him and whatever.'

'You really are serious, aren't you?' Sally murmured wonderingly.

'I really am.' Sophie nodded.

The more she thought about it, the more Sophie found she liked the idea of 'delivering' Max Hamilton's Christmas…

# CHAPTER ONE

'WHAT THE HELL—?' Max came to an abrupt halt as he stepped inside the entrance hall of his apartment and noticed first the stepladder and then the young red-haired woman perched on top of it. She seemed to be attaching something to one of the paintings.

The young woman, who seemed just as startled to see him, turned sharply, letting out a panicked squeak as the ladder wobbled precariously beneath her, causing her to lose her balance completely.

The squeak became an all-out cry of distress as the ladder continued to wobble before tipping over, leaving her with her arms windmilling ineffectively, her expression one of shocked horror as she hurtled towards the marble floor.

Max acted instinctively, instantly dropping his briefcase before stepping forward to hold out his arms in the hope of arresting her unexpected fall. He let out a loud 'oomph' as she landed hard against his chest, before taking him down with her.

Sophie was too stunned to be able to so much as think for several long seconds. And when her head finally cleared she didn't know whether to laugh in relief at her lucky escape from contact with the hard marble tiles or groan in embarrassment as she realised that she was currently sprawled inelegantly across her new employer.

So much for her reassurances to Sally that Max Hamilton would barely know she was there.

It didn't help that Max Hamilton smelt absolutely divine: a hint of sandalwood and spices, with a tang of lemon. No doubt from his cologne or aftershave.

Or that his breathtakingly sexy voice was now so close to her ear that his breath stirred the curls there as he spoke. It affected her just as much as it had yesterday. So much so that she had fallen off the stepladder the minute she'd heard him speak...

'Ouch,' he muttered beneath her now. 'I think I have a bruised backside at the very least.'

The wild red of Sophie's curls currently covered most of her face, something she was exceedingly grateful for as she felt the blush that now warmed her cheeks. She felt flustered, sprawled across Max Hamilton's chest, her thighs and legs also intimately entangled with his.

It didn't help that an image of that perfectly taut backside also instantly flashed into her mind. She had once seen a photograph in one of the gossip magazines of Sally's boss on a yacht somewhere in the Mediterranean, his only covering a pair of body-hugging black swimming trucks.

'Who are you? And exactly what are you doing in my apartment?' he now demanded irritably.

Obviously the bruising had done nothing to improve his temper.

Sophie struggled to disentangle herself, wrapping her arms about her drawn-up knees as she now sat on the tiled floor beside Max Hamilton. A Max Hamilton who was every bit as gorgeous as he had appeared in the photographs, despite the fact that he was eyeing her with narrow-eyed suspicion as he sat up beside her.

His overlong hair wasn't just dark; it was ebony, taking on a blue-black sheen beneath the overhead lighting. And his handsome face was so much more appealing in the animated flesh—straight dark brows over long-lashed and luminous green eyes, sculptured cheekbones visible beneath the tautness of his tanned flesh, with perfectly chiselled and sensuously kissable lips above a square and determined jaw.

Sophie dragged her gaze away from his mouth, only to look up and find herself instead held mesmerised by those piercing emerald-green eyes.

Eyes that now looked at her accusingly.

Sophie drew in a long and steadying breath as she rose to her feet, unnecessarily brushing her jeans down as she did so; she knew from being here for most of the afternoon that Max Hamilton's luxurious penthouse apartment was spotlessly clean. Courtesy of a cleaner, no doubt; Max Hamilton didn't give the impression he was the sort of man who would willingly wield either a vacuum cleaner or a duster.

She had been stunned when she'd first entered his penthouse apartment, on the twentieth floor of this art deco building. The apartment's decor was beyond opulent, with its pale silk-covered walls, original paintings and antique furnishings. Even the carpets were so luxurious she felt as if she were walking on air.

And walking was what she had done, for over half an hour, as she'd explored the whole of the apartment. Discovering there were half a dozen bedrooms, each with en suite bathrooms, two of them even having their own small sitting room— no doubt the master and mistress suite! There was also an indoor pool, huge gym, a sauna, a wooden panelled study, two huge sitting rooms and a dining room with a table that would easily seat a dozen people. As for the kitchen…! Sophie would get down on her knees and beg in order to possess a kitchen like the one in this apartment.

She hadn't seen the sort of opulence this apartment possessed outside the pages of one of those glossy magazines that were always to be found in doctors' or dentists' waiting rooms.

Her chin rose now as she looked down at the owner of all that opulence. 'My name is Sophie Carter.'

Max Hamilton rose lithely to his feet as he eyed her mockingly. 'Not Annie?'

'No, but I am an orphan,' Sophie answered tightly, not missing the reference to her fiery red curls and lack of height against his own couple of inches over six feet.

His mouth tightened at the rebuke in her tone. 'I'm sorry for your loss.'

Sophie ignored the condolence. 'I've been hired by your office to deliver your Christmas.' She chose the word deliberately, still irritated that this man found the prospect of having his sister and niece to spend Christmas with him something of a chore rather than the enjoyable experience it should have been. He obviously had no idea how lucky he was to have close family.

'You're the person Sally told me she'd hired?' Max had only been half listening to his PA earlier today, when Sally had informed him that she had hired someone to deal with all the arrangements for Christmas at his apartment with his sister and niece.

At the time he had been between several telephone calls from Cynthia Maitland, as she'd bemoaned the fact that he wouldn't be joining her in Aspen for Christmas, after all.

If nothing else, he had learnt a lot from those telephone calls: namely that Cynthia was becoming far too possessive about what had been, after all, only a casual affair between them. Learning that Cynthia now obviously had expectations—of their relationship and of himself—had been enough to leave Max feeling relieved to have an excuse to avoid her.

Max realised now that he should have paid more attention earlier to Sally, and that he had absolutely no idea who, what or where this petite red-haired woman had come from.

'Do you have a problem with that?' Huge brown eyes now looked up at him challengingly.

Not per se, obviously; it was only three days till Janice and Amy flew in to Heathrow, after all. But the young woman standing in front of him, with her mop of wild shoulder-length red curls framing a heart-shaped face dominated by freckles and those huge brown eyes and dressed in a red cable-knit sweater and hip and thigh-hugging jeans over heavy brown boots, looked barely old enough to have left school, let alone be responsible for organising his Christmas.

She certainly wasn't what Max had imagined when Sally had told him that someone would be going into his apartment today to start work immediately on his Christmas arrangements.

'There was no one else at the agency available?' he prompted uncertainly.

Sophie Carter smiled, instantly drawing Max's attention to wide and generous lips over small, perfectly straight white teeth. Sensuously generous lips that surprisingly gave him totally inappropriate thoughts!

'No,' she answered him dismissively.

'But...'

'It's quite simple really, Mr Hamilton—you either want me to organise Christmas for your family or you don't. But, as I understood it, your PA has now gone away for the holidays?' She lifted questioning auburn brows.

Max wasn't altogether sure he liked Sophie Carter's attitude. Or her, for that matter...

Likewise, he wasn't sure if she liked him, if her challenging tone, and that slightly contemptuous curl to her top lip, was any indication. But beggars couldn't be choosers, and Sally had vouched for his newest employee when he had confirmed she could call security at his apartment so that the woman could come in and start work putting up the Christmas decorations.

And, looking about him, he could see that Sophie Carter had done exactly that. There was already a real six foot tall Christmas tree standing in the entrance hall, not decorated yet, but there was an overflowing box of brightly coloured ornaments beside it, obviously in readiness.

There were also sprigs of real berried holly tucked behind the picture frames. That seemed to be what Sophie Carter had been doing when he'd entered the apartment and startled her into falling off the stepladder.

'It looks great so far,' he complimented lightly. 'I just— For some reason, I had expected you to be older.'

'You should have stopped while you were ahead, Mr Hamilton!'

That derisive smile grew wider, caused dimples to appear in her freckled cheeks.

Max grimaced. 'Was I ahead?'

'Probably not,' she came back drily.

He gave an irritated shake of his head. 'Have we met before?'

Sophie Carter gave a snort of laughter. 'That's not very likely, is it?'

Max raised dark brows. 'Why is that?'

She gave a dismissive wave of her hand that nevertheless managed to encompass the luxury of his penthouse apartment as well as his own appearance, as opposed to her own less than sartorial elegance in jeans, a jumper and heavy boots.

Max's own attention stayed on that slender artistic hand, the fingers long and delicate, the nails kept practically short. One of his particular hates was long, red-painted talons that could scratch a man's back to pieces when—

Now that really was an inappropriate thought when made in connection to the hired help!

'Do you do this sort of thing all the time or is this just a holiday job for you?' Max tried again.

She shrugged slender shoulders. 'I'm on Christmas break from my college course.'

Which meant she must be at least eighteen, Max realised. 'In?'

'Catering and business management,' she seemed to reveal reluctantly.

'So this is just a temp job to earn some extra money during the holidays?' he realised.

'Yes,' she confirmed tightly.

Max's brows lowered as he frowned. 'And have you done this organising Christmas thing before?'

'Many times,' she assured drily.

'Do you—'

'Perhaps you would prefer it if I stopped what I'm doing for now?' She spoke briskly. 'I can easily come back again in the morning. After you've left for work, of course.'

What Max would really like would be to know why it was that this woman seemed to have decided she disliked him before she had even met him. Because he was pretty sure that she had. After all, his first act had been to save her from what could have been a nasty, and painful, fall onto the marble-tiled floor of his entrance hall.

He shrugged. 'There isn't actually a lot of time left before Christmas.'

'No,' Sophie acknowledged evenly, more than a little disturbed at the realisation that she found Max Hamilton so immediate, as well as so fiercely, intrusively masculine.

She had known yesterday that just the sound of his voice sent shivers of awareness down her spine—that huskily sexy voice that made a woman think of silk sheets and naked, entwined bodies.

But the last thing Sophie had been expecting was to find the man himself so attractive that her knees felt weak and her hands trembled slightly. She could kind of see where Sally's friend Cathy had been coming from with this guy. It was just as well she and Sally had agreed not to admit to the family connection...

'It really is your choice, Mr Hamilton,' she added dismissively. 'After all, you're the one paying the bill.'

He considered her with those deep green eyes for several seconds before speaking again. 'Maybe the two of us should start again over a glass of wine. You are old enough to drink, I take it?' he added hastily.

'I'm twenty-four, Mr Hamilton. I've been allowed to drink for several years.' Sophie eyed him irritably.

'Twenty-four?' He looked startled. 'You don't look it.' He eyed her doubtfully.

'Well, you don't look like a man who is either too busy or too lazy to organise Christmas for his sister and niece, but obviously looks can be deceiving,' Sophie came back tartly.

And instantly had cause to regret that tartness as those hard green eyes narrowed to dangerous slits.

## CHAPTER TWO

'WHO ARE YOU?' Max Hamilton demanded again, his voice briskly authoritative now as he suddenly seemed to tower over her in the confines of the entrance hall of his apartment.

Sophie realised she had seriously overstepped the mark with her last comment. 'I apologise, Mr Hamilton. That was very rude of me and...there is no excuse for it.'

Except her physical reaction to Max Hamilton, of course. Which, given the circumstances of her family connection to Sally, she had no intention of allowing this man to so much as guess at. There was far more at stake here than her irritation with these unexpected feelings towards Max Hamilton. Sally's job, for one thing. And ensuring that his five-year-old niece, Amy, had an enjoyable Christmas for another.

'I believe a glass of wine for each of us is definitely in order.' Max Hamilton spoke determinedly, his tone brooking no argument as he stepped back with the obvious intention of having Sophie precede him into the kitchen just down the hallway.

She did so reluctantly, very self-conscious as

she wondered if Max Hamilton was looking at her own unbruised backside as she walked in front of him down the hallway. Probably not, when he had thought she wasn't even old enough to legally drink alcohol until a few minutes ago. She definitely bore no resemblance, in looks or sophistication, to those beautiful women he was always being photographed with in the papers.

And why did that even matter?

Just because Max Hamilton was the most sexily gorgeous man Sophie had ever set eyes on, with a voice to match, it didn't mean she was about to join the legion of women who were rumoured to have fallen in love with him over the last ten years.

Because the man was also a too rich and equally spoilt playboy and, worst of all, one who preferred to go skiing with friends rather than celebrate Christmas with his family.

As far as Sophie was concerned, that last mark against him was the worst one...

She watched him now from beneath lowered lashes, hesitating near the doorway as he crossed the kitchen to the wine cooler next to the huge stainless steel American-style fridge.

'You aren't driving later, are you?'

Sophie gave a tight smile. 'Public transport.'

He nodded. 'White wine okay with you?'

'Fine,' she confirmed distractedly.

He moved with a light predatory grace that Sophie found as disturbing as the rest of him. His legs were long in tailored dark trousers, the matching jacket of his suit fitting perfectly over those wide and muscled shoulders, the darkness of his tousled hair almost touching his shoulders at the back and falling onto his brow at the front.

It was testament to how much this man dominated the space around him that Sophie found herself looking at him rather than admiring the amazing kitchen she had literally drooled over earlier today.

She wasn't a great lover of modern kitchens, but she was willing to make an exception with this one; the kitchen units were high gloss black, topped with dark grey marble, as was the worktable standing in the middle of the spacious room. There was a matching breakfast bar, while all of the appliances were stainless steel, including a large range cooker that took up half of one wall. It was a chef's dream kitchen.

Sophie's dream kitchen…

And, if she hadn't already succeeded in blowing it by goading her new boss, she was going to enjoy the privilege of being allowed to cook in here over the Christmas period.

'Sophie?'

She looked up to find that Max Hamilton was looking across at her expectantly, having poured the two glasses of white wine and placed them on the breakfast bar, all while she was lusting after his kitchen!

'Sorry.' She stepped forward to sit up on one of the bar stools.

Not in the least elegantly, unfortunately; as Sophie knew from experience, there was no way any woman who was only five feet two inches tall could ever get up on a bar stool and look elegant or sexy whilst doing it!

Max Hamilton, meanwhile, looked both of those things as he moved to sit on one of the stools opposite and, as expected with his superior height, had absolutely no problem doing so.

He eyed her after taking a sip of his wine. 'Aren't you a little old to still be at college?'

The question was so unexpected that Sophie choked on the wine she had been sipping.

'Careful!' He moved with that smooth animal grace as he swiftly made his way round the breakfast bar before slapping her on the back.

Sophie glowered up at him as that slap caused her to spit out the rest of the wine. With her eyes streaming from choking and her nose leaking the excess wine, she must look oh-so-very elegant! 'I'm not sure whether I should thank you for that or not...' she croaked breathlessly.

'Just trying to help.' He grinned down at her unrepentantly as he pulled the white silk handkerchief from the breast pocket of his jacket and presented it to her with a flourish.

Sophie muttered under her breath as she took

the handkerchief and mopped up the tears from her cheeks before giving her nose a noisy blow.

'Sorry?'

She glared up at him. 'I said I can probably do without help like that.'

'Would you rather I had let you continue to choke?' Max held back another smile as he moved to sit back on the bar stool opposite, his expression deliberately innocent as he looked across at her enquiringly.

'I would rather— Oh, never mind,' Sophie dismissed impatiently. 'A minute ago you thought I was underage. I'll return this to you once I've laundered it.' She pocketed the used handkerchief. 'And then you say I'm too old to still be at college. Maybe I'm doing an advanced course?'

'Are you?' Surprisingly, Max found he was enjoying himself; Sophie Carter certainly wasn't boring!

As he so often found that he was bored when in the company of the beautiful women he habitually dated?

Well, yes, if Max was honest, he invariably found, no matter how beautiful or desirable and accomplished a woman was in bed, that when it came to actual conversation those women usually bored him almost to the point of falling asleep in their company.

Sophie Carter wasn't classically beautiful, but her skin was creamy smooth and the tight red shoul-

der-length curls, which should have clashed gar-
ishly with her red jumper but somehow didn't, were
somehow endearing, and those brown eyes were
huge enough for a man to drown in. Plus there
were those lusciously sensual lips…

Oh, for goodness' sake. She was only here in his
apartment to ensure that Janice and Amy had a good
Christmas. Well, as good as it could be, considering
that his sister and brother-in-law were currently at
loggerheads over something.

Max had no intention of getting caught in the
middle of that argument, whatever it was; he knew
from experience how volatile his younger sister
could be. He had leapt to Janice's defence too many
times when they were both in their teens, only to
find that he was the one left sporting a black eye or
a split lip, while Janice had made up with which-
ever one of her boyfriends she had previously fallen
out with.

'I only started catering college in September,'
Sophie replied softly, long lashes lowered over those
huge brown eyes.

'What were you doing before that?'

She looked up at him, those deep brown eyes
flashing her resentment at the question. 'What does
that have to do with what I'm doing now?'

Nothing at all. Except that Max knew that for
some reason Sophie Carter didn't want to tell him.

Maybe she had been married and was now di-
vorced and branching out on her own? Or maybe

she had needed to work for a few years in order to save up the money to put herself through college? Or—

'Perhaps you could tell me a little about your sister and niece, so that I have some idea what presents to buy them when I go shopping tomorrow?' Sophie's eyes were still slightly red from when she had choked on the wine, her nose too, and her lips were slightly puffy.

Max found his gaze lingering a little too long on those puffy lips.

'Mr Hamilton?'

'Call me Max,' he invited distractedly.

'I would prefer to keep our relationship on a purely professional footing,' she answered him primly.

And Max was rapidly coming to the realisation that he would much rather they didn't, that he found Sophie Carter extremely intriguing!

A knee-jerk reaction to having realised Cynthia Maitland's unwanted expectations of him?

Possibly.

Although he somehow doubted it.

As a self-made billionaire, Max had long ago become accustomed to, and irritated by, the pound signs that gleamed in a woman's eyes whenever she looked at him.

The only thing gleaming in Sophie Carter's expressive eyes when she looked at him was disapproval. For men in general? Or was it something specific about him, in particular, she didn't like or approve of?

And why the hell should it matter to him, one way or the other, what Sophie Carter did or didn't think of him?

It didn't was the answer to that question.

He shrugged. 'Janice likes silk scarves. And Amy is into horses rather than dolls. Or at least she was the last time I spoke to her.'

'Your sister's colouring?'

'Janice is tall, with the same colouring as mine. Except she's beautiful, of course,' he added drily.

Sophie's gaze dropped from meeting that probing green one as she inwardly acknowledged that Max Hamilton was extremely beautiful, in a purely alpha male and masculine way, of course. That overlong ebony hair was silky soft, his face all hard and masculine angles, his body appearing even more so beneath that perfectly tailored suit and white silk shirt.

Yes, Max Hamilton was most definitely a beautiful alpha male.

He was also way, way out of her league.

And, remembering the Cathy faux pas, that last realisation didn't even merit so much as a second thought! Certainly not while Sophie was still in Max Hamilton's disturbing company, at least.

'I think it's time I left now, and allowed you to get on with the rest of your evening.'

'I'm not going anywhere.'

Sophie eyed him irritably. 'Maybe I am?'

'Are you?'

She frowned. 'I don't mean to be rude, but I really don't think that's any of your business, Mr Hamilton.' As she had considered it absolutely none of his business that she had given up her original catering course four years ago in order to care for her very ill mother.

It might be none of Max's business, but he wanted to know anyway—wanted to know if Sophie Carter was involved with anyone right now.

'I really do have to go now,' she insisted as she stood up.

Max also rose to his feet, once again towering over her. 'You haven't finished your wine.'

She gave a self-derisive smile. 'I may not be driving, but I think I'll pass on the wine, after all, if you don't mind.'

Max found that he did mind, that he had been enjoying himself talking to the unexpectedly outspoken and equally as intriguing Sophie Carter.

Most women, he had found, tended to be an open book. At least, as far as their interest in him was concerned. Cynthia had gone one step further by actually expecting commitment, of course, but otherwise he knew it was his bank balance that was a woman's primary interest in him.

Not only did Ms Carter seem to disapprove of him—or his wealth?—but she also remained something of an enigma herself. It was a long time since

Max had found himself this interested in learning more about a certain woman.

And that woman happened to be the same one with whom he would be spending the run up to Christmas. 'Will you also be the one doing the cooking for us over Christmas?'

'The food is already ordered and due to be delivered before your sister and niece arrive on Friday.' Sophie nodded. 'Unless you would prefer to find someone else to do the actual catering?'

'Not at all,' Max assured smoothly. 'You don't have family or friends you would rather be with?'

'I already told you, I'm an orphan.'

That wasn't exactly what Max had wanted to know.

But perhaps Christmas this year, with the presence of the feisty Sophie Carter, wouldn't be just another day to him, as it had been for more years than Max cared to remember.

## CHAPTER THREE

'LET ME HELP YOU with those!'

Sophie almost dropped all the bags and parcels she was struggling to carry into Max Hamilton's apartment at hearing the unexpected sound of his voice somewhere in front and above her. Having spent most of the afternoon shopping—on his credit card!—she hadn't expected him to have returned home from his office just yet.

'Did you buy the whole of the toyshop or just half of it?' he drawled ruefully as he took the parcels out of her arms to reveal that he must have been home for some time to have changed into a casual black cashmere sweater and faded jeans, his over-long dark hair as sexily tousled as ever.

And, if that was even possible, he was looking even more deliciously gorgeous than he had yesterday in that perfectly tailored suit and silk shirt.

'Just half of it.' Sophie eyed him ruefully as she carried the shopping bags through to the elegant cream-and-brown sitting room, now dominated by an eight foot tall and fully decorated Christmas tree standing in the corner of the room beside the fireplace. 'Perhaps you would like to help me wrap them all up?' she added derisively.

He eyed her thoughtfully. 'I would, as it happens.'

Sophie gave him a startled look; she hadn't actually been serious in the suggestion—had considered it a threat rather than a genuine option. 'You would?'

'Why not?' He placed the parcels down on the three-seater sofa. 'You've obviously been busy already today.'

He gave the tree a pointed glance, coloured lights sparkling amongst the thick, green, sweet-smelling bowers and the red-and-gold decorations, with an elegant fairy adorning the top branch.

Sophie had also decorated the tree in the entrance hall today, but with a silver-and-red theme and a silver star twinkling on the top.

'I have to say, Sophie, that I'm really impressed with all your hard work so far.' Max Hamilton nodded his approval. 'The least I can do is to help giftwrap the presents after you've been out and chosen all of them.'

Sophie really had been joking earlier; she had no real desire to share wrapping Christmas presents with Max Hamilton, of all people.

Years of wrapping presents with her mother, enjoying the laughter, the pleasure and later the odd glass of wine, told her it was far too intimate a pastime to share with a man who made her feel nervous at the best of times. And so far there had been very few of those between the two of them!

Max didn't know whether to be amused or enchanted by Sophie's appearance in a red coat, the hood of the coat edged with white fur. She wore fur-trimmed gloves on her elegant hands, and there was even fur topping the calf-high boots worn over her jeans. She looked like a very petite and cuddly Mrs Santa Claus!

Enchanted probably wasn't a good thing when Max already found Sophie far too intriguing for their current situation as employer and temporary employee.

But she really had transformed his home in a short space of time, the smell of fresh pine having hit his nose the moment he'd entered the apartment an hour or so ago. The tree decorations were tasteful rather than garish, the coloured lights twinkling merrily when he'd switched them on, and there were yet more sprigs of fresh holly adorning the pictures in the sitting room.

There were even three beautifully embroidered stockings draped across the arm of one of the chairs, no doubt placed there ready to be hung up for Janice, Amy and himself on Christmas Eve.

And she had returned his handkerchief to him, ironed as well as laundered!

'I'm being paid—very generously, I might add!—to buy and giftwrap the Christmas presents for your sister and niece,' Sophie Carter reminded him tartly.

Max found himself irritated that she had deliberately reminded him of that fact. 'Nothing for me?' he drawled.

Those deep brown eyes widened. 'You would hardly be giving yourself a present!'

He quirked a mocking brow. 'Does that mean you didn't buy me a present, either?'

'Why on earth would I do th…? Very funny, Mr Hamilton.' She placed the half a dozen or so bags down on the sofa next to the parcels, along with the wrapping paper and labels, before straightening.

Max found himself wondering what sort of present Sophie Carter might buy him.

He usually received an expensive shirt, or maybe a sweater or aftershave, if there happened to be a woman in his life at Christmastime, but Sophie was a student, and obviously didn't have a lot of money, so what sort of gift would she choose? Something inexpensive but personal? Or maybe—

Damn it, Max had found himself thinking of his employee far too much today already!

Sally was well on her way to Canada by now and, without the help of his efficient PA, his own day had been even busier than usual. But still he had found time to sit and muse about the fiery-haired Sophie Carter…

He knew from their conversation the previous

day that she was an orphan, aged twenty-four and at catering college.

What he still didn't know was if she had a man in her life; the fact that Sophie was willing to spend Christmas cooking for his family would seem to imply that she didn't.

Max had deliberately chosen to spend his Christmases skiing the last ten years, since Janice had married Tom and moved to the States, and he had been only too glad to do so. Very occasionally he had taken a woman with him, but more often than not he had preferred to go alone, well away from all the festivities and anyone who knew him.

Sophie Carter didn't seem to have any choice but to spend Christmas alone, possibly without any presents to open up on Christmas morning either, except maybe something from friends?

It made Max feel guilty at the amount of expensive gifts she had gone out and chosen for Janice and Amy today. Totally illogically, he realised; it wasn't up to him to provide a happy Christmas or presents for every waif and stray who crossed his path. Even if he wanted to.

Which he didn't, he told himself firmly.

Max had been eighteen and Janice sixteen when their parents were killed in a car crash on Christmas Eve, hit by a drunk driver on their way home from doing some last-minute shopping for presents.

After that Max had only gone through the motions of Christmas for Janice's sake, and had been perfectly happy not to have to once his sister was married and living in New York.

He certainly didn't want to involve himself in the preparations for this Christmas any more than he needed to either.

'Yes, very funny,' he finally answered Sophie tersely. 'As you said yesterday that you're using public transport, you may as well get off home now; you can wrap the presents up tomorrow.'

Sophie had no idea what Max Hamilton had been thinking about for the past few minutes as he'd scowled darkly but, whatever it was, they weren't pleasant thoughts. He also seemed to have rethought his offer to help her giftwrap his sister's and niece's Christmas presents.

'Fine,' she accepted just as abruptly. 'Maybe you could just write out a dozen or so labels for Janice and Amy tonight, ready to go on the gifts tomorrow?'

'Of course.' He nodded, his expression arrogantly remote, now looking every inch the billionaire CEO he was.

'I'll just…' Sophie broke off what she had been about to say as his mobile began to ring. 'I'll leave you to get that.'

Max took the mobile from the pocket of his jeans and answered the call.

Leaving Sophie in something of a quandary as to whether or not she should just leave him to it. It seemed a little rude to just leave without saying goodbye, and yet she also felt as if he had already dismissed her. And not very politely at that!

As he didn't seem to be being polite to whoever had telephoned him either

'We've already talked about this, Cynthia, and the answer is still no.'

Cynthia?

'No, I do not want you to come over this evening so we can talk about it!' he snapped decisively. 'Why not? Because I already have someone here with me, that's why!'

That 'someone' being Sophie?

Which was hardly fair, or completely truthful either, when Max seemed to be implying that she was here on a personal basis rather than a business one.

'That sort of language is not in the least attractive, Cynthia. Goodbye to you too.' Max closed the mobile's cover with a decisive snap before putting it back in his jeans pocket. 'Well?' His brow was lowered and there was a scowl between his glittering green eyes as he turned to look challengingly across the room at Sophie, displeasure burning off him in waves.

Displeasure Sophie had no interest in having turned against her now that the hapless Cynthia had made an undignified exit!

'Well what?' She feigned an innocent expression.

An innocence that didn't fool Max in the slightest, if the contemptuous curl of his top lip was any indication. 'You seemed to have something to say on most subjects yesterday, so why not this one?' he bit out scornfully.

The phrase 'spoiling for a fight' came to mind.

'I don't think it's my place to have an opinion on the way in which you conduct your private life, Mr Hamilton.' Sophie gave a dismissive shrug.

'That didn't seem to prevent you from doing exactly that yesterday,' he drawled mockingly.

No, it hadn't. And he had done very little so far in their acquaintance to dispel any of those preconceived ideas she'd had of him being a selfish and self-obsessed individual, after accidentally overhearing his conversation with Sally two days ago. This latest conversation with a woman called Cynthia hadn't exactly endeared him to her either.

'My opinions are my own, I hope, Mr Hamilton,' she countered calmly.

His eyes narrowed to glittering green slits. 'I asked you to call me Max.'

She nodded. 'And I told you I would prefer to keep our association on professional terms.'

Max ran a frustrated hand through his hair, knowing his anger was directed towards Cynthia, and her inability to accept that things were over between the two of them, rather than at Sophie.

Hell, he and Cynthia had only been out together three or four times, and it had been pure coincidence that the two of them happened to be going to the same ski resort over the Christmas holidays. At least Max had thought it was, until Cynthia had revealed otherwise during their telephone conversations yesterday. He had certainly never given her, or any other woman, the idea that he was interested in settling down with them.

The slightly reproving expression now on Sophie Carter's face told him that she thought otherwise. And Max certainly didn't appreciate feeling as if he needed to defend himself, and his actions, to her.

'Exactly how do you expect to be able to continue doing that when you're going to be in my apartment over most of Christmas?' he taunted challengingly.

Sophie had been asking herself the same question since their conversation the evening before. But only in as far as she was an outsider looking in. 'Quite easily. I'll be busy in the kitchen most of the time, and you and your family will be in the rest of your apartment.'

'And what about your own meals?'

'They will also be eaten in the kitchen, once I've finished serving you and your family.'

Max really wasn't happy with the idea of Sophie waiting on them, let alone sitting in his kitchen eating her meals on her own. He doubted his sister would be too happy with that arrangement either, if she knew Sophie's circumstances, which he had no doubt she would within a day of meeting Sophie. Janice's years living in America had made her more open and friendly than her previous English reserve. Than Max's own English reserve.

'We'll see,' he answered non-committally now. He'd had more than enough arguments already this evening, this latest telephone conversation with Cynthia having left a nasty taste in his mouth.

As well as convincing Sophie that he was even more of a selfish bastard than she had already thought he was.

If that was even possible…

# CHAPTER FOUR

'WHAT THE HELL——?'

Sophie turned from where she had just taken a baking tray out of the oven at the sound of his harshly broken-off statement, only to instantly lower her gaze again as she saw that her boss was once again dressed in one of those perfectly tailored designer label suits, charcoal this time, his shirt a pale grey, as was the matching tie. His hair was tousled.

As if he had just got out of bed...

'I made gingerbread angels and snowmen for when Amy arrives tomorrow,' she supplied abruptly, thankful that her cheeks were already warm from baking, so that hopefully Max wouldn't notice that she was also blushing from the turn her thoughts had just taken from merely looking at him.

The two of them hadn't exactly parted well the previous evening, but even so Sophie had found herself thinking about Max—she now thought of him that way in her head, even if she refused to use that same familiarity to his face!—far too much once she had returned to Sally's flat.

She had wondered, too, about the woman, Cynthia, who had telephoned him and been rebuffed so coldly. Had she misjudged him over that? Perhaps this woman Cynthia had deserved the coldness of Max's brush-off? After all, Sophie knew nothing about his relationship with Cynthia; she could be a stalker for all she knew.

Sophie had half decided that she owed Max an apology today. And yet seeing him again, hearing his voice—and once again experiencing the shiver it gave down the length of her spine—she now thought better of it. She was far too aware of everything about Max Hamilton already and needed to keep him firmly at arm's length, rather than try to become friends with him. If any woman could ever actually be friends with such a physically immediate man.

Sophie doubted she could.

Although she found his continued silence now more than a little puzzling.

She looked across at Max searchingly, noting the grimness of his expression. His face was pale and there were lines around his eyes and mouth; his jaw was tightly clenched.

'Max?' she queried uncertainly, not sure if he'd just had a bad day at work—after all, he was minus his PA now that Sally had arrived safely in Canada!—or if she had done something to upset him since he came home?

But considering he had only been in the apartment for a few minutes, she had no idea quite what that could have been.

Even if she did say so herself, the decorations had been tastefully finished, and the presents were all gaily wrapped and placed beneath the brightly lit tree in the sitting room.

But Max had known she was going to do that this morning, had left the written labels in the kitchen for his sister and niece as Sophie had asked him to do, so that she could put them on the parcels today.

Some of the food had been delivered today too, the things that weren't perishable, but she had already put them away in the cupboards, so there was no clutter in here to annoy him either.

The only thing she could think of that might possibly have annoyed or irritated him was that she was once again still here when he returned from work. But, after today, she was going to be here most of the time over Christmas anyway.

Max gave himself a mental shake, aware that Sophie could have no idea why he had reacted in the way that he had to the smell of her cooking. 'I... It's just that I haven't smelt baking like this since my mother...' He broke off, mouth thinning into a tight line. 'Well, in a long time,' he completed abruptly.

Sophie eyed him quizzically for several seconds before prompting huskily, 'How long?'

Since his parents had died that bleak Christmas sixteen years ago!

Since his own and Janice's world had been shot

to hell by some drunk driver who hadn't bothered to stop at the red traffic light and had driven straight into his parents' car, killing them both instantly.

He deliberately hadn't thought about his mother's baking for years; the way the house would be filled with the smell of it for days before Christmas. And she had always, always, even when he and Janice were both in their teens, made gingerbread angels and snowmen for them to eat in the week leading up to Christmas.

Entering his apartment and being instantly assailed by that same smell had brought back all the nostalgic memories of those happier Christmases, as well as the more painful ones since.

He had forgotten—chosen to forget?—the days of his mother baking cakes and puddings ready for Christmas. The joy of helping her wrap up the family's Christmas gifts. The excitement of the whole family decorating the tree.

And in just a few short days Sophie Carter, with her Christmas preparations, had succeeded in bringing it all back to him with painful clarity.

It wasn't her fault, of course, just a sequence of unfortunate circumstances, Janice and Tom's marital difficulties having been the start of them.

Max drew in a deep breath before crossing the kitchen in two long strides. 'These look delicious— Ouch!' He let out a protest as Sophie smacked his hand away from taking one of the cooling gingerbread snowmen. 'What was that for?'

'They haven't been decorated yet,' she reproved. 'And you haven't answered my question,' she added intuitively as she looked up at him questioningly.

Sophie looked extremely cute with her hair tied up with a black band, the freckles endearing across her cheeks and nose, with a light dusting of flour on the top of the latter, and wearing a red Santa pinafore to protect her red shirt and black jeans while she was baking.

Cute?

Max didn't do cute!

He liked his women sophisticated, as well as tall and beautiful.

And Sophie Carter was none of those things.

Cute, but certainly not tall or sophisticated, and her face was intriguing—arresting?—rather than classically beautiful.

It had to be this family Christmas thing that was messing with his head, as well as the rest of his well-ordered life, because right now Max couldn't think of anything he would enjoy more than kissing that dusting of flour off the tip of Sophie's pert little nose, before laying siege to the sensuously pouting lips beneath. And to hell with the consequences!

Sophie wasn't sure she was altogether comfortable standing this close to Max. So close she could feel the heat of his body through the thin material of her blouse, and smell that insidious lemon and sandalwood aftershave as it invaded her senses.

She certainly didn't understand the emotion

burning brightly in the glittering green eyes looking down at her so intently as Max reached up and released her hair from the confines of the black velvet band.

Or the way all the air suddenly seemed to have been sucked from the room.

Just as all the air left her lungs in a whooshing sigh as that dark head slowly began to lower towards hers.

As if having Max Hamilton kiss her had been inevitable.

As if she had wanted him to kiss her.

Which was…

There was no more time for thought. No more time for reasoned protest. No more time for anything but sensation, as Max's arms moved about her waist while his lips now feathered lightly, caressingly, across the top of her nose, along the warmth of her cheek, before moving unerringly to claim her own slightly parted lips.

A questing, seeking, searing kiss, as Max's lips sipped and tasted hers again and again, his arms tightening about her waist as he pulled her in against him to mould the softness of her curves against his much harder body.

Sophie was so stunned she didn't know what to do with her own hands for several seconds as they lay flattened against the hardness of Max's silk-covered chest. Feeling emboldened as she heard him give a low and throaty groan, she slowly moved her hands up onto his shoulders and then over and into the dark thickness of the overlong and silky hair at his nape.

Max deepened the kiss, feeling the capitulation of Sophie's body as she leant into and against him, running the moist warmth of his tongue over her softly pouting lips as he tasted her before parting them and then venturing inside. He groaned softly as his tongue was instantly enveloped in the perfect heat of her mouth.

Much like his pulsing and rapidly lengthening erection would be welcomed into the moist and heated channel between her thighs?

Dear God!

Just thinking about making love to Sophie, of laying her naked on his bed, looking down at that glorious red hair, lit like a blaze of fire against the pillows behind her, her face flushed and aroused, before feasting on the creamy perfection of her body, was enough to cause his body to throb achingly.

Max deepened the kiss hungrily, his tongue thrusting rhythmically into her heat, even as the hardness of his thighs pressed against and into the softness of her abdomen, causing him to groan as he enjoyed the friction against his own sensitised and engorged arousal.

His arms tightened about her as he felt the tentative lick of Sophie's tongue against his own, a shy duelling that lit an even deeper fire beneath his already raging desire.

He couldn't remember ever being this physically aroused, this quickly, by any other woman. He had no thought for anything but Sophie, being closer to Sophie, making love to Sophie. His hands lowered to cup beneath her bottom and he lifted her up onto the uncluttered end of the table before unfastening the Santa pinafore and removing it completely, dropping it to the tiled floor, before he stepped in between her parted thighs.

Max groaned, his lips travelling across her cheek, down the length of her throat as he instantly felt her heat, drawing him in, the hardness of his erection pressing against and into that heat between her thighs, his body pulsing as he arched harder against the friction caused by her jeans.

'Max?' Sophie clung to Max's shoulders, dazed by the depth of the passion that had sprung up so quickly between them.

She felt weak too, at the feel of the proof of that passion pressing so intimately against her between her parted thighs. She also felt achingly aroused by the warmth of Max's hand caressing the naked flesh of her back beneath her blouse as his lips continued to explore and taste her throat, and then lower.

Quite when he had unfastened the front of her blouse Sophie had no idea, only becoming aware that he had done so as one of his hands moved beneath the smooth cup of her bra and she felt the warmth of his lips exploring the bared tops of her breasts.

Max raised his head to look down at her breasts with eyes of deep, dark green. 'This is beautiful,' he murmured admiringly as both his hands now cupped her beneath the red satin and lace of her bra. 'Do your panties match?' he enquired gruffly as the soft pads of his thumbs stroked unerringly across the pouting fullness of her aroused nipples, pressed noticeably against the satin material. 'Sophie?' he encouraged huskily as she made no reply.

Sophie moistened the dryness of her lips with the tip of her tongue before answering him. 'Yes. I— But it's a thong, not panties.'

His gaze flickered sharply up to meet hers. 'A thong?' he repeated in a strained voice.

Sophie nodded, knowing her cheeks were the same fiery shade of red. 'My mother told me that a woman can wear whatever she wants on the outside and still feel feminine and desirable if she's wearing sexy underwear underneath.'

Max raised dark brows. 'Your mother told you this?'

She smiled slightly. 'Yes.'

Max nodded. 'She was right.' He groaned, just imagining Sophie wearing only that red thong.

A tiny scrap of material that would barely cover the fiery red curls between Sophie's thighs at the front, and separate the firm and naked globes of her bottom at the back. Buttocks that he wanted to cup as he pushed that skimpy satin aside and thrust inside her—

'What the—?' Max bit out an expletive as he now heard the door to his apartment opening and the sound of voices out in the hallway.

Only three people, besides himself, knew the security combination for entering his apartment. Sally would be safely in Canada by now. Sophie was half naked in his arms. Which only left—

Oh, hell!

## CHAPTER FIVE

MAX PUT ALL thoughts of red satin thongs, and making love to Sophie, completely from his mind as he stepped back abruptly to pull the two sides of her blouse together, covering the fullness of her breasts. Hidden from temptation!

'You might want to button up,' he advised grimly as he turned away and strode towards the kitchen doorway, the sound of the voices in the hallway growing louder. As evidence that his unexpected visitors were on their way to the kitchen in search of him?

Something Max wanted to avoid, at least until Sophie had had the chance to refasten her blouse and straighten her appearance.

'Who…?'

'I suggest you do it now!' Max grated forcefully as he stepped out of the kitchen without so much as a backwards glance.

Sophie was too bewildered to immediately do as Max instructed. Although the sudden burst of happy laughter in the hallway, and raised excited voices, finally spurred her into action. She hastily got down from the table and refastened her blouse with fingers that shook slightly.

There was nothing she could do about her flushed cheeks, over-bright eyes or her slightly swollen and sensitive lips, but she picked up the black velvet band from the floor before pulling the wildness of her loosened curls back up into the confines of a ponytail.

Only just in time too, as a woman appeared in the doorway. A tall and beautiful woman with silky dark hair, shoulder-length, and eyes that sparkled a deep, warm green. Her patrician features more than a little familiar.

A woman who could only be Max's sister, Janice.

The woman and her daughter, who weren't expected to arrive until tomorrow.

Janice gave a warm smile. 'I'm sure my brother will introduce the two of us once he's managed to extricate himself from my husband and overenthusiastic daughter,' she drawled affectionately.

Sophie frowned at the mention of Janice's husband.

Wasn't it because his sister and her husband were having marital problems that Janice and Amy were joining Max in England for Christmas?

'Is that…?' Janice stepped further into the kitchen, very slender and elegant in a thick cream cable-knit sweater and black fitted jeans. 'My goodness, it *is* gingerbread,' she murmured wonderingly as she looked down at the biscuits on the cooling tray on top of the kitchen table.

'Janice...'

'Max, there are gingerbread angels and snow-men!' She turned excitedly to her brother as he spoke to her from the kitchen doorway, a little girl held securely in his arms. A beautiful little girl, who bore such a likeness to her uncle she could only be Amy. 'I'd forgotten just how evocative smells can be.' Janice gave a shake of her head as tears now glistened in her eyes. 'Max, do you remember—?'

'Yes,' he grated harshly.

Warningly, it seemed to Sophie.

Not that she had dared look at him again after that first glance, his expression grimly unapproach-able, the green of his eyes as chilling as an Arctic wind.

'I haven't smelt gingerbread like this in years,' Janice continued softly, completely undaunted—or simply unaware?—of her brother's lack of warmth. 'Not since the Christmas Mum and Dad died. Can you believe it's been sixteen years, Max?' she added sadly.

'Yes,' he rasped harshly.

Sophie looked sharply across the room at Max. She had thought the loss of her mother six months ago was bad enough, but his parents had both died at Christmas sixteen years ago? At the same time? Which surely must mean that their deaths couldn't have been due to illness or natural causes?

Which also explained why Max had said he hadn't smelt gingerbread baking 'in a long time'? And the reason he had looked so grim when he'd arrived home earlier and smelt it in his apartment.

Could his parents' deaths also be the reason that Max usually chose not to celebrate Christmas?

It would certainly explain his aversion to anything to do with the festive season.

As it explained why he chose to go skiing every year rather than join in any of the Christmas festivities.

And why he didn't possess so much as a single Christmas decoration, let alone a tree.

And the fact that he'd had to ask Sally to have 'Christmas delivered' to his apartment.

Perhaps Max wasn't such a bah humbug, after all, and it was more the case of the festive season holding such sad memories for him that he preferred to avoid everything to do with it?

Sophie felt slightly guilty now for judging him without knowing all the facts. If he had just explained—

But of course Max wouldn't explain himself to her. Why should he? She had been employed by him, and was being paid by him, to 'deliver Christmas' to his apartment, and then only because of the expected arrival of his sister and niece. Of course Max wouldn't feel a need to explain himself to someone whom he considered merely an employee.

Although quite where their earlier intimacies

now put them in regard to maintaining that distance, Sophie had no idea!

She glanced across at Max from beneath lowered lashes, her heart giving a leap in her chest as she recalled the feel of his lips against hers, along the column of her throat and across the bared tops of her breasts. Breasts he had also cupped and held, caressed. Her nipples tingled now, tightening inside her red satin and lace bra, just thinking of the intimacy of those caresses.

She had also told him she was wearing a matching red satin thong, for goodness' sake.

Her cheeks flushed just thinking about that part of their conversation...

In the circumstances, it really was just as well that she had persuaded Sally into not revealing that Sophie was her cousin!

Max gave her a hard and mocking grin, as if he were fully aware of some of her thoughts before he turned his attention back to his sister. 'Perhaps we should just make the introductions, Janice?'

'Oh. Of course.' His sister dragged her gaze away from the gingerbread to turn and look at Sophie with curious eyes. 'I'm Janice Hilton, Max's sister.' She smiled warmly at Sophie. 'And that's my daughter, Amy, in Max's arms. And this—' she turned to smile at the tall, blond-haired man who had just entered the kitchen and moved to stand beside her before draping his arm about her shoulders '—is my husband, Tom.'

'I think Sophie has already guessed that much,' Max drawled ruefully.

'Sophie?' Janice echoed lightly, Max knowing by the sharpness of the curiosity in his sister's avid green gaze that she was more than a little interested in knowing who—or what—Sophie was to him.

Which was a question Max would also like an answer to.

Until tonight he would have said that Sophie was a temporary—intrusive!—and paid addition to his household. An irritating necessity if he was going to give Janice and Amy a family Christmas with all the trimmings.

Until tonight?

*Be honest with yourself, at least, Hamilton*, he inwardly berated himself; he had found Sophie intriguing from the beginning. Had found her conversation amusing as well as interesting. And although she bore absolutely no resemblance to those model-beautiful women he usually dated, Sophie undoubtedly had her own attractions.

Her eyes were such a deep and dark brown a man could drown in them, for one.

Those freckles across her nose and cheeks were a temptation to kiss them, for another.

Her lips were full and pouting, and extremely kissable.

As for the creaminess of her breasts…!

Max hadn't been able to resist kissing them either. Or touching them. As for caressing them?

Sophie's breasts were extremely responsive, the nipples plump and full. As delicious and succulent, in fact, as two ripe berries, and Max had wanted to gorge himself on them.

The fact that Sophie's lips were red and slightly puffy from the heat of their kisses, with a slight redness on her chin and down her neck, thanks to the five o'clock shadow on his own jaw, was evidence of how close he had come to doing exactly that.

Lord knew how far things would have gone between the two of them if Janice and family hadn't arrived so unexpectedly.

Which raised the question—what was Tom doing here with his wife and daughter?

Not that Max wasn't pleased to see his brother-in-law, or that Janice and Tom were so obviously back together, because he couldn't have been happier on both those counts. He had always liked Tom, and it had to be better for all of them, but especially for Amy, if Janice and Tom had resolved their differences. Max just wished he had known about the reconciliation before the three of them had actually arrived.

Not that it made a lot of difference in the grand scheme of things, because Janice had already informed him out in the hallway that the three of them would now be spending Christmas with him rather than just two, and that they'd arrived a day early so that they could surprise him.

Any explanations about the reconciliation, if

Janice and Tom cared to give any, could be made after Amy was safely in bed. And, if not, then Max considered it was none of his business.

'Sophie Carter,' Max answered his sister briskly now. 'Employed by me, to answer my "organising Christmas for you" prayer,' he added drily.

'Oh.'

Max chuckled ruefully. 'Try to look a little less disappointed by that explanation, sis,' he drawled mockingly. 'You're embarrassing Sophie.'

Sophie was beyond mere embarrassment right now. Way beyond, after the intimacies she and Max had indulged in before the arrival of his sister and her family.

Max had also, in just a few brief words to his sister, placed Sophie firmly in the role of employee.

'It's time I cleared up in here and left you all to enjoy the rest of the evening together,' she announced briskly as she moved round the table to start putting the now cooled gingerbread into a storage box ready for decorating tomorrow morning. 'Unless you would like me to prepare something for dinner before I go?' she offered with a politely enquiring glance in Max's direction, letting him know that she had no delusions about what had happened between them earlier and could be just as coolly businesslike as him.

And, with the arrival of his sister and her family, that was exactly what Sophie intended to be in future, as far as Max Hamilton was concerned!

'I seem to have done nothing but eat since we left New York,' Janice refused lightly. 'How about everyone else?'

'I'd like to go and look at the big tree and then go to bed, Mummy,' Amy answered tiredly.

'I'm good too, thanks,' Tom also refused.

Which left only Max...

Only Max?

Sophie gave an inward quiver as she realised that he—maintaining a distance from him—was going to be her biggest problem over Christmas.

## CHAPTER SIX

SOPHIE LOOKED AT MAX enquiringly, even as she inwardly willed him to say no to her offer to stay and cook dinner for him. Because she dearly wanted to leave now; she needed to get out of Max's apartment, away from Max, in order to go home and regroup.

If that was even possible after what had just happened between them.

But she had to at least try.

Max Hamilton was a billionaire and she was a struggling student. Max was sophisticated and she was far from being that. Max was a rich and handsome playboy with a legion of women in his past—and present?—and she hadn't so much as had time to go out on a single date in over three years. Also, Max was an experienced lover and she was still a virgin!

'Let's go and look at the tree in the other room, hmm, Amy?' Tom Hilton was the one to lightly break the silence. 'I'm pretty sure I saw presents beneath it!' he teased his young daughter.

Amy gave a squeal of excitement even as she struggled to be put down from her uncle's arms, before grabbing hold of her father's hand and dragging him out of the kitchen and down the hallway to the sitting room.

There was a continued and awkward silence in the kitchen once father and daughter had left, causing Janice Hilton to look between Sophie and Max curiously.

'Er... Perhaps Amy would like to help me decorate the gingerbread in the morning?' Sophie prompted when she couldn't stand the silence any longer.

'That's really kind of you; I'm sure she would love it.' Janice smiled warmly. 'Remember, Max, how we always used to?'

'Not now, Janice!' her brother rasped harshly.

'Perhaps not,' she accepted with a wistful sigh. 'I think perhaps I should go and join Tom and Amy in the sitting room now, and leave the two of you alone to talk,' she added with a rueful glance at the stony-faced Max. 'Nice to meet you, Sophie.' Janice paused in the doorway. 'Oh, and did you know you have white powder—possibly flour!—on the back of your jeans, Sophie?'

Sophie's cheeks blazed with warmth as she looked over her shoulder and saw the flour on the backside of her jeans, glaring at Max as the other woman left the room to join her husband and daughter in the sitting room. Obviously, the flour had got there when Max had lifted her up onto the kitchen table.

'Don't blame me!' He held up his hands defensively.

Sophie looked up from brushing the flour off the back of her jeans, certain that her face must look very hot—and even more bothered!

'And who else should I blame, when you're the one that lifted me onto the table in the first place?'

'I don't remember you protesting at the time,' Max came back mildly, outwardly amused by Sophie's embarrassment, but inwardly irritated too— because he very much doubted he had heard the last on the subject from his sister.

Brown eyes glared daggers at him. 'And I don't remember being given much opportunity to protest.'

Max returned that gaze quizzically. They both knew her statement wasn't completely truthful, that Sophie could have demurred at any time— when he first kissed her lips, when his tongue and lips had searched out the delectable hollows of her throat, when he had clasped her bottom and carried her over to the table, when he had unfastened her blouse, cupped her breasts and caressed them—and Max would have stopped.

At least, he hoped that he would.

Sophie, with her blazing red hair and refreshingly unusual and freckle-faced beauty, had a way of turning his well-ordered world upside down. Of turning him upside down. So much so that things like caution and self-control seemed to fall by the wayside the moment he was with her.

As they did now.

His body was still hot and aching, telling Max all too clearly that he wanted to continue where the two of them had left off. Something that was impossible, and would be for some time, now that his sister, brother-in-law and niece had arrived to stay.

'Never mind,' Sophie dismissed abruptly before visibly forcing the tension from the slenderness of her shoulders. 'Now that your brother-in-law is here, would you like me to go present shopping for him too, before I come back here in the morning?'

Well, at least she intended coming back in the morning; there had been every chance that she wouldn't, after their earlier intimacies.

'Fine.' Max nodded. 'I— You don't have to go right away,' he continued huskily. 'You could always stay and have a drink with all of us? It will give you a chance to get to know Janice, Tom and Amy better.' He instantly had cause to regret his impulsive offer, as Sophie now eyed him suspiciously.

'I— No, thanks,' she refused abruptly, her gaze now refusing to meet Max's. 'It's late and I— Henry will be expecting me home any minute,' she finished determinedly.

'Henry?' Max repeated sharply. 'Who the hell is Henry?' His voice had deepened accusingly as he continued, without waiting for her to answer, 'Damn it, I asked you the other day if there was anyone you should be spending Christmas with.'

'And I told you there wasn't,' she maintained stubbornly.

His eyes narrowed. 'You don't want to spend Christmas with the man you're obviously living with?' Max couldn't remember ever feeling this angry in his life before.

Sophie lived with a man called Henry!

This innocent-looking little sprite, with her honest brown eyes, smart—and utterly delicious!—mouth, lived with a man called Henry.

Sophie realised she had made a mistake the moment she'd mentioned Henry's name, but at the time she had been too flustered by thoughts of her and Max together just minutes ago, too desperate to leave Max's apartment, to escape him, to think properly before speaking.

And now that she had spoken there was no way she could either retract the statement or admit that Henry was a cat; there was every chance that Max knew his PA had a cat called Henry, and that he would then add two and two together and come up with the correct answer of four. Namely, that Sally knew Sophie rather better than he had previously been informed. Which would not only be embarrassing for all of them but might endanger Sally's job as Max's PA.

'Henry and I are currently sharing a flat, yes.'

'And just how long has this arrangement with Henry existed?' Max demanded to know harshly.

Sophie shrugged uncomfortably, not fooled for

a moment by the softness of Max's tone. The dangerous glitter in those green eyes told an altogether different story. 'Just the past few days.'

'The past few days?' Max echoed incredulously. Disgustedly. 'And you don't want to spend Christmas with the man you've only just started living with?'

She shrugged uncomfortably. 'I need the money you're paying me more—'

'Damn it, you almost allowed me to make love to you just now,' Max rasped accusingly.

'I don't recall there being much "allowing" about it. You just took,' Sophie came back defensively as she forced herself to meet Max's gaze, uncomfortably aware of the contempt he now felt towards her as that emotion glittered uncensored in those dark green eyes.

Contempt as well as disgust.

And it would be wholly deserved contempt and disgust if Sophie really were living with a man called Henry and had earlier allowed, and responded to, Max's kisses and caresses.

As it was, there was no way she could explain who Henry really was, not without also implicating her cousin in the deception they'd carried out.

'Perhaps it is time that you left.' Max spoke evenly.

'Yes.' Sophie could no longer meet those contemptuous green eyes.

Max's mouth twisted mockingly. 'After all, you really don't want to keep Henry waiting any longer.'

She gave a pained frown. 'Max—'

'Yes?'

Sophie inwardly quaked at the unmistakable disgust Max managed to engender in just that one word. 'Never mind.' She gave an uncomfortable shake of her head. 'As I said, I'll be a little late in the morning, as I have to shop for those presents for your brother-in-law.'

He gave a dismissive shrug of those powerful shoulders. 'I'll be at work anyway.'

Her eyes widened. 'But your family is here and it's Christmas Eve!'

He nodded tersely. 'And?'

And she had already known that Max Hamilton hadn't become a billionaire without working as hard as he played. That taking Christmas Eve off work to spend the day with his family probably hadn't even occurred to him, let alone been a real possibility.

'And nothing,' she accepted distantly. 'I was only being polite by informing you why I might be a little late in the morning.'

His mouth twisted with hard derision. 'I think the two of us have gone way past being "polite" to each other, don't you?'

Yes, they probably had, Sophie accepted heavily.

There was no probably about it.

Max had seen her breasts earlier, covered only by that red satin and lace bra, for goodness' sake.

Had kissed and caressed them until they still ached with arousal. And he had so obviously fantasised about seeing her in the matching thong too, once she'd told him she was wearing one.

Yes, the two of them were way, way past being polite to each other.

## CHAPTER SEVEN

IT WAS WITH great reluctance that Max let himself into his apartment the following evening, all too aware that, for the next two days at least, there would be no escaping Christmas.

Or Sophie…

A fact instantly brought home to him as he stepped into the marble entrance hall, the delicious smell of food cooking telling him she was probably in the kitchen right now.

He was still utterly furious with her for omitting to tell him that she already had someone in her life. A 'someone' called Henry.

At the same time as he hadn't been able to stop thinking about her since they'd parted last night. Images of her, of kissing her, touching her, had disturbed his sleep last night, and totally wrecked his concentration at work today.

Damn it, a masochistic side of him wanted to spend time with Sophie. To enjoy looking at her. Talking with her. And to laugh too, as she gave him yet another one of her cheeky set-downs in response to something he had either said or done that she disapproved of.

How sad was that? That he was inwardly aching for even the disapproval of a woman he had met for the first time just three days ago?

Utterly pathetic was what it was.

Sophie was ten years younger than him. A student, for goodness' sake. And she wasn't tall and slim, or sophisticated—those fiery red curls were completely untameable!—or in the least classically beautiful.

Or, it seemed, available.

Max freely acknowledged, to himself, at least, that it was the latter which had annoyed him the most.

Because Sophie lived with another man. A man called Henry.

A man Max had been resisting the urge, all last night and today, to seek out and strangle with his bare hands.

How caveman was that?

It was unbelievable that Sophie had managed to get beneath his skin in such a short space of time and he had felt positively primitive just thinking of her sharing an apartment—a bed!—with another man.

'Uncle Max!' An excited Amy appeared in the entrance hall, looking cute as a button in a green velvet dress, with a matching ribbon in the darkness of her curls. 'Uncle Max, come and see how beautiful the tree looks today!' She grinned happily as she took his hand and pulled him into the sitting room.

Max came to a halt just inside the doorway, fingers tightening about the handle of his briefcase as he saw that Sophie wasn't in the kitchen, after all, but down on her hands and knees next to the tree in the sitting room, adding yet more gaily wrapped presents to the dozens and dozens already piled high around the base of it.

His mouth went dry as he saw Sophie was wearing fitted brown trousers today, with a matching brown sweater. The former outlined the perfect curve of her bottom as she bent over, causing him to wonder if she was wearing another thong today. The latter clung to the soft swell of her breasts as she straightened to her knees to look across at him guardedly. Those fiery red curls cascaded, unchecked, down onto the slenderness of her shoulders and about her flushed face.

For a man who had always enjoyed coming home to the peace and solitude of his apartment, Max felt a warmth inside at seeing Sophie here with his family.

With very little effort on his part, he could get used to finding her waiting here for him every evening when he came home from work.

A realisation that sent a cold shiver of apprehension down the length of his spine.

He didn't want or need any woman waiting for him when he came home from work, this evening or any other. He knew only too well how easy it was to lose the people you cared about. The people you loved. Which was why he had never fallen in love with any of the women he had dated.

Why he had deliberately chosen to go out with women he knew there was no chance of him ever falling in love with?

Perhaps.

No, not perhaps—that was exactly what he had done for the last sixteen years. Since losing his parents so suddenly, he had learnt in a single blow just how fragile life could be, and how painful it was to lose the people you loved.

He wouldn't—couldn't—allow a fiery-haired urchin like Sophie Carter to penetrate the hard shell he had kept over his emotions for so many years.

'Are you planning to change before dinner, Max?' Janice prompted pointedly.

Max gave himself a mental shake as he realised he had been staring at Sophie this whole time, and that his expression must have been as unpleasant as his thoughts, if the pallor of her cheeks was any indication.

His expression remained grim as he turned away to look at Janice. 'How long do I have before we eat?'

It was impossible for Sophie to miss the fact that Max had chosen to ask his sister that question, rather than the person actually cooking the evening meal. As a means, no doubt, of letting her know exactly where she fit into the scheme of things.

Just as it had been impossible for her to have

mistaken the look of displeasure on Max's face, and the way his fingers took a white-knuckled grip of his briefcase, the moment he entered the sitting room and saw her sitting there with his family.

Well, if he thought for one moment that she had imagined she might be included in their family Christmas, he was mistaken. She knew her place, and it wasn't here but in the kitchen. She was only here now because it was the first chance she'd had to slip the token presents beneath the tree that she had bought for the Hilton family.

Although, after his behaviour just now, she was starting to regret that she had felt guilt pressure her into buying a present for Max too.

And it had been far from easy to find something suitable for him; what did you buy a man who was a billionaire and already had everything, or had the means to buy anything and everything that he could ever want or need?

The choice of a pop-up book on horses had been easy for Amy. And she had found a pretty, but in-expensive, scarf ring made out of jade for Janice. Tom had been a little more difficult, but Sophie had finally settled on an autobiography she had thought might interest him. Which had just left her with Max to buy for.

Just!

Everything she had looked at had seemed either too personal, or too ordinary, or just too obviously inexpensive for a man as rich and overwhelmingly powerful as Max Hamilton.

Until she remembered the book she had bought for her uncle's birthday a couple of months ago, a humorous book written by one of the more outspoken politicians. A book her uncle had greatly enjoyed, and recommended for any cynic. Which, Sophie had decided, described Max Hamilton to a T!

Not only was he cynical, but he was also sarcastic and arrogant and, at times, just plain hurtful.

'Sophie?' Janice queried softly.

Sophie had decorated the gingerbread snowmen and angels with Amy once she'd arrived this morning, and the Hiltons had been out for the rest of the day, doing last-minute shopping that morning and then taking Amy ice skating in the afternoon. But nevertheless Sophie had spent a little time alone in the kitchen with Janice earlier this evening. Enough to know that she liked the other woman very much.

Enough to know that the relaxed and friendly Janice was nothing like her arrogant and disdainful older brother!

'Dinner will be served in an hour or so, Mr Hamilton,' Sophie informed him stiltedly before stiffly crossing the room, her head held high as she moved past him to return to the kitchen.

It didn't take a mastermind to realise that Sophie was annoyed with him again, Max acknowledged ruefully as he watched her leave. Even the red of her hair had seemed to crackle with angry disapproval.

No change there, then.

'You weren't very polite, Max,' Janice admonished him softly.

'No,' he acknowledged without apology, in no mood to explain himself to either of the two women presently in his apartment. 'I'll just go and shower and change into something more casual before dinner.' He didn't wait for his sister's response as he followed Sophie out of the room.

He had every intention of turning right, in the direction of his bedroom suite, walking down the carpeted hallway to his rooms, closing the door and taking a shower, preferably a cold one, after leaving the sitting room.

Instead, he found himself turning left and heading in the direction of the kitchen. And Sophie.

Max stood unobserved in the doorway, watching her as she concentrated on stirring something in a saucepan on top of the hob. She was listening to Christmas carols playing softly on the radio while she worked. The wildness of her fiery red hair was once again gathered up into a brown band at her crown, and the Santa pinafore was also secured about the slimness of her waist and looped over the back of her neck.

A neck that looked very slender and vulnerable as she bent over her task.

A vulnerability that Max was totally unable to

resist as he crossed the kitchen on silent feet until he came to a halt, standing just inches behind her. He was instantly aware of the lightness of her perfume—a mixture of spring flowers and a headier spice. Just as he was also aware of the warmth of her body.

A combination that drew him in like a magnet.

The first Sophie knew of Max's presence in the kitchen was when she gave a start of surprise and then stiffened as she felt his arms move about her waist and link together over her abdomen as he pulled her gently back to rest against his chest. 'What…?'

'I want to apologise for my boorish behaviour to you a few minutes ago, Sophie.'

'What's so different about a few minutes ago?' she challenged as she attempted to separate his hands and release herself. 'I had just assumed it was par for the course where you're concerned,' she added ruefully. The warm feel of Max's breath against her ear indicated that his head was lowered to her level, as proof that he was standing far too close for comfort. If Sophie needed any further evidence of that, when the length of his chest and thighs was pressed so intimately against her back.

His chest rumbled against her spine as he gave a husky chuckle. 'You really are very bad for my ego.'

'It's been my experience so far that your ego is already more than big enough for one man. Now would you kindly release me?' Sophie added firmly. 'Or do I have to hurt you?'

Max couldn't stop his burst of laughter at her threat. Sophie was at least a foot shorter than him, and must weigh a good hundred pounds less too; the idea of her being able to physically 'hurt' him was ludicrous.

Besides which, holding her had filled his head with a calm he hadn't felt in almost twenty-four hours.

'Max?' Sophie prompted warningly as he made no move to do as she asked and release her.

Max turned her round to face him; his lids were lowered to hide the expression in his eyes. 'I like holding you.'

'That wasn't the impression you gave last night.'

'You had just told me you're living with another man,' he reminded her sharply.

Sophie's eyes widened. 'Another man' seemed to imply that Max somehow thought of himself as a man in her life. Which was laughable. Yes, he had kissed her, and those kisses had got a little…well, a lot…out of control, but once Christmas was over she was never going to see him again. Despite the fact that she could clearly feel the length of Max's arousal pressing against the softness of her abdomen.

'And that situation hasn't changed since last night.' She put both her hands against his chest and pushed. To absolutely no effect. 'I should warn you,

Max, I'm a first dan in ju-jitsu and I'm not afraid to use it.' She tilted her back to look up at him challengingly.

'That's admirable.' He smiled mockingly. 'Unfortunately for you, I'm a fourth dan, so what do you think your chances are in a fight between the two of us?'

Not very high, Sophie acknowledged with an inner wince, knowing how wide the gulf was between a first and fourth dan; no wonder Max had such a fit and lithe body for a man who supposedly spent all of his time sitting behind a desk adding to his billions. He obviously didn't spend all of his time doing that!

'Maybe we could have a practise together in the gym here some time over the next couple of days?' He quirked one dark brow.

Sophie had no intention of becoming hot and sweaty with Max, in the gym here or anywhere else, ever!

She gave him a sweetly insincere smile. 'I'll pass, if you don't mind.'

He gave what she easily interpreted as a smug smile. 'Thought you might.'

Maybe, if he hadn't given that self-satisfied smile, she might just have repeated her request that he release her and then backed off.

Unfortunately, he did smile smugly. After that, Sophie had no intention of backing off.

# CHAPTER EIGHT

'WHAT ARE YOU DO—?' Max barely had time to gasp his surprise before the fingers on both of his hands were bent back painfully and he suddenly found himself flat on his back on the kitchen floor, with Sophie looming menacingly above him as she lay across his chest and twisted his wrists to hold his hands above his head. 'Are you insane?' He stared up at her incredulously.

'Getting there, I think,' she acknowledged as she spoke between gritted teeth, at the same time implying that he was the one driving her there.

Now that he was over the initial shock, this situation had tipped over into the realms of hilarious, if Max thought about it. And, at this precise moment, it seemed that he had all the time in the world to do exactly that.

Not that he couldn't have released himself if he had wanted to, dislodging Sophie from on top of him. Because he certainly could have. As a fourth dan to Sophie's first, he could have done that quite easily. He just chose not to do so for the moment.

There was something extremely arousing about having Sophie throw him to the floor before lying on top of him like this. In a position of dominance, her face only inches from his and flushed from her exertions, her eyes glittered down at him darkly in warning. So much so that the blood was pounding hotly through Max's veins, making him uncomfortably aware of the increasing heat of his desire for the woman positioned above him.

A woman whom he sensed was becoming as aroused as he was, noting her nipples hardening against him and the heat deepening between her thighs, the fullness of her lips parting invitingly as she breathed heavily.

A woman who was already involved with, and had admitted living with, another man.

Max eyes narrowed. 'Exactly what is Henry to you?'

Sophie was thrown by the unexpected question. 'I don't see what…'

'Do you share a bed with him?'

She instantly thought of the way Henry had tried to sneak up onto her bed to sleep last night—something strictly forbidden by Sally, spoilt pet or otherwise. 'No,' she answered honestly.

'Have sex with him?'

'No!' She gasped her answer this time, compelled to make the denial even though she knew it was really none of Max's business, even if Henry had been the man he thought rather than her cousin's cat.

'But the two of you do live together?' It was

obvious from Max's disgusted tone that if the two of them had been living together then they would definitely be sharing a bed and having sex.

'Only because it's convenient for a couple of weeks,' she admitted reluctantly.

'So the two of you aren't romantically involved?'

'I'm not—'

'Would you say he's a friend rather than a boyfriend?' he persisted.

She eyed him warily now. 'Max...'

'Answer the damned question.' His eyes glittered as hard as the emeralds they resembled as he glared up at her.

Sophie returned that gaze rebelliously, even though she now seriously doubted the wisdom, or sanity, of her actions. Not only could this be extremely awkward if any of the Hilton family should walk in on them, but she had just manhandled Max Hamilton, the powerful billionaire, to his own kitchen floor before throwing herself on top of him.

A move which, sanity aside, should have put her in a position of power. It should make her the one in control of this volatile situation between the two of them. And yet Sophie knew from the dangerous glitter in Max's eyes that she wasn't either of those things. That it was Max who held all the power. And the control.

Because her traitorous body was enjoying their close proximity far too much, her breasts full and aching, her nipples engorged. As for the increase in the aching heat between her thighs...

'Yes,' she finally answered Max challengingly.

That dangerous glitter intensified in his eyes for several seconds before it was dampened down, controlled. 'So last night you deliberately chose to let me continue to think that the two of you were lovers?'

'I really don't see...'

'Oh, you're going to see, Sophie,' Max promised her grimly. 'In just a few minutes you're going to see just how dangerous it is to play those sorts of games with me.'

She gasped. 'I wasn't playing games.'

'It's far too late for protests now, Sophie,' he bit out harshly.

'Only just, from where I'm standing,' drawled an amused voice from across the room.

Sophie's face was stricken as she turned sharply to look at the woman now standing in the kitchen doorway. At Max's sister, Janice Hilton, as she stood in the kitchen doorway.

Sophie was mortified to be caught in such an uncompromising position with her boss.

'I came to see if you needed any help, Sophie,' Janice continued lightly, her green eyes alight with the humour she was obviously fighting a losing battle to keep contained. 'But obviously you have the situation well under control.' She arched pointedly amused brows at the fact that Sophie had her brother pinned to the kitchen floor.

Sophie closed her eyes as she inwardly prayed for the floor to open up and swallow her.

A prayer that wasn't answered, of course, because Max was still lying on the kitchen floor beneath her when she opened her eyes again, and Janice was now grinning her enjoyment of this situation as she continued to look down at the two of them.

Sophie couldn't even glance in Max's direction now, to see his reaction to his sister's arrival in the kitchen. She continued to look at Janice instead as she quickly released Max before scrambling inelegantly to her feet.

'I— This isn't what it looked like.'

Her cheeks were ablaze with embarrassment, no doubt clashing dreadfully with the red of her hair.

'I was just— I just…' She stopped talking, chewing on her bottom lip, at a complete loss to know exactly what explanation to give for what she and Max had been doing a few minutes ago.

'I'd be as interested as Janice to hear what it was you were just doing, Sophie.' Max rose lithely to his feet to stand beside her, his anger of a few minutes ago having completely evaporated, replaced by humour at Sophie's obvious embarrassment.

Not that he didn't think for one minute that he wasn't going to come in for his own share of questions from his little sister once the two of them were alone together. Still, it was worth it just to see the way Sophie was now squirming with discomfort.

Sophie turned to glare at him with angry brown eyes. 'I believe we can do without your warped sense of humour right now, thank you very much.'

'Need I remind you that you were the one who dragged me down onto the kitchen floor?' Max mocked drily.

'And it's a pity I didn't decide to knock you on the head at the same time,' she snapped back.

'She's absolutely priceless, Max.' His sister chortled her obvious enjoyment of the situation.

'That's one way of describing her, yes,' Max answered his sister drily.

He wondered if anyone had ever spoken to him in the completely uninhibited way that Sophie always seemed to. Not for many years, if at all, he acknowledged. And yet he found that he liked Sophie's blunt honesty, the way she felt absolutely no fear or hesitation in saying exactly what she thought, both to him and about him.

'I— We had just discovered that we both practise ju-jitsu,' Sophie put in desperately, 'and I was demonstrating one of the moves I've just learnt to Max.'

'Lame, Sophie. Very lame,' he repeated mockingly. 'Now, if you wouldn't mind disappearing, Janice? Sophie and I still have a few more moves we need to discuss before dinner.' He arched a pointed brow at his sister.

'I don't mind at all. But I should keep those "moves" to a minimum for now, if I were you,' Janice advised, her eyes still openly laughing at them.

'I doubt Amy would understand if she were to walk in and find that the two of you had recommenced making those moves together on the kitchen floor.'

'Go,' he bit out tersely, waiting until Janice had left before turning back to Sophie, his eyes narrowed. 'We don't have time for this right now, Sophie, but rest assured, this isn't over,' he warned her softly.

'Oh, it most certainly is over,' Sophie told him heatedly, knowing it should never have begun. That she should never have allowed Max to annoy her to the point she had physically attacked him.

'I don't think so.' Max eyed her contemplatively. 'What I do think is that you should stay here tonight, Sophie,' he added huskily.

She gave him a startled look. 'What? Why?'

He shrugged. 'It's Christmas Eve, public transport is going to be awful and you'll be coming back here early tomorrow morning anyway, to prepare lunch. And there are certainly plenty of bedrooms here for you to choose from,' he added ruefully.

It was Christmas Eve, and as yet Sophie had no idea how she was going to get home tonight, let alone to come back here in the morning; none of the trains and buses were running, and she doubted there would be a deluge of taxis running on Christmas Day either. If any.

But stay here for the night?

In Max Hamilton's apartment?

She didn't think so.

Besides which, Sophie had a distinct feeling that Max had already decided which bedroom, given the option, *he* would choose for her to stay in.

And then there was Henry to think of.

She gave a shake of her head. 'I can't.'

'Why the hell not?'

Her mouth firmed at the dismissal in his tone. 'I have to go back to the flat tonight. Henry...'

'Isn't your lover. Or your boyfriend.' Max's eyes glittered darkly.

'Neither are you,' Sophie retorted heatedly.

And instantly wished that she hadn't.

Max had held her a couple of times, had kissed and caressed her and she had wrestled him to the kitchen floor once, but that was the extent of their relationship. Max might give every impression of behaving like a jealous lover right now but, from those stories Sophie had read about him in the media over the years, he didn't do the boyfriend thing. Ever. He did sometimes escort a lover, but never anything approaching the permanence of being called any woman's boyfriend.

As the woman Cynthia had found out to her cost? It was a distinct possibility.

Just as it was a distinct possibility—a certainty—that Sophie would never see Max again after Christmas.

'I apologise for what happened just now.' Sophie sighed wearily. 'I'm just a little... Thank you for your offer of staying here for the night, but my answer has to be no. Now, if you wouldn't mind, I need to finish cooking dinner,' she dismissed briskly, avoiding even looking at Max.

Max continued to look searchingly at Sophie as she turned to inspect the contents of the saucepan she had been stirring when he'd first entered the kitchen just a short time ago.

He easily noted the way her face had now paled. That weary droop to her shoulders. The slight trembling of her hand as she gave the contents of the saucepan a stir.

And knew that he should just leave this alone. Should just leave Sophie alone. That he was playing with fire. That desiring her, wanting to be with her, might just consume him. If it hadn't already done so.

At the same time as he knew that he couldn't leave this, that just the thought of Sophie returning to spend the rest of the evening with some other man, even one that she had acknowledged wasn't her lover or her boyfriend, was going to keep him awake for most of the night again. Most? He knew from experience that it was going to be all night!

Which basically meant it wasn't going to happen.

# CHAPTER NINE

'I'LL DRIVE YOU HOME later tonight and you can pick up some clothes for staying here for the rest of Christmas, at the same time as you explain the situation to Henry.'

Sophie eyed Max warily as she slowly turned to look across the kitchen at him. Instantly feeling a melting sensation deep inside her, a longing, an ache for him.

Did that mean she was falling in love with Max Hamilton?

That inner melting sensation could be lust, but the fact that her heart gave a jolt in her chest every time she so much as looked at him would seem to imply that she felt something more than that. Something Sophie was sure she had never felt for any of those boys she had dated casually before her mother became so ill.

Perhaps because they had been boys and Max was so obviously a man?

A decisive and determined man who had now decided, and was just as determined, that she was going to stay here in his apartment for the rest of the Christmas holiday.

In his bedroom?

It wasn't such a huge leap to take when she considered the passion that seemed to flare up between the two of them so easily, along with his threat earlier that *this wasn't over*. In truth, Sophie wasn't sure she would have the strength to resist if that was what Max had also decided.

She straightened. 'I'm not sure what situation you're referring to.

'Also,' she continued firmly as he would have spoken, 'as I've already said, thank you for the offer, but I really can't stay here.' There was no way she could possibly leave Henry on his own in Sally's flat for the next two days and nights. Or allow Max to realise it was Sally's apartment she was staying in...

'Because of Henry,' Max guessed.

Her chin rose. 'Yes.'

His eyes were narrowed to glittering emerald slits. 'What aren't you telling me?'

Sophie gave a humourless laugh. 'There are so many things I haven't told you—and that you haven't asked—that I wouldn't even know where to begin.'

His mouth thinned. 'I've asked about Henry.'

'And I've told you all that you need to know about him.'

'I beg to differ.'

'You—'

'I do know that you're twenty-four years old,'

Max continued determinedly. 'That both your parents are dead. That you're currently taking a catering and business course at college. That you're already an amazing cook, if those smells coming from the oven are any indication,' he added appreciatively. 'That you claim not to have a current boyfriend or lover.' He scowled darkly before his brow cleared as he looked at her. 'That you have an understated and yet totally mesmerising beauty. And the most amazingly soft and kissable lips.' His voice had lowered huskily, seductively. 'That your breasts are extremely sensitive to my touch...'

'That's enough,' Sophie cut in uncomfortably, Max's last two claims embarrassing her, as the previous ones had surprised her. Max thought she was beautiful? That aside, he did know a lot more about her than she had realised.

As she knew a lot about him?

She knew that he was thirty-four years old. That both his parents had died around Christmas sixteen years ago, probably in an accident of some kind. That he was a self-made billionaire who shied away from relationships, perhaps because of the early loss of his parents, resulting in a fear of emotional commitment?

That he was without doubt the most attractive man Sophie had ever met in her life. That he had the most amazingly soft and sensuous lips. That the hardness of his arousal—a direct response to her proximity?—had been pressed against her just minutes ago.

'We have plenty of time to fill in the other details later, surely?' Max urged huskily.

Such as the fact that Sophie was falling in love with him?

She somehow doubted that was something Max wished to hear. From any woman. 'I'm sorry, but my answer is still no,' she refused again stubbornly.

His jaw tightened. 'I am driving you home, Sophie, and you are staying here for the rest of Christmas.'

'You—'

'It's settled, Sophie,' he added decisively, putting an end to the conversation by turning sharply on his heel and leaving the kitchen.

And a very flustered and equally frustrated Sophie.

SHE REMAINED FLUSTERED and frustrated for the rest of the evening, Max insisting she would sit down in the dining room with the family to eat dinner with them. An invitation that was echoed by the whole of the Hilton family, thus making it impossible for Sophie to refuse without making a scene.

She felt most uncomfortable removing her pinafore and sitting down at the table with all of them to enjoy the first course of homemade pâté, followed by the main course of salmon and assorted vegetables, and then a delicious chocolate concoction made from her own recipe, in deference to five-year-old Amy.

Even more disturbing was having Max sitting next to her, looking devastatingly attractive in an emerald-green cashmere sweater and black tailored trousers, and insisting on serving her food to her. As if she really were a guest rather than the hired help.

As if she were Max's very personal guest.

Having Max behave so attentively towards her made Sophie a little uncomfortable, but if the Hiltons noticed it then they chose not to comment on it. They were a gregarious family, the conversation never flagging, and Max became equally relaxed in their easy-going company.

To add to the excitement of the evening, Janice made the announcement that she was expecting her second child as they lingered at the dinner table drinking coffee and eating the chocolates Sophie had made. Amy was ecstatic at the thought of having a baby brother or sister, but Sophie noticed that Tom and Max seemed less enthusiastic as they shared a concerned glance.

Causing Sophie to wonder, with the timing of the announcement and Tom and Max's attitude to the news, if perhaps this second pregnancy had something to do with the couple's earlier marital problems.

A question she put to Max when he drove her back to the flat later that evening.

Sophie had lost that part of the argument, at least.

As she had fully expected she might, after Max had been so insistent earlier this evening, and noticeably hadn't drunk any wine with his meal. Because he'd had every intention of driving her home, no matter what her objections. The Hiltons had added to the pressure of her accepting Max's offer of driving her home by assuring her they had every intention of clearing away after dinner.

In the end it was just easier for Sophie to accept Max's offer rather than trying to find a firm who had an available taxi that would come out this late on Christmas Eve. Most of London's taxis would be busy driving people home from parties and clubs this evening.

However, she had no intention of losing the argument regarding staying at Max's apartment for the rest of Christmas.

She had cautiously given Max an address that was in the general area of Sally's flat, rather than specific to it; there was absolutely no reason why Max should ever have bothered himself to learn where his PA lived, but Sophie thought it best not to take any chances.

'Janice isn't supposed to have any more children,' Max answered Sophie now with a grimace as he drove his car through the busy London streets. Christmas lights were blazing everywhere and a light sprinkling of snow had started to fall to add to the magic of the evening.

'What does that mean?'

He shrugged. 'She had a difficult time with Amy's birth and the doctors advised that she not have any more children. Tom offered to have a vasectomy at the time, but Janice wouldn't allow it. Any more than she would agree to have this pregnancy terminated when it was confirmed last month, which is why she and Tom argued and Tom moved out for a couple of weeks, hoping to shock her into changing her mind. It didn't, so Tom's just given up. My sister can be extremely stubborn when she wants to be,' he added with a frown. 'And yes, it's a family trait,' he said drily as he saw the knowing rise of Sophie's brows.

'I would never have guessed,' she drawled mockingly, before sobering. 'Is Janice going to be all right?'

'Tom and I will ensure that she is,' Max confirmed grimly; he had no intention of losing his sister too. 'Which street and building?' he prompted as they entered the area of London where Sophie had said she was staying.

'Anywhere around here will be fine—'

'It's snowing heavier than ever, Sophie, so which street and which building?' Max repeated evenly.

'There's really no need for you to—'

'Sophie.'

Just her name, even spoken in that flat, undemanding tone, and Sophie knew that Max expected her to answer him without further argument.

Unlike the argument she knew was going to

ensue when she told him she wouldn't be driving back with him.

But he was right about the snow; it was falling more heavily. The roads remained clear because of the amount of traffic on them, but the pathways were definitely being covered in a layer of light and fluffy, and no doubt slippery, snow.

Her mouth firmed as she made her decision. 'Take the next left and the building is halfway along that street.'

'Thank you,' he accepted tightly before following her instructions.

Sophie's trepidation grew as they neared Sally's building. So far, Max didn't seem to have made any connection between the name of the road and his PA, and Sophie could only hope that he never did.

She had absolutely no idea what his reaction would be if he were to realise, at this late date, that it was Sally's flat she was staying in, and that Henry was in fact her cousin's cat.

To be fair, Sophie could have had no idea a situation like tonight would ever happen when she had persuaded Sally into letting her be the one to 'deliver Christmas' to Max Hamilton's apartment. She really had thought she would just do her job, get paid and never see Max Hamilton again.

Instead of which, Sophie was now caught up in a situation that could prove disastrous for Sally, and was more than a little dangerous to her.

## CHAPTER TEN

'I'M GETTING COVERED in more snow the longer you keep me standing out here, Sophie,' Max drawled pointedly as she made no effort to get out of the car once he had parked next to the pavement and come round to open the passenger door for her.

She shot him an irritated glance. 'There was absolutely no need for you to get out of the car in the first place.'

'There's every reason when you're coming straight back with me. And sooner rather than later,' he added with a grim look up at the heavily snow-laden sky.

'I'm not…'

'Get out of the damned car, Sophie,' he bit out impatiently. 'We can argue about this again once we're inside out of the cold.' Max was enjoying the snow, if he was honest; it snowed so rarely in London, but especially at Christmastime, that it was rather lovely to see.

Unless it was just that he was turning into a romantic sop as a result of this unexpected and inexplicable attraction he had felt towards Sophie from the beginning? An attraction that only seemed to deepen with each day that passed.

He could think of a few people, mainly female, who would definitely find the idea of him becoming a romantic sop highly amusing.

Sophie gave him a disgruntled glance as she finally climbed out of the car, pulling up the white fur-lined hood of her red duffel coat over her hair as she did so.

'You look like Mrs Santa Claus.' Max grinned appreciatively as he closed and locked the car door before taking a firm hold beneath her elbow and walking with her across the pavement to the front door of the four-storey building.

Sophie shot him another quelling glance as she paused after unlocking the door into the building. 'As I said, there is absolutely no reason for you to come up with me because I'm not coming back with you.'

'And I said we'd talk about that again once we're inside,' he reminded with deceptive lightness.

Sophie's frustration grew as she watched how the falling snow was settling lightly on the darkness of Max's hair and the shoulders of his dark brown sheepskin jacket. The stubborn expression on his face said he had every intention of accompanying her up to the flat. And going inside.

She quickly did an inventory of Sally's flat inside her head. As far as she could remember, it had been clean and tidy when she'd left this morning, and Sally kept all of her photos of herself and Josh in her bedroom so there were no incriminating photos of her cousin around in the main room. Henry was a bit of a problem, but with any luck he would have settled himself somewhere for the night and be comfortably asleep.

'I'm really not coming back with you, Max,' she repeated firmly.

'And I'm really not going to continue arguing with you about this in the middle of the street,' he came back mildly as he pointedly pushed open the door to the building before standing back and waiting for her to enter.

Another argument Sophie knew she had lost as she strode inside the warmth of the building, frowning as they stepped into the lift together. She once again went through every room in Sally's flat in her head, desperately trying to remember if there was anything in the main rooms to give away the identity of the owner.

Max studied Sophie between narrowed lids as he leant back against the opposite side of the lift, noting the flush to her cheeks and the way she was fidgeting with the keys in her hand. 'Nervous about introducing me to Henry?' he taunted.

'No!' Her eyes flashed darkly.

'You're definitely nervous about something.'

'I'm annoyed, actually, because of the way you bullied me into this. I'm not a child, Max, and I don't appreciate being treated like one, either,' she added impatiently as he stepped out of the lift beside her into the hallway.

Max had no doubt that Sophie was spoiling for another argument. Just as he was convinced that her reaction to his insistence on driving her home and accompanying her up to the flat she was staying in was slightly...off. Out of proportion to the situation, because there was no way she would be able to get back to his apartment tomorrow if the snow kept falling as heavily as it was.

'Nor do I have any intention of introducing you to Henry,' she continued stubbornly as she came to a stop outside one of the doors.

Yes, definitely off, Max decided.

'What's the big deal, Sophie?'

She was behaving far too edgily for Max to be one hundred per cent convinced as to her claim of having only a platonic relationship with this guy Henry.

Not that he thought Sophie had ever lied to him—on the contrary, she could be too damned honest for comfort at times. It was just that the more she tried to fob him off, the more determined Max became to meet this Henry and judge the situation for himself.

He gave a shake of his head. 'I really can't see what your problem is about the two of us meeting.'

'I don't remember asking to be introduced to your friend Cynthia,' Sophie came back heatedly.

'Ah, I'd forgotten, you must have heard my side

of that telephone conversation with her a couple of days ago,' Max acknowledged ruefully. 'Cynthia had ideas about our previous relationship that in no way coincided with my own,' he dismissed grimly. 'I've only been out with her a few times, and I haven't so much as seen her for over a week.'

'You don't have to explain yourself to me,' Sophie assured dismissively.

'Any more than you need to explain yourself to me in regards to Henry?'

'Exactly.'

Max's eyes narrowed at her vehemence. 'Is Cynthia the reason you've been so determined to keep your distance from me?'

Sophie gave an inelegant snort. 'That doesn't seem to have worked out too well for me so far, now does it?'

Max gave a satisfied grin at the truth of that statement; he didn't seem to be able to keep his hands off Sophie for longer than a few minutes at a time, and she wasn't exactly fighting him off either. 'The difference being that I'm no longer even seeing Cynthia, whereas you're actually sharing an apartment with Henry,' he pointed out softly.

Sophie drew in a frustrated breath. 'You really are the most persistently stubborn man I have ever...'

'Ever what?' Max prompted huskily as Sophie

broke off the statement abruptly, her cheeks blushing a fiery red.

*Ever known she was falling in love with*, Sophie inwardly acknowledged, disgusted by her weakness.

The only man she had ever known she was falling in love with.

Max Hamilton, of all men.

She had to be a masochist to have ever allowed such a thing to happen.

Allowed it?

It had crept up on her these past few days without her even realising it was happening.

And now it was too late, she acknowledged with an inward groan.

Because, as Max steadily held her gaze with his as his head slowly began to lower towards hers, Sophie knew that she was already in love with him.

Her knees actually went weak at the first touch of Max's lips against hers, and she might even have collapsed at his feet in their handmade Italian leather shoes if she hadn't reached up to grasp onto the collar of his jacket.

It was certainly impossible for her to pull back from responding to that dizzying kiss. Or to resist when Max continued to kiss her as he took the keys to the flat out of her hand. Although she did manage to make a throaty murmur of protest as he unlocked the door and gently pushed her inside.

'No Henry,' Max murmured with satisfaction as

the darkness and silence of the apartment told him that the two of them were alone.

Unless Henry had already gone to bed? Which, as far as Max was concerned, was just as good as the two of them being alone.

'I've been wanting to do this again for hours,' he acknowledged throatily before backing Sophie up against the wall, capturing both her hands in his and raising them above her head before taking hungry possession of her mouth.

The hardness of Max's arousal pressing up against her caused a responding ache and dampness between Sophie's own thighs as she returned the heat of his kisses, their lips tasting, tongues duelling, teeth biting, the two of them hungry for each other. For being closer still, as Max easily dispensed with both of their coats before pressing into her hotly.

Sophie was breathing hard by the time Max finally raised his head to look down at her with glittering eyes. 'Bedroom?' he prompted economically.

Definitely not the bedroom, Sophie had enough sense left to decide; not only were there recriminating photographs of Sally and Josh in there, but Henry's noticeable absence gave her the feeling that he was currently curled up asleep on the bed. No doubt in feline protest at being left on his own for much of today!

'Sitting room,' she substituted breathlessly.

'Take me there,' he encouraged throatily as he took a firm hold of her hand.

Sophie found her way down the hallway in the darkness—darkness was good, less chance this way of Max seeing anything he shouldn't.

Besides, it wasn't completely dark in the sitting room, the layer of snow on the ground outside causing a reflection of light to glow eerily through the windows, giving everything a strange grey effect, including Max and Sophie.

'Remember that ju-jitsu move you made on me earlier this evening?' he prompted huskily.

Sophie looked up at Max as she replied uncertainly, 'Yes.' Max's teeth gleamed down at her in a grin in the darkness even as Sophie felt her feet leave the floor, the breath knocked out of her lungs as she landed flat on her back on the sofa. 'Max!'

'Fair's fair,' he murmured with satisfaction, taking his weight on his elbows as he slowly lowered himself down on top of her, the two of them touching from chest to thighs as he claimed her lips once again.

Sophie felt surrounded by Max even as she gave herself up to the pleasure of that kiss. To his heat. His smell. The sheer immediacy of him.

She was completely lost to that pleasure as she felt the warmth of his hand cupping her breast beneath her sweater. The soft pad of his thumb was a light, and then harder, caress against her already roused nipple. His lips roamed the length of her throat, tasting, biting and murmuring his approval as she let out a low groan of pleasure as he pushed up her sweater. She had only the thin barrier of her bra between her flesh and his as Max suckled one of her nipples into the heat of his mouth.

'White or cream?' he murmured seconds later as his kissed his way across to its twin.

'Cream.' Sophie didn't even pretend not to understand him.

'Are you wearing a matching thong?'

'Yes.'

'I need to see that!' Max groaned, heat having coursed through his body, his arousal hot and pulsing, just visualising Sophie in a thong.

His gaze held hers as he moved slowly down her body until he knelt between her parted thighs. He unfastened the button and zip of her trousers before folding the material back, his breath catching in his throat, mouth going dry, as he revealed the scrap of cream lace covering the neatly trimmed thatch of curls between her thighs.

'You're beautiful, Sophie,' he murmured huskily as he sat back to slide her trousers down to her thighs, able to see the thong more clearly now—a small triangle of lace which barely covered those fiery red curls, with an inch-wide band of lace about her waist.

'Turn over,' he encouraged throatily even as he shifted sideways to allow the movement. 'Please, Sophie,' he urged gruffly as she hesitated.

Sophie's cheeks were as fiery red as her curls as she allowed Max to remove her trousers completely before she rolled onto her front, looking back over her shoulder as she heard Max's indrawn breath.

'You have the most gorgeous bottom, Sophie,' he complimented even as his hands moved to caress it.

'Max...' It was Sophie's turn to gasp, her fingers clenching, nails biting into the cushion beneath her, as she now felt the cool touch of Max's lips against the heat of her skin.

'Beautiful,' he murmured admiringly, his breath a hot caress against her flesh as he kissed the base of her spine. 'Can I—? What the hell?' He gave a sudden harsh cry.

Sophie was too lost in her pleasurable euphoria to realise what had happened at first, and then it took her a minute or so to realise that Henry had chosen that moment to show himself by launching himself onto Max's back.

Claws out, no doubt!

# CHAPTER ELEVEN

Sophie was sitting on the edge of the sofa, still struggling to pull her trousers back on and fasten them by the time Max had located and flicked on the light switch. He stood looking searchingly around the room for whatever it was that had attacked him, green eyes narrowing as he located the black cat sitting on the back of one of the armchairs. The cat's back arched as he gave a disapproving hiss in the direction of their late-night visitor.

'Bad cat, Henry,' Sophie scolded, fully dressed again now as she moved to shoo him off the chair and he ran and hid beneath the coffee table.

'Henry is a *cat*?' Max exploded disbelievingly.

Sophie froze as she realised her mistake. A mistake that could cost her dearly. Could cost Sally dearly too, if Max made the connection between them at last.

'Sophie?' Max prompted harshly.

She gave a pained wince, feeling the colour drain from her cheeks as she slowly turned to face Max and instantly saw that the indulgent lover of a few minutes ago had been replaced with the cold and arrogant Max Hamilton, billionaire CEO and owner of Hamilton Enterprises.

'I'm waiting for an answer, Sophie.' The softness of his tone sounded even more dangerous than his previously harsh one.

She moistened her lips before speaking. 'I'm… I'm cat-sitting for…for a friend while she's away over Christmas.'

'That wasn't what I asked!' There was no sign of so much as a crack in Max's icy veneer.

Sophie swallowed before confirming heavily, 'Yes, Henry is a cat.'

'And you deliberately let me think——'

'I never lied to you.'

'You lied by omission!'

'You *assumed* Henry was a man.'

'And you allowed me to continue to assume it.'

'Yes.' She sighed at the cold accusation in his tone.

'Why?'

'I just… I thought it best… It just seemed the wisest thing to do, in the circumstances!'

Those arctic green eyes narrowed to icy slits. 'And what circumstances are those? Damn it; why couldn't you have just told me that Henry was a cat and be done with——' He broke off, becoming very still as he now eyed Sophie speculatively. 'What's your friend's name?' he prompted softly.

Yep, there was definitely going to be trouble,

Sophie acknowledged with another wince, in all probability for both Sally and herself.

'Answer me, Sophie!' Max snapped harshly.

'This is all my fault. Sally had absolutely nothing to do with it.' She rushed into speech. 'She— We— I thought it best if you didn't know of the connection, then if anything went wrong, if I made a mess of things, there would be no comeback on Sally.'

Max continued to look at her coldly. 'What connection would that be?'

Trust Max to have latched onto that part of her statement!

Just one glance at the cold implacability of Max's expression and those icily glittering green eyes was enough to warn Sophie against even attempting to continue to deceive him about her family connection to Sally. Any further prevarication really wasn't an option when he was already so angry. And it could result in her getting Sally fired from her job as Max's PA. If that hadn't happened already, as far as Max was concerned.

Her gaze lowered from meeting his piercing green one. 'Sally is my cousin.'

'Your cousin?' he repeated softly.

'She and my Aunt Rachel and Uncle William are the only relatives I have, yes,' Sophie confirmed huskily.

'In that case, why didn't you go to Canada and spend Christmas with them?'

'I wasn't... I didn't feel up to travelling all that

way yet, let alone— I offered to look after Henry instead,' she stated firmly.

Max continued to look at the top of Sophie's bent head for several long seconds before he turned away abruptly. He moved to stand in front of one of the windows, his clenched fists thrust into the pockets of his trousers as he absorbed, and tried to make sense of, this conversation.

Sophie was the cousin of his PA, Sally.

She was cat-sitting her cousin's pet while Sally and her parents were in Canada meeting her fiancé's family.

Leaving Sophie to 'deliver Christmas' to Max's apartment.

His shoulders tensed as he slowly turned. 'You either overheard my conversation with Sally that day in her office, or Sally repeated it to you.' It was a statement rather than a question.

'Sally would never do that,' she assured him heatedly. 'I—I was meeting Sally for lunch that day and I overheard the two of you talking. I thought it best to wait outside in the hallway till you'd finished,' she admitted gruffly.

'And in the meantime you eavesdropped on a private conversation!' Max's top lip curled back contemptuously.

'Not intentionally! I just— I had arrived at Sally's office a little early for lunch and the two of you were talking and I didn't want to interrupt. I couldn't help overhearing what you were discussing and—'

'I should take a breath, Sophie,' he advised scathingly.

She gave an impatient shake of her head. 'Sally had nothing to do with the decision not to tell you of our family connection; that really was all my idea. Sally was short of time and I had nothing else to do over Christmas except look after Henry, and so I offered to organise Christmas for you and your family.'

'To "deliver Christmas" was how you described it that first day, if I remember correctly,' Max rasped harshly. 'A direct quote from part of my conversation in Sally's office that day. Which is no doubt the reason you were so damned contemptuous towards me when we first met.'

'I thought you were just a Bah Humbug. I had no idea then of the reason why you've avoided celebrating Christmas for so many years,' she defended uncomfortably.

But she had realised the reason now, Max accepted, after Janice's indiscreet comments about their parents both dying at Christmas sixteen years ago.

None of which changed their current situation in the slightest.

'Perhaps in future that will teach you not to make snap judgements about peo—' Max broke off his scathing comment to look at Sophie searchingly.

'You said that Sally and her parents are your only relatives?'

She gave a puzzled frown. 'Yes.'

Max remembered that Sally had taken a week's compassionate leave during the summer so that she could spend some time with her cousin, whose mother had just died after a long and painful illness. And then there had been another day off following that week, so that Sally could attend her aunt's funeral.

And Sophie's unfinished comment just now regarding her desire not to travel *yet*.

Was it possible that her aunt had been Sophie's mother?

'When did your own parents die, Sophie?' he prompted huskily.

She frowned. 'I don't see…'

'Humour me,' Max bit out abruptly.

'My father died fifteen years ago, and my mother…my mother died six months ago,' she acknowledged huskily, her gaze not meeting his even though her chin rose challengingly. 'It's because she was so ill for so long that I didn't finish my original college course.'

Max was angry with Sophie for not telling him of her connection to Sally. And even more furious with her for allowing him to believe that Henry was a man.

At the same time he couldn't help but feel compassion for her recent loss. Because it was recent;

losing a beloved parent was an ache, a hollowness that could never be truly filled. And he, of all people, should know how it felt to lose your parents, and to spend that first Christmas without them. Especially so when it had been just Sophie and her mother for so many years.

There were also his own strange, as yet inexplicable desires, feelings even, for Sophie. Feelings he was just too angry at the moment to even try to comprehend. Feelings that made him even angrier about this situation, if anything.

One thing he did know, no matter how cross he might be with Sophie right now—he had no intention of leaving her here to spend Christmas alone with that hissing, spitting fur ball!

He drew in a deep breath. 'Does Sally have a travel basket for Henry?'

Sophie looked startled. 'Sorry?'

'You may well have cause to be before this Christmas is over,' Max warned grimly. 'But all I'm interested in knowing for now is whether or not you have a basket we can put that monster into—' he shot Henry a quelling glance as he saw the black cat had slunk out from beneath the coffee table and was now eyeing him balefully '—while we drive back to my apartment.'

Sophie wasn't just startled now; she was dumbstruck. Was Max seriously suggesting that she should not only continue to spend the rest of Christmas with him and his family at his apartment, but that she should also bring along the belligerent Henry to join them, too?

Because he wanted her to spend Christmas with him?

Doubtful, after this recent conversation.

It was more likely to be because she had been hired to 'deliver Christmas' to him and his family and Max still expected her to do exactly that.

'The snow is falling heavier than ever, Sophie,' Max rasped at her continued silence. 'Which means we have to leave soon if we're going to get back at all.'

It was the latter, of course, Sophie accepted heavily. She really shouldn't harbour any illusions of it being anything else, despite their earlier intimacy.

She might have fallen in love with Max in just a few short days, but he certainly didn't feel anything approaching that emotion for her.

And he never would…

## CHAPTER TWELVE

'WHO WOULD HAVE thought that a five-year-old could make a lapdog—or, in this case, cat—out of the fur ball?' Max mused as he entered the kitchen of his apartment. He'd just spent several minutes in the sitting room watching Amy carry Henry around in her arms as if he were a baby while the cat looked up at her adoringly. 'He's a disgrace to the feline race!'

Sophie couldn't help but laugh as she turned, her face flushed, from taking warmed mince pies from the oven, ready for an afternoon snack.

The last twenty-four hours had gone more smoothly than she could ever have hoped for, following that awful scene between herself and Max at Sally's flat yesterday evening.

Present opening this morning had been fun. How could it not be, in the company of a five-year-old who still believed in Father Christmas?

To Sophie's surprise, she had received gifts not only from Janice and Tom, and a separate one from Amy, but there had also been a present under the tree for her from Max. A beautiful pashmina in shades of russet and brown, which she had been convinced Janice must have chosen for him until the other woman assured her that she hadn't.

Sophie's heart had given a leap at the thought of Max having gone out to buy a present for her. A pleasure that had been instantly dampened by the blandness of his expression when she had given him her heartfelt thanks for the gift, and he had distractedly thanked her for his own present of the book from her.

Sophie had kept herself busy in the kitchen all morning and Christmas lunch had been a great success. The turkey had been cooked to perfection, along with an assortment of roasted vegetables, with Christmas and chocolate pudding to follow—the latter was for Amy—accompanied by Sophie's own special brandy cream and ice cream.

Sophie had still been a little uncomfortable as the family once again insisted that she had to sit down and join them for the meal. She was so very aware, still, of the gulf that now yawned between herself and Max.

But she needn't have worried because Max had gone out of his way to be polite to her today.

Too polite, if Sophie was honest with herself. She much preferred the rude irascible Max to this polite stranger.

She eyed him warily now. 'Can I get you anything?'

'I think the two of us should talk, don't you?' He leant back against the kitchen table, arms folded in front of his powerful chest as he studied her from between narrowed lids. He looked very handsome in a black silk shirt and faded blue jeans, his dark hair as tousled as ever.

Sophie gave him a nervous glance as she placed the mince pies onto a plate. 'If this is about me not telling you of my family connection to Sally...'

'It isn't. Although I'm interested to know why you made that decision.' His eyes had narrowed questioningly.

Sophie chewed on her bottom lip. 'Sally mentioned that you once had a problem with a friend of hers who took over as your PA while Sally was away on holiday.'

'Cathy Lawrence,' he muttered with feeling.

'Yes.' She winced at those obvious feelings of disgust. 'I was the one who persuaded Sally into not revealing our own family connection. Just in case I messed up too,' she added awkwardly.

His eyes darkened with amusement. 'The difference being that I would have welcomed you throwing yourself at me every chance you got.'

'Instead of which, I threw you.' Her cheeks burned with remembered embarrassment. 'Onto the kitchen floor,' she reminded him with a wince.

Max shrugged his broad shoulders. 'I deserved it.'

'But...'

'Stop worrying, Sophie; I assure you, there will be no repercussions on Sally for any of this. The opposite, in fact,' he added huskily. 'This Christmas has been more than I could ever have hoped for. It's been magical,' Max continued softly. 'And that's mainly due to you.'

'Me?' Sophie echoed softly. 'I didn't do anything that you didn't pay me to do.'

Max's mouth tightened. 'We both know you've gone way above and beyond what I asked for,' he corrected huskily. 'In fact, none of this—' his glance encompassed the whole of his apartment; the sound of his niece's laughter heard from the next room, the decorations, the wonderful, and deeply nostalgic, smells of the Christmas food cooking '—would have been possible without you.'

'I'm sure you would have managed well enough without me, hired someone else to...'

'That's the whole point, Sophie.' Max straightened as he looked down at her intensely. 'I've realised this last few days that I don't want anyone else. That managing is exactly what I've been doing for so many years. Without you.'

She shot him a nervous glance from beneath lowered lashes. 'I don't understand.'

He smiled at her with sympathy; after the shock and, yes, he admitted it, anger of realising that Sophie had hidden from him that she was Sally's cousin it had taken him twenty-four hours of soul-searching to reach his own conclusions as to why he felt so angry. He couldn't expect Sophie to understand how he felt after just a couple of minutes of conversation. Or expect her to feel the same way about him as he now felt about her.

The only encouragement he had was that he knew Sophie responded to him on a physical level, at least. The rest would have to be worked at.

Which was a pretty scary thought for a man who had never in his life felt the least inclination to work at a relationship with a woman before now.

Before Sophie.

He smiled slightly. 'I love the book you bought me for Christmas, by the way. I've been meaning to buy it for months, I just never got around to it, was always too busy doing something else.'

'I'm glad you like it.' She still eyed him warily. 'As you can see, I love my pashmina.' She was wearing it about her neck right now, the russet and brown colours looking wonderful against the red of her hair.

'I'm glad.' Max nodded. 'Sophie...' He gave a grimace as he paused impatiently.

'Yes?'

Max straightened his shoulders determinedly. 'I may as well come straight out with it and just tell you how I feel.'

'How you feel about what?' Sophie looked completely bewildered by his intensity.

She might look even more bewildered in a moment, but it was a risk Max had to take. That he was determined to take. 'Everything you've said and thought about me was correct. I've avoided celebrating Christmas for years because of my parents' deaths on Christmas Eve sixteen years ago. I found it an irritation; I even resented having to organise Christmas here this year for Janice and Amy. And I have a reputation when it comes to women. Have never so much as contemplated a serious relationship with one.'

'Max...'

'Until now,' he completed firmly. 'Until you,' he added huskily as he reached out to take both her hands in his. 'Sophie—' He drew in a deep steadying breath. 'Being with you these past few days, feeling my apartment become a home rather than just a place for me to sleep. Laughing with you, arguing with you, kissing you...'

'Oh, please don't!' She groaned her embarrassment.

He gave a wide smile. 'I love kissing you and touching you, Sophie. Just as I love laughing and arguing with you. In fact, I love it all so much, I love *you* so much, I want to go on doing it for the rest of my life.'

Sophie had ceased breathing as she gazed up at Max searchingly, wonderingly, sure she must be dreaming. Or that she had somehow fallen over and bumped her head and was imagining all of this. Because Max—Max Hamilton, billionaire CEO and owner of Hamilton Enterprises, a man who had avoided emotional involvement for all of his adult life—couldn't possibly have just told her that he loved her. Could he?

She gave a disbelieving shake of her head. 'You were so angry with me last night.'

'I was angry with myself,' he corrected. 'And totally confused by the depth of that anger. It's taken me until now to admit why that was. Sophie, I'm no good at this sort of thing, have no idea how to go about courting you, wooing you, winning you, let alone persuading you into loving me as I love you.' He drew in a deep breath. 'But I would dearly like you—in fact, I'm begging you—to give me a chance to at least try.'

Sophie couldn't speak, could still barely breathe, as she felt the hot tears gather in her eyes. Tears of happiness, not sorrow. Because, miracle of miracles, Max had just told her that he loved her.

*Max loved her!*

It was too huge, too immense, too intense for her to be able to fully take it in.

'Sophie, please,' Max groaned throatily at her continued silence. 'At least tell me you'll give me that chance. I couldn't bear it if— These past few days, being here with you, coming home to you, have shown me that it, and you as my wife, are what I want for the rest of my life.' He stared down at her intently.

'You want to marry me?' she gasped breathlessly.

'Of course I want to marry you.' Max looked

down at her sternly. 'What did you think I meant by courting, wooing and winning you?'

'I didn't think— Didn't know— Oh, yes, Max, I'll marry you!' She threw her arms about his neck as she launched herself into his arms. 'I love you too, Max. I love you so very much.' She beamed up at him. 'I didn't dare to hope, to dream, that you would ever feel the same way about me.'

Max looked down at her searchingly, his face lighting up with joy as he saw the truth of that love shining in the warmth of her eyes and her expressive face.

Miracles did happen, Max realised emotionally.

And Sophie was his own personal miracle.

A miracle he fully intended to love and cherish for the rest of his life.

EXACTLY A YEAR LATER, Sophie's main Christmas present to Max was to tell him that in approximately seven months' time they would be bringing yet another miracle to the happiness of their married life together. That she was expecting a cousin for Amy and her six-month-old brother, Barney...

\* \* \* \* \*

# *Snowed in with Her Boss*

## MAISEY YATES

*USA TODAY* bestselling author **Maisey Yates** lives in rural Oregon with her husband and three children. She feels the epic trek she takes several times a day from her office to her coffee-maker is a true example of her pioneer spirit. In 2009 Maisey sold her first book to Mills & Boon® Modern™. Since then it's been a whirlwind of sexy alpha males and happily-ever-afters and she wouldn't have it any other way. Maisey's favourite time of year is Christmas, when she can focus on family and friends. Visit her website at www.maiseyyates.com and look for her on Facebook.

# CHAPTER ONE

"PLEASE, SIR. WE NEED just one more shovelful of coal for the fire. Only, the bookkeepers are freezing, even with their fingerless gloves and stocking caps."

"What are you talking about, Amelia?" Luc Chevalier looked up from his desk at his assistant, who appeared, if possible, more doe-eyed than usual, her dark brows crinkling in the middle, her hands clasped in front of her chest.

"Embellishing my request for time off."

"It is not cold in this office. Neither do I have a...fireplace in here, and if I did, I wouldn't burn coal. I would burn wood."

*"A Christmas Carol,"* she said, blinking her owlish blue eyes. "I feel like a Dickensian street urchin." She sighed, brushing her bangs out of her eyes.

"I cannot give you time off."

"Think of Tiny Tim."

"I sincerely doubt anyone called Tiny Tim is depending on your presence over the holidays."

"You don't know that," she said.

He cleared his throat and shuffled the papers on his desk. "I do, actually. You have two sisters. You have no brothers. Your father's name is Michael. And unless you have a new nephew named Tim, there is no Tim."

"How do you remember all that? It makes it seem like you care."

"Not especially," he said, "it's just that I don't forget."

"Charming. Luc, it's Christmas. I need some extra time off."

"What is the date today, Amelia?"

"It's December 21."

"Then it is not Christmas. Christmas is one day. Not a week. Not four months as store displays might have you believe. One day. You will be off work in time on Christmas Eve to enjoy any religious services you may need to attend, and you will be off on the day of the holiday itself. But not the entire week before."

"Don't you have some sort of feast to get to? Family gathering?"

"You're well aware that I do not have a good relationship with anyone in my family, as my father is a terrible human being and my brother is barely a notch above him. I do not take holidays with them. I do not take holidays at all."

"Bah. Humbug," she said.

"In continuation of your *A Christmas Carol* theme. Very clever."

"Though, I feel, underappreciated in this setting."

"Which setting?"

"Your office. With a man who hates Christmas, the sound of children's laughter and classic literature."

"That's ridiculous," he said. "I'm quite fond of classic literature."

"Har. Har. Please, Luc."

He cleared his throat and stood up, watching Amelia's blue eyes widen slightly as he did. "I'm sorry, but I found out only an hour ago that I need to go to Aspen to speak to Don Fleischer about the acquisition of the resort. I can't afford to sit it out and wait until after Christmas."

Luc was relatively new to real estate. He was coming off being the CEO of one of Europe's largest investment firms. But after finding out his father was stealing from clients, he'd walked, after burning the generations-old institution to the ground.

His father had caused him enough pain over the course of his life, yet he'd continued to work for the old man and he had no idea why.

But he was done with that. He'd taken the money he'd earned off investments and started new, away from Chevalier Financial.

And that meant he couldn't let things simply sit just because some people felt the need to inject their lives with frivolity and trees inside their living rooms. He didn't get it, particularly, but then, the only function Christmas had ever served in his life was that it got his father out of the house nearly every night for the month of December for social engagements.

He'd always appreciated that about the holidays, anyway.

"Wait...what? We're going to Colorado?"

"Yes. You'll be compensated for travel, as always, and I will have you back in time for Christmas. Actual Christmas, and not these vague days leading up to it that everyone seems to want to spend in a red-and-green haze."

"Luc...my family is..."

"You can bring them back key chains. And a mug. I will give you spending money for cheesy, location-based souvenirs."

"Luc, I don't..."

"It is not a request, Amelia, it's part of your job."

She balled her hands into fists and raised them up, shaking them, the ring on her left hand glittering in the light. "Blast you, Luc Chevalier."

"Every year, Amelia. For the past three years. And you still act surprised?"

"You don't make me go on a last-minute business trip every year."

"No, but we have this discussion about Christmas every year. Though, this is the first year you've borrowed from *A Christmas Carol*. The year you stole from scripture to try and convince me was a particular low."

"On earth, peace and time off among men."

"We leave early tomorrow. We're taking the private plane, and I will have those candy cane lattes you like."

"And the candy stir sticks?" she asked.

"Yes, the candy stir sticks."

She sucked her lush bottom lip between her teeth and chewed on it for a moment, and he allowed himself some time to enjoy the sight.

He hadn't enjoyed a woman in…far too long. Starting up a new company meant there was no time for sex. Though, sex and his assistant should never be a part of the same train of thought. No matter how long it had been.

A good assistant was a lot harder to find than a good time in bed. And his very engaged assistant was off-limits for even more reasons than just employment.

"And scones?"

"In several flavors, though I believe cranberry is your seasonal preference."

A smile made the corners of her lips turn upward. "You remembered."

"Again, because I don't forget. Don't be flattered by it."

"I've known you for nearly four years and you've never once flattered me on purpose, Luc."

"But what does it really matter since you still end up getting the coffee you like?"

She lifted a shoulder. "I guess it doesn't. Though, don't think it atones for the fact that you're making me fly more than halfway across the country when I have Christmas shopping to do."

"You can shop online. During business hours. You do it, anyway."

Her eyes widened, her mouth dropping open in a perfect rendition of shock. "I do not."

"You do. On your phone. I've seen you do it."

"Vintage fashion goes fast. I have to be able to buy it when it comes up."

"And you have to be able to…I don't know, personally assist me when I need it."

She rolled her eyes. "When do I not, Luc?"

"You always do, which is why you still work for me. And speaking of the fact that you still work for me, perhaps it's time you went and did a little of that."

"Oh, Luc, Santa is going to bring you so many presents."

He smiled in spite of himself. Amelia had that way about her. She wasn't the type of person he would normally employ. Much less the type of person he would employ to work so closely with him.

She wasn't quiet or professional. She didn't seem to observe any sort of conventional dress code. Though her red shoes, black dress pants and oversize charcoal sweater, open at the front with a white button-up shirt dotted with birds were indeed office appropriate in the strictest sense, they were *not* conventional.

She also wasn't one to work with quiet efficiency.

Rather, she was one to work while whistling, or singing. She had a nice voice, soft and old-fashioned, like having a black-and-white movie flitting around the office.

And he should mind. She should drive him crazy. She should disrupt his peace of mind and his Zen, though many would argue he actually possessed no Zen. And yet, Amelia didn't bother him in the least. He found her a strange, if somewhat comforting presence.

She wasn't quietly efficient, but she was efficient, and sometimes her singing "A Few of My Favorite Things" was a nice signal that her efficiency was in full swing.

"Santa would be better off giving presents to someone who needs them," he said. "If I want something, I go out and get it. I don't need to wait for it to be brought to me."

She pursed her lips. "Yep. Well, I'm off to go and do all that work I have to do. Since I won't be in the office for…how many days?"

"We're only staying over one night, Amelia. You'll be back home in plenty of time for Christmas. Don't make your eyes all big."

"They're just like that," she said, blinking slowly.

He let out a deliberate sigh, then scooped the papers up from his desk and handed them to her. "No, they aren't. You definitely make them larger in different situations. You're doing it now, don't try and play innocent."

Dark-fringed eyes widened farther. "I am not."

He raised his brows and she raised hers back. "Off with you," he said, smiling again, because she just had that way about her.

"I'm off, Mr. Chevalier." Somehow when she said "Mr. Chevalier" it had a way of sounding less respectful than when she called him Luc.

"Good," he said.

"'Ohh, tidings of comfort and joy!'" she sang as she walked out.

"Well, that's going to be fun on a three-hour plane ride," he muttered, sitting back at his desk.

He might be adding alcohol of some kind to his latte. There was only so much holiday cheer he could stomach.

# CHAPTER TWO

AMELIA BRUSHED HER bangs out of her eyes, trying to undo the damage done by the wind as she'd boarded Luc's private plane.

She should be used to the opulence by now, but she wasn't. How could you get used to opulence on this scale? A giant plane, for two people and staff. It was bigger than her apartment, and definitely plusher. But then, she doubted Luc got anything at thrift shops.

She sat down on the couch and tried to ignore the dull buzz that filled her ears. Shell-shocked was about all that described her this morning. Not heartbroken, which was weird. Or not weird. But angry. And she was rarely angry.

But she was now. She felt...empty. And tricked. And in some ways relieved. But also confused.

*It's you I want to spend my life with. This isn't who I want to be.*

Well, what was she supposed to do with that? *Thanks for all this right around the holidays, Clint.*

She fiddled with her engagement ring, a heavy weight settling on her chest.

"Where is my latte?" she asked the empty room.

Luc chose that moment to stride—yes, stride, he was big on the striding—into the seating area of the plane. Her heart did a funny little jump thing. Like it did when he surprised her. It wasn't her fault. He was dead sexy, and no matter her current circumstances, she noticed. She noticed big-time.

From his lean, well-muscled build, to his smooth mocha skin, dark eyes and sensual lips... Oh, yes, Luc Chevalier was not a man a woman could ignore. Even a woman like her, who was ensnared in a relationship so complicated she didn't even want to look at the man she was engaged to, and should not want to look at any other man, period.

Stupid Clint. And his stupid issues. Issues that were hers because that's what happened when you cared for someone. When you'd loved them since you were sixteen.

Nine years. Nine years of being together, of buying into all kinds of stupid things she never should have, and now...well, she had no idea what.

Things with Clint had seemed simple at first. Then she'd started working for Luc and things had become immeasurably more complicated. She'd had a man in her life providing her with companionship, being the son her parents had never had and in general treating her like a sister while he was supposed to be her future husband. All while her boss slowly drove her crazy with the promise of lust and sex that had certainly not been a happening thing in her relationship.

Of course, Luc had never actually promised *her* sex. But he…exuded it. One look at him, and you knew, just knew, what those big, capable hands could do. Probably. It was all hypothetical for her. But her imagination was really good. It always had been. Heck, after all these dry years with Clint, it had to be. Honed, sharpened, etcetera.

He'd convinced her that waiting until marriage was romantic and right. And she'd felt…as if it showed how serious he was. As if it made her special. Of course, it might have been had he not been burning off *his* sexual needs with other people.

While she'd had nothing but fantasies. And scones. And shoes.

Lots and lots of shoes.

And complications. After this morning there were complications she'd never foreseen. Her entire life felt upended. Her family… Oh, this would destroy her family. Clint was the son her parents had never had and her marrying him was so darn approved of it was almost comical.

"Your latte will arrive after takeoff," Luc said, sitting in the chair opposite her, his masculine scent teasing her nose and making her stomach tighten. Working with him was hard on a girl's hormones. "Buckle up."

She obeyed, not even bristling at his commanding tone, because hey, she was used to it.

Honestly, it was a good thing he was as grumpy as he was. That sort of helped to counterbalance his sexiness. Okay, she lied. Sometimes his grumpiness was even enticing. Because it made every smile she eked out of him an achievement. It made him seem like a locked box holding something special inside and sometimes she got little glimpses of it, and it made her want to just…wrench him open sometimes.

But that was inappropriate. One should not want to wrench their boss open.

Yet she always had. Her fascination with Luc, with his moods, and his smile, and his good looks, had been there from day one. Her ring had kept her insulated against taking any of it too seriously or too far. But there had always been a little more to her feelings for him than was strictly appropriate.

A little flutter of excitement when he walked into the office in the morning that had absolutely no business being there.

The engines fired up, and they started moving down the runway. There were a lot of perks to one's boss having a private plane, but the efficiency and speed were top on the list. They achieved liftoff only a few minutes after she boarded, and she didn't even have to sit next to anyone with questionable hygiene.

Luc's hygiene was impeccable. He smelled like… well, he smelled like everything good and spicy. The man, ironically, smelled like Christmas.

"Thanks for that, Luc. So are you going to let

me in on the agenda for the next couple of days and why I'm so necessary?"

"You're necessary because you always are," he said, his accent caressing the words like a touch. A very sensual touch. He spoke very good English but there was a French flavor to his speech that never failed to make her feel all shivery.

"Well, thanks for that. But specifically, what function am I fulfilling?"

"I need you to help keep track of things. And to give your opinion. When I decide on what I want to offer, I'd like your take on things."

"But you're an expert on real estate. Surely you don't need my opinion."

"I do. I need people to want to come and stay in a resort. Obviously, it's being sold because it's not profitable at the moment, or at least it's not doing what Fleischer wants it to. Or else why would he sell? So I have to make the decision as to whether or not I can make it do what he can't."

"And you want my opinion for that?"

"Yes."

"I'm flattered. Look, that's the second time in two days you've flattered me. You're losing your edge."

"You can unbuckle now," he said, a command, not a request. Why did it make her go all shivery?

"Okay," she said, undoing the buckle because she wanted to, not because he'd told her to.

She leaned back in her seat, and the stewardess

appeared with a red-and-white mug, and a small plate with a scone. She also had Scotch for Luc.

"Wow. That's roguish of you. It's early."

"It's evening in Paris."

"And we're in New York."

"I'm still on Paris time."

"Have you been back to Paris in four years?"

He smiled and she gave herself a mental back pat.

"No." Then he unrepentantly lifted his glass to his lips and took a drink.

She admired him for it, if she was completely honest. He was a master at not giving a damn about what other people thought, or what the rules or conventions were. And to someone who was so bound to those same things, it was both awe-inspiring and terrifying.

She wished she could be like that for one fleeting moment. That she could say to hell with convention and reason. To hell with Clint and their past. To hell with what he was asking her to do. And with what her family might think.

But that wasn't her.

"I'll just stick with my latte."

He held his drink out. "You don't care to make it more interesting?"

"A full-fat latte is interesting enough," she said. "Trust me. Why are we leaving so early?"

"We have a breakfast meeting with Fleischer."

"A breakfast meeting?"

"Yes, after which we will spend our time enjoying the resort. I think he's hoping to drive the price up."

"By showing you a nice relaxing time? Doesn't he know you'd rather chew glass? Oh, no, he's probably going to foist holiday cheer on you!"

"Luckily," Luc said, leaning back, one long leg stretched out in front of him, the other bent at the knee, "I am immune. You, on the other hand, had better be careful."

"I'm already radiant with cheer," she said, smiling and fluttering her lashes at him. This, at least, felt normal. She'd forget all that other crap for now. No one ever teased Luc, she'd noticed that when she'd first come to work with him. But she did. She treated him like she did everyone else, well, with some added respect because he signed her paychecks, but her parents had always taught her that race, gender, class or general uptightness were never a reason to treat anyone differently.

So, in spite of the fact that he was as rich as God and scary as all get-out, she treated Luc like she did everyone. And weirdly, he seemed to like it. At least, she still had a job. So at the minimum he tolerated it.

Which she would accept.

"You do sort of radiate," he said, taking another drink of Scotch.

"Why don't I feel complimented?"

He lifted a shoulder. "I don't know. I need you to check on some properties while I deal with some final schematics approvals for the new build. And no singing."

"No singing?"

"Drink your latte."

"But I want to sing." She didn't really.

"No," he said, taking another sip of his Scotch as he took his laptop out of the bag that was positioned next to him, "singing."

She pulled a face and took her computer out, too. "I can sing in my mind."

"No, you can't."

"You don't own my thoughts, Luc Chevalier," she said, opening up her laptop and typing in her password.

"No, I meant you're incapable of singing in your head. You will be belting out something ridiculous in about five minutes. It's best if we put a moratorium on music."

"I can so sing in my head." She had a feeling she wouldn't, though. Not with her thoughts as crammed with gloom as they were.

They both put their heads down and started working. And it didn't take long for her to fill the empty space left by reading boring work reports with a Christmas carol. A few moments later Amelia felt her lips start moving and then...

"'God rest ye merry...'" She looked up, at Luc's dark, judgy gaze. She cleared her throat and looked back down. "Bah humbug, Mr. Scrooge."

But she didn't sing again. She worked. And she kept on that way until the plane landed in Denver.

"That landing was terrible," Amelia said as they got into the limo that was waiting for them in front.

"It always is here," he said. "It's all the mountains."

"Damn mountains," she muttered, putting her purse in her lap and curling up against the door, more for a little distance from Luc than from genuine trauma over their rough landing.

Luc reached over, his finger brushing her cheek. A bolt of heat crackled across her skin and went down deep. "Are you all right?" he asked, his deep voice traveling along the path forged by the fire that had gone before it.

It was a one-two punch. His touch and his voice. If he added something else to the mix she was toast. She moved more tightly into the cold plastic embrace of the door handle.

"I'm fine," she said. "I get a little nauseous on rough touchdowns like that, but honestly, it's nothing to be concerned about because... Since when are you ever concerned?"

"Since you look like you're about to vomit on the leather seats."

"So touching."

She whipped her phone out of her purse and opened up one of her flash sale shopping apps, scrolling through the daily deals.

"See? You do shop at work."

"It's early!" she protested. "And we went back in time."

"You're still on the clock until five."

"You're harsh," she said, touching a picture of a pair of candy-apple-red shoes.

"You have shoes that look just like that," he said.

"No, I don't."

"You do."

"I don't!"

"You wore them yesterday."

She rolled her eyes. "Those are cranberry. These are more of a true red."

"And today you have on Muk Luks."

She looked down at her knee-high furry boots, with the leather laces and fuzzy balls. "Yes. I do. It's cold here out west. It's snowing."

"Which is what you want with a ski resort," he said. "At least we have that."

"Yeah, otherwise it's just a bunch of rich idiots scooting down a mud hill."

"Yes, well, you don't want that."

"Mmm."

The limo wound up the side of a mountain, on a freshly plowed two-lane road lined with snow-covered evergreens.

In Manhattan, there were places on the streets where your vision was walled in by buildings. Beyond the gray steel in front of you was the glass and metal beyond it, and above, there was a small pocket of yellow-coal sky.

But here…here it was trees. Trees along the roadway, over the mountains and, beyond that, more trees, with a shocking blue sky streaked with white clouds.

It was like being thrust into Oz after the black-and-white haze of Kansas.

The road ended on the mountaintop at a large lodge, constructed of heavy wooden beams and a green sheet metal roof, covered in patches of bright snow.

"Sold. Can I live here forever?" she asked.

"There are very few shops," he said.

"Online shopping."

"Are you still online shopping?" he asked.

"No," she said. "Because as someone pointed out, I do have very similar shoes."

"You should have brought ski boots."

"We're only going to be here a day."

"Yes, and we're due at breakfast now."

"Now? I am in Muk Luks, Luc, as you pointed out."

He made a very dismissive French sound that rippled through her, not like the sexy electricity from before, but like annoying, static electricity. "They'll do fine. You're in the mountains, after all. And you look as beautiful as ever."

*Don't blush. Don't blush.* "You think I'm beautiful?"

Oh, wow. What in the world was that? How

needy could she get? Asking if he thought she was beautiful.

Though, considering the beating her ego had taken recently…she did feel in need.

He looked her over, his dark gaze assessing. "Yes. Because you are beautiful, and I can see."

"Oh, well. That's nice."

"I am nice."

"Pah!"

Luc got out of the limo and walked around to her side, opening the door for her. "Look," he said, "nice."

"Well, you aren't horrible."

"Damned with faint praise."

"I bet that doesn't happen often."

A smile curved his lips. "That depends."

"On what?"

"On whether or not they're mad that I didn't stay around for the morning after."

"Ah," she said, getting out of the limo, her head a little swimmy. She really didn't need to think of Luc in that context. Not so near her…thinking about him in that context. "Well, that has nothing to do with this."

"Of course not. Ready for breakfast?"

"Obviously I expect a Denver omelet."

"We're not in Denver."

"But we're a lot closer than usual. So I assume it will be superior to the New York Denver omelet."

"One hopes," he said.

They walked across the paved drive and through the front doors into the expansive lobby. An older man dressed in a suit, with black hair that looked as though it might have been dusted in snow, stood there with a woman at his side. She was near his age, Amelia guessed, and perfectly put together in a blue pantsuit that Amelia herself would never be caught dead in, but could respect.

"Mr. Chevalier." The man, Don Fleischer, she presumed, extended his hand.

"Mr. Fleischer," Luc said, confirming her initial thought. "And this is?"

"My lovely wife, Anna."

"Pleasure," Luc said, his lips wrapped around the word as if it was decadent chocolate. Why was his voice so sexy?

Anna Fleischer was not unaffected. And really, who would be? The other woman flushed slightly and extended her hand to shake his. "Very nice to meet you."

"I'm very pleased to see you've brought your girlfriend—or is that fiancée," he said, his eyes dropping to her left hand, "with you. I prefer to have something of a family meeting, rather than a true business meeting. And I particularly like it when a man includes his partner in important business affairs."

"Naturally," Luc said, moving nearer to

her, his arm sliding around her waist. "I would hardly make such a decision without the woman I love by my side."

## CHAPTER THREE

AMELIA STIFFENED, HER EYES widening. "Uh…"

"You must be starving, Amelia, darling," Luc said.

She curled her hand into a fist, feeling conscious of the ring on her finger, the one that had been there for four years. The one she'd spent most of the day considering removing.

And now it had gotten them into this.

Though, why Luc was touching her instead of correcting Fleischer she didn't know.

She felt as if she'd stepped into an alternate dimension. What was the man going on about? "I did have the scone on the plane."

"Just one scone," he said. "I thought you wanted an omelet."

Don laughed. "We do have good omelets. Right this way into the dining area."

Amelia and Luc followed, Luc with his arm still wrapped around her waist. He was making her all warm. And it was weird.

Then when they reached the table he held the chair out for her. She sat, giving him the best and most subtle side eye she could manage.

The breakfast really was a personal visit, peppered with talks of business. Luc was adept at mainly keeping the personal topics relegated to Don and Anna, and to use those moments to push through to a discussion about the running of the resort. They were moving to be in warmer climates, to be nearer to their grandchildren, but the resort was special to them and wouldn't it be nice to have another couple interested in taking it over?

Luc, to his credit, did remind them that he owned many properties, and would likely not personally run things in Aspen. But they were both sold on his charm, so neither seemed to mind.

Amelia, for her part, mainly sat quietly, shoveling egg, ham and cheese into her mouth. It was a good omelet. That, at least, in this crazy mixed-up world, was a surety. Cheese would never fail her.

Every once in a while she would nod enthusiastically in agreement with Luc, because that much she knew would be appreciated. That she did as part of her job. The touching stuff, though, was not a part of her job, and every time he brushed his fingers over her knuckles she had to fight the urge to leap up out of her chair and shake the warm fuzzies off her hand.

She didn't, though. She sat still. And she was pretty sure she was accomplishing the playing it cool act.

"Well," Don said, standing when all the plates

were clear. Everyone else at the table followed suit. "I suppose I should let you get to your room."

"I…It is no trouble at all to have Amelia put in her own room," Luc said, stumbling over his English. She'd never heard him do that before.

Anna laughed. "We're not that old-fashioned, Mr. Chevalier. We put you in the Aspen Suite. Of course we didn't realize Amelia was coming, but it is the best room in the lodge."

"Faaaabulous," Amelia said, heat rising in her cheeks and other…places.

"Everything was taken up already," Don said.

"Oh, very kind of you," Luc said, smiling. "Now…which floor?"

Don handed him a card with a code written on it. "The top floor. And you have a passcode to get into the room."

"Fantastic." Luc took it and tucked it into his suit jacket pocket. "Shall we?"

"We shall," she said, smiling far too brightly as she walked with him to the elevator. They got inside and when the doors slid shut, she rounded on him. "What the?"

"I could have corrected them, but to what end? We're here for a day, to look the place over and to try and get the best deal possible. Forging something of a…personal relationship with the Fleischers is obviously the way to go. And will make my somewhat low offer look okay."

"This is awkward. Like…fourteen-year-old boy

walking by the Sports Illustrated Swimsuit edition in public, while wearing sweatpants, awkward."

"That is some kind of awkward."

"Isn't it?" she snipped.

"Amelia, you and I have worked together for four years, I'm sure we can sleep in close quarters for an evening without being terribly bothered by it. Unless you're bothered by it."

"What? Me? Pfffft." She blew out a breath. "Bothered. Why would I be bothered?"

"You seem bothered."

She crossed her arms under her breasts and determinedly stared the elevator doors down, as if that might make it move faster. "Nope," she said. "Not. Bothered, that is. Not even a little. You're my boss and…and…a friend kind of, when you aren't being a grumpy.… Well, you're grumpy most of the time but…why would it be weird? It's not weird."

"Then everything should be fine. I just saw no need to rock the boat."

She took a deep breath and let it back out again, everything suddenly kind of unsteady. "But you lied. About us. And I don't…I don't really like that."

"Why?"

"Because. Just…you know, forget it." She waved a hand in dismissal. "It doesn't really matter."

"Fantastic," he said.

The doors slid open and Luc walked out without waiting, then strode down the hall to the room, punching in the code quickly. She followed, try-

ing to process why exactly she was suddenly in
annoyed territory, rather than just slightly uncomfortable territory.

*Shades of Clint?*

No. This had nothing to do with Clint, and all
the garbage happening with him. That was a separate drama and would have to wait to be dealt with.
Probably while they were all spending Christmas
together. His parents and hers, and…just great.

Anyway, for her to be bothered by Luc's little lie
on that level would sort of require her to have feelings for Luc. And for him to be tricking her into
thinking he had feelings for her. Which was not
what was happening. So really, it was nothing like
Clint. So she should just chill.

She walked into the suite and breathed a sigh of
relief. It was large. With more than one room. There
was a couch right in the main room, and there was
what she assumed to be a bedroom off to the left.
There was another door to the right that might just
be another bedroom.

"There," he said. "This will actually be quite
convenient, because if I need you for anything,
you'll be right there."

She nearly choked over the image that put in
her head. Of Luc needing her. In the night. His big
hands, dark on her pale skin as they skimmed her
curves and…

"Yeah," she said. "For work stuff."

"What else would I mean?"

"No…personal stuff."

He arched a dark brow. "Amelia, does this make you uncomfortable? Because the last thing I want to do is make you uncomfortable."

"No," she said. "I'm fine. It's a nonissue. We're adults. We can manage."

"Let me tell you," he said, dark eyes blazing as he took two steps closer to her, his expression intense. "I know some men just take what they want, with no thought to how it might affect other people, but I am not that man."

"I know," she said, feeling breathless now.

"That is for men like my brother."

She swallowed hard, her heart beating fast. "Yes, I know. Your brother the fiancée-stealing jerk."

"Have you heard the story?" he asked.

"From you? Only every time his name is mentioned in the news. I also read the article in *Vanity Fair* about The Wedding That Wasn't."

"You didn't even work for me then."

"No, but I read that kind of thing. I'm interested in society and pop culture and it was…a big deal."

"I know, Amelia, it was my wedding. Trust me, I know."

She blinked. "You must have loved her a lot."

Luc paused, shoving his hands in his pockets and looking at Amelia, who looked especially wide-eyed, yet again, since their encounter with the Fleischers downstairs. Not that he could blame her, especially.

It had been a definite change in direction, but as he'd said to her in the elevator, he saw no reason to correct Don, not when it might work to their advantage in some way. He had no way of knowing, and it would be best if he could simply give himself every tool to work with.

Of course, somehow, all of that had led to a shared suite, and to her asking questions about Marie.

"No," he said, his tone harsher than he'd intended. "I did not love her a lot. I daresay I didn't love her much at all. It was a business arrangement." Which was partly true. But she'd been the woman he was prepared to spend his life with and, in the end, she'd betrayed him.

And even more painfully, his brother had betrayed him. Yes, he knew Blaise had his own baggage. Raised mainly in Africa with their mother, Blaise's life had been completely different from Luc's. Luc had spent his childhood in a mansion in Paris.

And in his mind, he'd always seen Blaise's stealing Marie before the wedding as some kind of revenge. Revenge for a charmed life that had never been as charmed as Blaise had imagined. As anyone might have imagined.

His father had been—was still—a tyrant. A mean drunk. Distant at best and violent at worst.

But all anyone ever saw was the facade. The mansion. The man in the suit.

Luc knew differently.

And while he'd paid lip service to forgiveness, while he'd told Blaise years ago to just forget it, forgiveness had never truly taken root in him. Because Blaise couldn't return what he'd stolen. Because Luc could never forget.

"Well, if you didn't love her then…" Amelia looked at him, pain in her blue eyes. "I hope she knew, Luc. Because I think it's pretty bad form to use a woman like that. To use anyone like that."

"She knew," Luc said. "Though, in the end she said it wasn't enough. The day before the wedding. Do you suppose she could have come to that conclusion faster? Do you suppose she might have… ended things with me before she jumped into bed with my brother?"

Amelia frowned. "Fine. Point taken."

"I was not using her. I believe I just pointed out to you that I'm not one who does that."

"And…your brother was using her?"

"My brother is with someone else now."

Blaise and his wife, Ella, had been married for four years. Surprisingly, or rather not, Luc had not attended the wedding.

"I know," Amelia said, pointing toward her breasts. At least, that was where his eyes went. "This dress is hers."

"You're wearing one of my sister-in-law's designs?" he asked.

"I wear Ella Stanton clothes all the time. She's a genius. I like to mix her with vintage."

"I'm not sure how I feel about that."

"So I can't sing in my head and you don't know how you feel about me wearing a certain designer? What next? Are you going to order me to take the dress off?"

She froze as soon as the words left her mouth, her gaze clashing with his.

He took a moment to appreciate the way her dress formed to her figure. One thing was certain, his sister-in-law was talented. The gray sweater dress made the most of every curve, covering skin, but tantalizing all the same.

And he wondered what exactly she might look like unwrapped for his pleasure. He'd done his best never to go there with her, really, he'd succeeded. She wasn't his type. She was open, smiley and chipper. She wasn't all self-contained and polished like an ice sculpture, not in the least.

She was all cheer and broad gestures. And she was not his fiancée. She was engaged to another man, and he would be damned if he ever sunk that low.

He would never be like his brother. Would never be like his father. Both seemed to do whatever they wanted in regards to women, but not Luc.

He ignored the fierce twist in his gut and turned toward the bar in the corner. "I could use a drink."

"It's still before noon."

"Not in New York."

"Blah!" she said. "So…what, I have to pretend to be your fiancée now?"

"Only until tomorrow," he said, walking over to the bar and pulling out a bottle of whiskey.

"This ring," she said, holding her hand up, "would be a pretty poor showing for a billionaire."

"I've only just started up the company, maybe I'm saving my money?"

"Bah," she said. "I would throw this back at you if that were your offering!"

"But it was Clint's offering, and you don't seem to mind it coming from him."

"Clint," she said, "is not a billionaire. He is a thousandaire, with an okay job. All things considered, this ring is pretty good."

"Such a double standard."

"Yeah, well," she said, "you're also a lot more demanding than Clint is, so…I think you'd owe me for putting up with your shenanigans."

"Shenanigans?" he repeated.

"Yeah, your shenanigans. This? This right here? This fake engagement brouhaha is the definition of a shenanigan. It may even be high jinks."

"High jinks?"

"Madcap ones!"

He almost laughed at her. She was…she was just so very much. An explosion of color and movement, all the time. The ring, the one they'd just been discussing, caught the lights, glittering. Reminding him of the fact that he couldn't notice. Not really.

There was a knock at the door and Luc put down his drink. Amelia was just standing there. "I've got it," he said, "don't worry."

"Was I supposed to assist you in door answering? I'm not a butler."

He turned and headed to the door, opening it. "Yes?"

There was a woman in a black uniform there, with a cart in front of her. "May I come in?"

"Sure," he said, stepping aside and allowing her entry while he examined the items on the cart. An ice bucket, champagne, a bowl of chocolate-covered strawberries. There was also a white envelope with his name on it.

"Compliments of Mr. Fleischer," she said. "He wanted you to experience the romance package the resort offers, both so that you could appreciate just what sort of draw couples might feel to the location, and for you and your fiancée." She bowed slightly. "Enjoy."

*"Merci,"* Luc said as she walked back out of the hotel room. Then he turned to Amelia who was uncharacteristically quiet. "What is it, Amelia?"

She shook her head. "Shenanigans."

"Why not enjoy?" he asked. "You wanted time off. Doesn't this feel like time off?"

"But I'm with you, and not my family or my…" she trailed off, worrying her lower lip.

"Am I so bad?"

"You are so my boss is all. Nothing personal." She reached into the strawberry bowl and took out a piece of fruit, lifting it to her lips.

There was nothing wrong with watching her eat a strawberry. Just a moment of enjoyment. It wasn't touching. It wasn't violating her engagement or their working relationship.

It was just him taking a small moment, the first in a while, to remember that he was a man and not just an entrepreneur.

She parted her lips and closed them over the tip of the berry, her eyes closing.

He was getting heated watching that. And that was not appropriate workplace behavior. Even when that workplace was currently a romantic suite.

Romance meant nothing to him, these surroundings meant nothing. This woman meant nothing.

She hummed, low in her throat, the sound sending a kick of desire through him and proving his previous thought a lie. She did mean something. At least to his long-neglected libido. Fascination—which honesty compelled him to confess he'd felt for her from the moment they'd met—was twisting into something else. Something more intense. Something darker. Something he really couldn't afford to feel.

"Nothing personal at all," he said, taking a strawberry from the bowl and popping it into his mouth. Then he poured himself a glass of champagne and picked the envelope up from the cart and opened it. "Look at that. A brochure of all the activities we're entitled to partake in today."

"Goody. Since this is supposed to be vacationy, let me see."

He handed her the glossy, trifolded paper and waited while she perused it. She reached into the bowl and took out another berry, this time putting it into her mouth whole. Her dark brows knit together. "A massage," she said. "Hmm. Well—" she looked up at him "—I could use one. My muscles are knotted. I'm a little stressed."

"You're stressed?" he asked.

She blinked. "A little."

"You've been singing a lot of Christmas carols for someone who's stressed."

"Well, I acquired a lot of my stress today." Her eyes narrowed.

"Point taken."

"A ride on the tram over the mountain, to a restaurant at the summit. Wow. That sounds…high."

"Do you have a problem with heights?"

"Not at all," she said. "If you do, maybe I'll take the tram ride, and you can get the massage except… I really do want the massage."

"We can't do things separately," he said.

"Well, then, the massage is off the…massage table. Because I'm not getting oiled up with you." Her cheeks turned pink. "Well, that was a little bit more…out there than I meant it to be." She cleared her throat. "How about this tram? We can ride it to the top for lunch."

"Is food all you think about?"

"Hey, I've now watched you pour two alcoholic beverages very early in the day, so if we're going to get judgmental you're going to lose this round, my friend."

"All right, lunch it is."

"I'm thinking cheeseburger."

"Really?"

"Yes, Luc. Really. Because cheese doesn't ask stupid questions. Cheese understands."

"Well, then let's journey to the mountaintop for your understanding cheese."

"You're absurd," she said, "this entire thing is absurd."

"Well, we're living it. So we might as well enjoy it."

She worried her lip for a moment, then slapped her hands down on her thighs. "Yes, dammit, I will enjoy it. I'm owed some enjoyment. A little time off without my family. Still with my boss, but hey, I'll take what I can get. Let's go get that burger."

# CHAPTER FOUR

"WELL, THAT REALLY was high. So this had better be quite the hamburger," Amelia said as they waited for their food.

The tram had taken nearly an hour, which Amelia had seemed honor-bound to fill up with Amelia-like chatter. About birds, and trees. And how blue the sky was.

And all he'd been able to think about was how her lips had looked wrapped around the strawberry. And from there, his mind had gone to how her lips might look if they were wrapped around his—

Yes, he'd had to adjust his thinking quite often. Among other things.

"I imagine it will be," he said. "Since it's closer to Denver."

"That doesn't apply to all food, just foods with Denver in the name." She rolled her eyes and took a French fry out of the basket in front of them.

"That makes more sense than what I was thinking."

"Do you have culture shock yet from leaving Paris and all its pastries behind?"

He lifted a shoulder and took a fry from the basket. "No. New York has everything I want. Plus it's missing a lot of things I'd rather not deal with."

"Your family."

"Exactly."

"What happened with your dad? I mean...we've never talked about him. I know it was a huge deal in Europe when you left the firm."

"Because my father is a tyrant, and why I worked with him for as long as I did is...well, it is a mystery to me. I was raised to take over the firm, and I did. I was raised to marry a suitable woman, and for a while it seemed I would do both. I had Marie, who was so very perfect to be the queen for the Chevalier kingdom. Until it all came crashing down. And there was a point where I was still working to keep my father's empire running, while my brother went out and did what he pleased...and I asked myself why I was still working so hard for something I didn't even care about."

"You got an answer, I take it?"

"No. I got no answer. And that was when I decided to leave. If you don't know why you're working sixty-to-eighty-hour workweeks, you shouldn't be working them."

"I don't suppose."

"I also found out my father had been stealing money. From the business, from clients. So after I set the law on him, I left."

"You were the one who...who broke all of that open?"

"Yes. I am. Don't tell me you secretly imagined I might be involved in the crime?"

"I seriously never did," she said. "You're too much of a rule follower."

Luc frowned. Under normal circumstances he wouldn't mind being called a rule follower. But for some reason, coming from her just now, it sounded very unexciting. And as though it might be the real reason he hadn't had sex in nearly a year.

"Well, I'm glad to think you don't believe I could be a criminal," he said.

"Though," she said, "I'm starting to think that I can be very stupid about people."

"Why is that?"

"Just...reasons."

Right then, a waiter set their plates in front of them. Two very large cheeseburgers. The view, which was all snow-capped trees and gray rock jutting up beyond them, was at odds with the food. One was common, the other altogether unique. Wild.

Then there was Amelia. She seemed more a part of this than Manhattan somehow. Perhaps because she defied the clean, sleek steel of the city. Because she was nonuniform and bright. Because she was modern and vintage, and Christmas carols and snark.

"What are your reasons? I just told you my secrets."

She shook her head. "Mine are not really...mine. I know that doesn't make sense but...it's true."

"Fair enough," he said. "We're not really on a date, after all. Just testing out the food."

"And it is good," she said, taking a bite of her cheeseburger.

"Well, I'm glad it was worth the trek."

They ate in silence. Well, relative silence. Sometimes Amelia hummed while she chewed.

"Ready to head back down the mountain?"

"Uh, sure, I guess so."

He left the voucher that had been included with the brochure on the table and they walked back to the tram. "Ready?"

"Yep."

He walked into the yellow car and held his hand out. She took it and he lifted her inside. Her hands were so soft. Warm.

The attendant slid the door shut, and the car began to move along the cable, out of the station and back over the trees, over the valley that ran between the mountains.

"Wow," she said. "This is incredible. Also, though, when you look straight down it makes you slightly dizzy."

"Then don't look down," he said.

"It's kind of a rush," she said, leaning toward the window, her forehead pressed against the glass. "Smoother than an airplane. And it feels more real. It feels a lot more like flying in some ways."

"You were the kind of girl who would dream of

flying, I think," he said. He wasn't sure why he'd said it. He only knew it was true.

She looked at him and smiled, a dimple in her left cheek dipping inward. "I did. I made myself cardboard wings and used glue and gold glitter to make them sparkle. I was fifteen. It wasn't so socially acceptable."

"You seem like you don't care much for convention, anyway."

"You know, I don't in some ways. I mean, society can take a flying leap. But in other ways... I know what it's like to have family expectations of you. I mean...sure it wasn't running a bank or anything but...I'm really close to my parents and I know they see me a certain way. That they see my future a certain way. And if they were tyrants or criminals, then maybe I could walk away, but they aren't. I love them. And I'm just always afraid of disappointing them."

"How could you possibly disappoint them?"

She lifted a shoulder. "There are ways, I'm sure. It's just...in my family there are a lot of emotions."

"You have sisters," he said.

"Yes, I do. And you know that because a Chevalier never forgets."

"True enough."

They rode the rest of the way in silence, which was beyond unusual for Amelia, her face pale, her cheeks and lips a stark pink in contrast, her gaze focused on the view. She looked oddly serious. And sad. It made his stomach twist.

The car touched down at the other station, and he helped Amelia out. "Ready for the massage?"

"What did I tell you about the massage?" she asked.

"Do you really want to skip this? We're testing out the facility."

The dimple deepened, blue eyes glittering. "Fine. I guess I'll suffer the indignity for a little deep tissue relief."

He reached out to take her hand, and she pulled away. "What?" he asked.

"I—I shouldn't."

"Clint?" he asked.

"Kind of."

"Just hands," he said, and he didn't know why he felt compelled to convince her of that. Didn't know why he felt the need to talk her into letting him touch her.

"Just hands," she said, extending hers.

He wove his fingers through hers, the shock of her skin on his not lessening since the last time he'd touched her. This whole thing with her was much more problematic than he'd anticipated.

They walked out of the tram terminal and into the lodge again, heading up the stairs that led to the spa.

It was all exactly what he wanted to see as a potential buyer. Very little needed to be done to the property to make it perfect. The same rustic elegance that was evidenced in the rest of the place carried through, craftsman-style details, beautiful inlaid wood and exposed beams.

And at the center was a giant Christmas tree, white lights glittering against the deep green.

With the right marketing, this resort could be much bigger than it was. He didn't see why it wasn't yet on the radar of celebrities looking for a place to stay and ski. In his mind it was well suited to that. All it needed was a bit of rebranding.

A woman greeted them at the front and ushered them into a small room that had a wall entirely made of glass, which overlooked the broad expanse of wilderness at the back of the resort. There was utter privacy, with a sense of openness.

Yes, this could be a very popular destination.

Amelia looked pointedly at the two white robes, hanging on the little room divider.

"I take it that's what we're supposed to wear?" she asked.

"I think so. You can get behind the shade if you like."

He felt as if they were potentially playing with fire. In fact, he knew he was. He knew that this had gone somewhere beyond simply playing the part of happy couple, and assessing the value of the resort. Frankly, he could have donned a suit, walked in here and told Don Fleischer he was prepared to offer and that he wanted to inspect the facilities, and yet he hadn't.

And he wasn't going to. Not when...not when this was happening. Not when, for the first time in his memory he felt a rush of excitement and the thought of what might happen.

Sex was a certainty for him—dry spell aside—when he went out, if he wanted sex, he got it. Women were always willing. The combination of money, power and looks was his ticket into many bedrooms. And there was no thrill. There was no tightening in his stomach, no rush of anticipation. No sense of the unique or unknown.

Sex was a known quantity. How could anything about it be suspenseful? It was simply arousing, and then, satisfying.

This wasn't even sex. This was just the anticipation of being near her while she was dressed in nothing more than a robe. This was just the desire to see a bit more skin than she'd shown while in her dress.

The desire to be in this intimate setting with her.

It wasn't about release. It wasn't about getting naked and getting it done as quickly as possible. He wouldn't even touch her. It was just about the moment.

For some reason the moment had become everything.

Amelia disappeared behind the divider and he turned toward it, undoing the top button on his shirt. He could hear her rustling around behind the screen, hear her clothes being removed.

And he could imagine it.

Every whisper of fabric over skin had his imagination on overdrive, until his body ached. Until he was so hard he couldn't talk himself down.

He put on his robe quickly and sat on the massage table, his hands in his lap.

A moment later, Amelia emerged, her cheeks the color of ripe strawberries. Which were fresh on his mind for several reasons.

She sat on the massage table across from him, forcing a smile. "So now we wait?"

"Yes," he said, unable to stop himself from taking a visual tour of her body. The robes were thin, the room warmed by a fireplace in the corner.

The V of pale skin than ran from her elegant neck down to the curve of her breasts was enticing. Begging for touch. Begging, at least, for him to sit there and appreciate her.

She took a deep breath that jarred his heart and sent a kick of heat through his veins. The thin fabric of her robe molding tightly over her breasts, revealing the outline of her nipples.

*Mon dieu.*

He needed to get a grip. Preferably in private and on himself.

He was a thirty-five-year-old man, not some horny teenager. It was his own fault for putting off sex as long as he had.

She took a breath, her lips parting as if she was about to say something when the door opened. Two massage therapists came in, smiling and greeting them both, before turning on some sort of wooden flute music.

That he could do without. He wasn't a meditation sort of guy.

"Go ahead and lay down on your stomach," his masseuse said. "We can lower the robe down past your shoulders and work on your back."

He looked over at Amelia, who scrambled to lay facedown on the table before turning her head away from him and shimmying her shoulders, working the top of her robe down, baring her back, her breasts covered by her position.

He looked away from her and did the same.

And for the next several minutes tried not to die of extreme overarousal.

It wasn't the touch of the woman working on his muscles. He barely felt that. It was the sounds Amelia was making. Amelia didn't do anything quietly, so he didn't know why he should be so surprised that, when being massaged, Amelia sounded as though she was eating very good chocolate, or having very good sex.

"You're very tense, Mr. Chevalier," his masseuse said, right about the time Amelia moaned, long and low into the table.

Yes, he was. And he had a feeling he was going

to leave this appointment with more knots in his back than when he'd come in.

"Mmm...yessssss."

*Merde.*

She was actually going to kill him. There was no point even denying it now, as he lay facedown on the massage table trying to fight the hard-on from hell. He wanted her. He wanted her naked and under him, and over him.

His assistant. A woman with a ring on her finger.

He was, in that moment, everything he hated and still wanting her was stronger than the shame.

The half-hour session seemed as though it lasted four times as long. When they put hot rocks along the line of his spine, and hers, he was ready to beg to be thrown in a snowbank. She liked the hot rocks very much, and she was not shy about voicing her approval.

Finally, it was over. Amelia's moan of completion and disappointment sent one final lick of flame over his skin.

"That ends the session. Now we'll leave you two to get dressed. If you need anything else during your stay, we're here to see to your needs."

No they were here to ignite impossible needs, he thought bitterly as he sat up, his robe pooling around his waist.

Amelia sat up when the door closed, her dark brown hair tumbled over one shoulder, her cheeks flushed, her robe clutched tightly in her fists, closed snugly over her breasts.

She looked like a woman who'd just been tumbled. Or, rather she looked like a woman who needed to be. Or maybe it wasn't her. Maybe it was just him. Maybe he was the one who needed it, and he was reading the signs wrong.

But he didn't care just now.

"Amelia," he said, his voice low, rough, almost unrecognizable even to his own ears. "I am your boss. And this is a vulnerable situation for you." He was tripping over his English now. He wasn't sure if what he was saying made sense. All of his thoughts had reverted to French. And he was trying to translate the words coming out of his mouth as quickly as possible. "But, and forgive me, you are oiled up and you're naked. And I want…. If you want me to stay over here, I want you to say so. Now."

Amelia could only stare at Luc, her heart in her throat, her entire body shaking.

The massage had her feeling loose, and very languid, which was a word she didn't think she'd ever embodied before.

And he was right. They were naked. And oiled up. And yeah, she'd said that would never happen. But right now it was happening. And he was looking at her as though she was a woman. A woman he desired. Not a woman he cared for. Not a woman he hoped might fix him.

His eyes burned with heat and passion, the kind

that had never, ever been directed at her before, and until that moment, she hadn't realized it had been missing.

But it was. And suddenly she felt parched for it. Needy. Desperate.

"I don't want you to stay over there," she said, her words coming out in a rush.

"Well, thank God for that."

## CHAPTER FIVE

IT WAS INSANE. And it was wrong. Wrong, wrong, wrong. She hadn't made any decisions about Clint yet, and technically, regardless of the circumstances, they were still engaged. Which meant that she should tell Luc to get back on his side of the room.

And she should flee to the safety of the divider. Flee and put her clothes back on and lace her boots up tight so that she was too much trouble to undress.

That thought made her heart hiccup in her chest. Undressing? Was that where this was going? Was that what the look on his face meant? That undressing was imminent? That kissing was imminent?

He stood up and moved to the table, putting his palms flat on the table, on either side of her thighs, his dark eyes intent on hers.

"Just...kissing right?" she asked.

"Just kissing," he said, lifting one hand and cupping her chin with his thumb and forefinger. "Just lips."

"I think...I think I can handle that." Except she wasn't sure at all. Because he was Luc, her boss, her almost-friend. And she hadn't been kissed by anyone other than Clint in…ever. And it had been years since it had made her stomach knot up and her breath shorten. Years since it had mattered at all.

Clint had gotten comfortable like socks. And now that she knew his secret, she understood why. And she felt…unattractive. She felt unwanted. She felt as if he was keeping her around for comfort. And she wasn't wrong. He wanted an ideal, a certain lifestyle. And she suited that.

*It didn't stop him from finding passion with someone else.*

No, it hadn't stopped him from finding passion with someone else. And catching him with a slightly damp, freshly showered man in a towel in his living room early this morning—was that really only this morning?—had explained a lot. But it was his response that shocked her, that kept the ring on her finger and made her feel as if…as if somehow she was the one doing the betraying if she suddenly had a problem with the status quo.

If she wanted something more than what they had.

Well, she did, dammit. She wanted to be wanted. She wanted to be kissed. If nothing else, she wanted to be kissed.

So she was the one who closed the distance between her and Luc. She was the one who angled her head and touched her lips to his.

His mouth was warm and firm, skilled. He opened to her, his tongue touching the tip of hers, sending a bolt of lightning straight down to her stomach, and parts lower.

He tightened his hold on her chin, holding her still as he deepened the kiss. She wanted to wrap her arms around him. To pull him against her, to press her breasts to his chest and do something to alleviate the ache that was building between her thighs.

But she was afraid to do that. Afraid to deviate from his plan. Because obviously he had one. He was so clearly in control of it all, his lips so practiced and perfect on hers.

He was, without a doubt, about a thousand times the kisser Clint was.

And it didn't even make her feel guilty to think that.

He released his hold on her chin and put both of his hands on her hips, tugging her forward, stepping between her legs as he did, his mouth hungry on hers.

She was starving for this. Not just for the physical contact, but to be wanted. To have a man touch her as though it were essential to his well-being. To have him taste her as though she was dessert and not the salad he had to have to stay healthy.

That was what she was to her fiancé. And she realized it with blinding clarity, as Luc tugged her tight against his body, bringing the part that was aching for him into contact with his hardened arousal.

Oh…wow. Yes, this had been lacking entirely in her life for…ever.

She wrapped her arms around his neck, throwing herself into the kiss completely. Because she deserved it. Because she was so tired of being socks and salad.

Because she was tired of waiting for a man who just didn't want her.

Luc slid his hands around her, cupping her butt and urging her forward. She went, wrapped her legs around his hips, everything lining up even more perfectly now. She gasped as a bolt of pleasure went through her, as her entire body shook with need. Need that she hadn't even known had been in her.

She'd never considered herself an overly sensual person but she was doubting that assessment now. She slid her hands down over his chest, beneath his robe. Felt the hardness of the muscles there, the heat of his skin, and his raging heart, hammering against her palm.

He wanted this, too. He was shaking. He was losing control. He was hard for her.

The realization sent a surge of power through her. For the first time, she felt as if she had power as a woman. For the first time, she realized what she could do to a man. There was nothing wrong with her. The relief she felt…there were no words.

She moved her hands lower, and Luc pulled away, wrapping his hand around her wrist, tugging her arm upward, his focus on her engagement ring, his eyes fierce.

"No," he said, his voice ragged. He moved away from her, running his hands over his face. "That should not have happened," he said, bending down to collect his folded clothes from the chair. "It should never have happened."

"Wait…" she said, reeling from the change in activity. He'd just been kissing her, drinking her in as if she were water in the desert, and now suddenly he was…across the room, and now behind the divider. Dressing. "What?"

"You are engaged," he bit out, his tone uncompromising.

She stood up and eyed the screen. "Yeah, I am. And it's my engagement, so I think it's my…problem," she said.

"But I am your boss, and that means I need to exercise a little bit more restraint than that."

"Oh, boo. Why is it that everything I do is so… Why does everyone else get to just dictate the terms?" She wrenched her robe off and tugged her clothes on. "Why is it my function to make everyone else comfortable while…while I just atrophy?"

She jerked open the door to the massage room and walked toward the elevator. She got in and leaned back against the wall while the doors closed, her vision blurring as tears filled her eyes.

She was going crazy. Her neat and orderly existence had started to crumble this morning and she had no idea what she was supposed to do about that.

Except just…watch it fall.

Which was not what she wanted to do. She wanted to scream. And punch someone. And punch herself. Because she was an idiot.

She growled when the elevator doors opened, and stalked down the hall to their room. And realized that she had no key.

"Argh!"

She kicked the door and turned, leaning back against the wall and sliding down to the floor, her knees drawn up to her chest. Her woolen tights would have to be enough to protect her modesty.

As if it mattered since she'd just crawled on her boss like a sex-starved maniac. Because she *was* a sex-starved maniac. There was no modesty left. No shame. She was embarrassment.

He'd kissed *her*. And he'd made her feel special, and sexy for a moment. And then he'd pulled back and been regretful. As if her status with Clint was more important than what she wanted, no matter what she said. Which…under normal circumstances she might have appreciated. But not now. Not in the throes of feeling as if she'd wasted nearly a decade of her life in the service of what benefitted Clint.

The elevator doors slid open and Luc walked out into the hallway.

"You don't have a key?" he asked, looking down at her.

"No, Mr. Chevalier, I don't have a key."

"I do."

"Oh, well, nice for some." She slid back up the wall, vaguely aware that the wall texture was going to make her hair look ratty.

He put the card in the slot and the light turned green. "You're angry with me," he said, pushing the door open.

"Ding ding ding! Someone get the man a prize!" She walked into the hotel room ahead of him and sat on the couch, huffing loudly.

"Amelia, I'm not going to do this. This is what Blaise did to me. And I have too much respect for—"

"For a man you don't even know? More respect than you have for me?"

"What's the point, Amelia? We work together. Every day. And there is no good way for this to end. Either you start your marriage out with a lie or…"

"But that's my problem! It's not your problem."

"No, it is, because I don't want to be that man. I *refuse* to be that man."

"What I want is just…so small to everyone, isn't it? If I'm not making people comfortable and helping them live their convenient little lie then who am I?"

"What?"

She closed her eyes, fighting against the misery that was threatening to swamp her. "Clint cheated on me. I found out this morning."

"What?"

"It gets better. Or worse. The thing is...the thing is that he wants me to stay with him. Because he's sorry. And he was weak and he apologized. He said he still loves me."

"Amelia..."

"But...the thing is, he told me that he's gay."

She might have laughed at the look on Luc's face if she wasn't so miserable. "Oh."

"Yeah, well, it...definitely cleared some things up for me. But the thing is, I don't know what to do with that. We've been together for nine years. And my parents love him. And his parents love me. And there's this expectation that we're going to be... I mean, I've known Clint since I was a kid. And they've always expected us to end up together. I expected us to end up together. But..."

"I'm unclear as to why he wants to marry you," Luc said.

Amelia sucked her cheeks in, then released them with a smack. "Uh...I'm going to go ahead and give that some additional context and say this has more to do with his sexual orientation than the fact that you're actually stymied as to why a man would want to marry me."

"That is what I meant."

"Ah, well, yay me. Knocking 'em out of the park today." She let out a long breath. "He told me, after a lot of apologizing, after his *friend* left, that...that it's not what he wants for his life. That he wants the life we've been building toward for years because he thinks that would be better." She bit her lip. "And what do I do?" she asked. "What do I do? He's… I love him, Luc. And I don't think I'm in love with him, if I'm terribly honest, but he is my best friend. He really is. And I'm angry because he didn't tell me. And I'm angry because if I turn away from him now…because he's made me feel like doing anything other than what we planned is a betrayal on my part. And the only thing I really do know is that kissing you felt really good. I just wanted to feel good for a while because otherwise, frankly, today has kind of sucked."

"I'm not sure what to tell you," he said.

"Then don't tell me anything. Thankfully, we're going home tomorrow. I'll deal with Clint. And we can pretend this never happened. I'm under duress, so just…ignore it all." She looked at the champagne that was still sitting in the ice bucket. "I am gonna take this." She snagged the bottle. "And I'm going to go to my room."

"Dinner?" he asked.

"I think I'll skip it. Suddenly I'm not very hungry."

Amelia turned and walked into the bedroom, shutting the door firmly behind her. Tomorrow, they would fly back to New York. Then it would be Christmas. And she would just…go home to her family and pretend that nothing bad was happening. They would all spend Christmas together, even Clint and his parents, and then after the holidays she would figure out what to do.

# CHAPTER SIX

LUC DIDN'T SLEEP at all. He spent the entire time tossing and turning and trying to ignore the fact that he was hard as hell for a woman who was off-limits.

Engaged. Personal assistant.

Though, he had to admit that her revelations about her fiancé had put a new and morally interesting spin on the engagement.

Clint hadn't been faithful to her. And really, in his opinion, she shouldn't marry him. And he had a feeling she would arrive at the same conclusion. But for now, she was still wearing the ring and that felt... Well, considering his past it was a complication he couldn't ignore.

Which meant he would continue to ignore the hard-on. Particularly difficult in the morning. He gritted his teeth and went to his suitcase, tugging out a pair of jeans and a T-shirt, putting them on as quickly as possible. He wasn't going to shower. He would only end up thinking of her. And he would end up doing something he would probably regret. Their employer/employee relationship might be able to survive an ill-advised kiss, but if he let himself get off at the thought of her, if he made fantasizing about her acceptable that would be a can of worms that was hard to close.

He snagged his phone off his nightstand and saw a warning banner on the lock screen. He entered his passcode and opened it.

"Dammit," he said, walking out into the living area. "Amelia," he said, belatedly realizing that he probably should have gotten his arousal under control before he tried to be in the same room as her.

"What?" She emerged from the bathroom, freshly showered, her cheeks pink, damp hair curling around her face. She was wearing a sweater that looked as if it might have started life as a blanket, and a pair of tan pants with leather patches on the knees. In short, she should look sort of ridiculous, and she didn't. She was still sexy, even dressed as some insane version of a jockey.

"There is a weather-related issue. I'm going to call the airport."

"A weather-related issue?" She scurried to the window and swore. "I should say so!"

He followed her line of vision, looked outside at the swirling white flurries that were falling down. "It doesn't look promising."

A few moments later, he'd confirmed that it wasn't good. "Planes are grounded today," he said. "Even if we could take off from here, we can't land in New York."

"What! But…tomorrow is Christmas Eve and… and I am going to kill you! I'm being hyperbolic but…but seriously, Luc, all I wanted was Christmas and now I am stuck in freaking Colorado with you! And you won't even kiss me!"

"Because I can't control the weather, and because kissing would be a bad idea."

"Sure," she said. "If I don't get home for Christmas I am going to be unhappy. And," she said, looking at him defiantly, "I'm going to sing."

"What?"

"If I am here on Christmas Eve I am going to sing all night. I'm going to sing about wise men, and mangers and I'm going to sing about Santa coming to town and you won't be able to stop me."

"I did not intend to get you stuck here."

"Well," she said, her eyes widening, "I am stuck here. I just am. With you. In one room that now seems very small. So I would just…just like to make you as uncomfortable as I am."

"You don't think I'm uncomfortable?" he asked.

"You're the one driving this train. You dragged me here. You didn't correct Don when he assumed we were engaged. You made us get massaged in the same room when I had said that I didn't want to get naked and oiled up with you. You kissed me, then you acted like you wished you could unkiss me. And now we're stuck here. So you don't have the right to be more uncomfortable than me. Not when you're the one making decisions for everyone."

"I am trying to make the right decisions," he said, his voice low, "you're my employee, and even if nothing else stood between us, that would be enough. It's wrong for me to touch you, wrong for me to take advantage of you."

"Take advantage of me? As if I'm a child rather than just your assistant?"

"I sign your checks. There is every chance that an advance from me could feel forced on you."

"But it doesn't!" she exploded, striding across the room toward him. "The thing is, I don't want it to feel forced on you. One thing I am really sick of is having my advances just be a turnoff. That's how he acts. He used to kiss me and now…barely. If ever. I thought we were just in a rut, but it turns out he doesn't want me. Well, I'm not going to force myself on men who don't want me."

"Amelia…"

"But answer one question for me, Luc, please."

"What is that?"

"Is it me? Is something wrong with me? Am I fundamentally unsexy in some way?"

He closed the distance between them, wrapped his arm around her waist and tugged her close. She blinked, her jaw dropped, her eyes especially wide. And she felt good. She felt *so* good. Her soft curves, her breasts…he didn't want to say no.

He didn't want to toe the line or do the right thing or any other cliché. He wanted her. And the rest didn't seem to matter. For once in his life, he wanted to be the one who didn't care about the rules.

Where had they gotten him? Under his father's

heel. He'd lost his intended bride to his brother. He'd been in a job he'd hated for more than a decade. What was the point of doing the right thing when it never got you what you wanted?

He didn't want right. He wanted Amelia.

"Does it feel like there's anything unsexy about you?" he growled, putting his hand on her butt and pulling her in tight, letting her feel the hardened ridge of his arousal.

"I…I thought this was wrong."

"It is," he said. "In so many different ways I can't name them all. But I think it's going to happen. One night, I might have been able to handle. Even two nights, maybe. I bet I could resist you for two nights."

"You aren't resisting," she said, her voice breathless.

"Because I don't want to."

"Neither do I," she said.

"You have to understand," he said, "this isn't going to be anything else. I don't want marriage, and I don't want a wife and children. I don't want forever. All I want from you is sex."

She let out a sharp breath. "Thank God, because the other guy wants me to be his wife, bear his children and he doesn't seem to want sex at all. Frankly, a man who only wants sex seems like a much simpler undertaking."

"I'm glad to hear you say that."

Then he kissed her, her lips soft against his, her

body melting into him. It was rare for him to know his lovers these days, at least in a real way. Before Marie, he'd dated women, he'd had relationships, but after that he'd had sporadic affairs.

Amelia was different. He knew her. He was conscious of the fact that it was Amelia's lips he was kissing. That it was Amelia who made soft sounds of pleasure as he moved his hands over her curves.

There was no room for right or wrong now. There was only want.

Amelia felt as if she couldn't breathe, but at the moment, she didn't really care. All she knew was that she'd gone from enraged to turned on out of her mind in three seconds flat.

This was exactly what she needed. He was exactly what she needed. How had she missed that? For four years, she'd worked next to a guy who did more for her just by asking her to make him coffee than Clint had done by kissing her, and she still hadn't realized.

Friendship wasn't enough. The desire to make his life better wasn't enough. Without this, they couldn't have a marriage. She couldn't marry him.

So that decision was made, and she could stop thinking and just revel in the feeling of Luc's lips on hers. She didn't ever want to stop kissing him. She hadn't known it could be this good, this deep. She hadn't known she could feel it down to her toes and every place in between.

That a kiss could make you lose track of time

and sanity. That it could make you so damn hungry you felt weak in the knees.

He growled and backed her up against the wall, his hold on her firm, the kiss so deep, so hard. As if he was trying to prove what she already knew. That his kiss was in a whole different league from every one that had come before it. As if he was trying to wash away every other touch with heat and fire.

It was working. Oh, dear Lord, it was working.

He pushed his hands beneath the hem of her top, warm palms skimming over her stomach. Yes. Yes, yes. This was what she wanted. She wanted it all, she wanted it now. With him.

She hadn't exactly imagined that her first sexual experience would be with Luc, but then, she'd spent the past few years imagining that her first time would be on her wedding night with the man who'd wanted to say vows to her before he ever took her to bed.

But that had all been a sham. A way for him to put off what he didn't want. A way for him to try and make what he was doing sound like it was somehow better, all while she starved for human touch.

It didn't matter that this wasn't what she'd imagined. This was better. It was Luc. She spent five days a week with the man, assisting him, working with him. Talking to him. And, yeah, he was grumpy. And she didn't always understand him. And she didn't always like him.

But he was a friend. And she trusted him. In that moment, it hit her just how much. She could never just go to a bar and find a stranger to give her what she wanted, it wasn't in her. It was so much better to be with him.

And okay, it wouldn't be forever, but that was okay. She was still trapped in limbo. Still felt emotionally attached to the man she'd planned on spending the rest of her life with, while her body was firmly on team Luc.

He put his hand on her thigh and gripped it tight, pulling her leg up over his hip, blunt fingertips digging into her skin. She loved that. Loved how he touched her with such intent, with such desperation. There was no hesitation. There was nothing but pure, raw need.

A need that echoed inside her.

He leaned into her, pressing her back more firmly before reaching down, taking hold of both of her legs and lifting her, helping her wrap her legs around his waist before pulling them both away from the wall.

He didn't break the kiss as he carried her into his bedroom and deposited her on the bed. Then he pulled away, his hands gripping the bottom of his shirt before he wrenched it over his head, revealing well-defined muscles. Just the right amount of black hair dusted over his dark skin.

"Oh, my," she said, her heart kicking into high gear as his hands went to the snap on his jeans. Really, she should probably be taking her clothes off, too. But kissing was where her experience ended and she knew for a fact that wasn't the case for Luc. It made her feel fluttery. And now, for the first time, she felt really truly nervous.

A half smile curved his lips. "Like what you see?" he asked, lowering the zipper on his pants and pushing them, and his underwear down his lean hips.

Her mouth dried, making it impossible for her to swallow. Nearly impossible for her to speak.

"Uh...yes," she said, taking a visual tour of his body. Broad chest, slim waist and...and the most male part of him. Thick and very aroused.

She bit her lip, trying to fight against the rising tide of virginal panic.

"You don't sound convinced," he said.

"Maybe you should kiss me again," she said. "Because I do less thinking and more feeling when you do that, which I think is probably good."

He smiled and put his knee down on the bed, leaning over and claiming her lips again. And just like that, the nerves evaporated. Like water hitting up against a wildfire. There was no way they could win, not when his touch burned everything away. Everything but this.

He tugged her shirt up over her head, leaving her in nothing more than her black bra and those leggings she'd put on earlier, which now didn't seem quite so appropriate. Though, not any worse than the black cotton panties that were beneath. Nothing about her ensemble said vamp, that was for sure.

"I'm not really, uh..." He pushed her pants down her legs and pulled them off, leaving her in her unsexy undergarments. "There is no lace here," she said. "Sorry. I wasn't exactly expecting...this."

"You don't need lace," he said, his voice rough, his finger tracing the tender skin just beneath the cup of her bra. "You only need to be you."

That made her want to cry, and she wasn't sure why. Except maybe that just being her had never really felt as if it were enough. She'd always felt the need to bring extra. To go above and beyond and make herself valuable to the people in her life. But he seemed fine with just Amelia. In plain black underwear.

Heck, he seemed more than fine.

His dark eyes glittered as he flicked the catch on her bra open, letting it fall down her arms and onto the bed, exposing her breasts to him. "Perfection," he said, lowering his head and flicking his tongue over her nipple, his breath cool on her wet skin when he pulled away. "Absolute perfection."

Pleasure zipped down to her core, her internal muscles tightening. Oh, she wasn't going to survive this. After twenty-five years of celibacy this was surely going to kill her. The dam that had held back all of her passion, all of her desire, for so long was going to burst and drown them both.

He shifted, pressing his lips to the valley between her breasts, then to her stomach, just above her belly button, continuing on down below it. He moved his hands down her thighs, sliding them inward and parting her legs for him.

She looked at him, watched him watch her with utter and complete concentration, tracing the delicate skin of her inner thigh with the tip of his finger, around the border of black cotton that hid her most private place from view.

"I feel like this is the moment I've been waiting for since the day we met," he said. "And for some reason, I didn't realize it until now."

She sucked in a shaky breath as he gripped the sides of her panties and tugged them down, pulling them off and throwing them to the floor.

They were naked. Together. She'd never been naked with a man before. She was a lot less embarrassed than she'd imagined. Because it felt natural. It felt right. She never would have thought that he was the one it would feel like this with. And how could she? She'd always imagined this moment with someone else. But she could see that it wouldn't have been right. Because it wouldn't have been this, it wouldn't have been Luc.

He leaned in and kissed her thigh, following the path he'd moved his finger over a moment ago. And her breathing stopped. Her brain stopped. Everything in her paused, waiting to see what he would do. Hoping he would do what she thought he might, and kind of hoping he wouldn't because it seemed like such an intimate thing.

But then he did, his tongue sliding over her, then dipping inside her before tracing back. She put her hands on his head, holding him to her, trying to keep back the moan that was rising in her throat. But when he added his finger, she stopped trying.

She gasped, any thoughts of embarrassment or nerves gone now. Nothing mattered but this. But being wanted by him. But having him enjoy her body like this.

He continued to pleasure her with his mouth, pushing her higher, further than she'd ever thought possible, a knot of tension building in her stomach, getting tighter and tighter, until she thought it might break her. Until she thought there was no way she'd be able to survive.

He pushed another finger inside her, moved in time with his tongue, and it all broke free. The dam burst, the flood of pleasure far more overwhelming than she could have imagined, far more satisfying. Far more devastating.

He moved then, reaching for the nightstand drawer, and the box of protection that was inside. He tore it open, his hands shaking. For her. He was still hard, the evidence that he'd enjoyed what he'd done to her openly displayed.

She watched him roll the condom over his length before he came back to her, kissing her lips as he moved into position, the head of him testing the entrance to her body.

It suddenly occurred to her, through her postorgasmic haze, that this was going to hurt. But it was too late for her to brace herself. He entered her fully, a sharp, hot pain ripping through her as he did.

She whimpered, putting her fist over her mouth and trying to stifle the sound. He didn't seem to realize the sound was from pain, though, and that was actually fine with her.

He pulled back before thrusting in again, and this time, it didn't hurt quite so much. And each time he came back to her, it hurt less, until eventually, it felt good again. Until tension started building, deep in her again, the promise of another release.

She gripped his shoulders, then moved her hands down over his back, feeling the play of muscles as he moved in her, reveling in the closeness.

He slid his hand beneath her butt and cupped her, pulling her up tightly against him, the slight readjustment bringing all the right things into contact with each other. Every thrust, every movement taking her closer to the edge.

She wrapped her legs around his hips, arching against him, guided by his firm hold on her bottom.

Then he kissed her, hard, deep. And took her straight over the edge. She clung to him, because if she didn't she was sure she was going to lose touch with the bed. Hell, with the earth.

He pulled his mouth from hers and buried his face in her neck, speaking French against her skin as he froze above her, his muscles shaking as his own release rocked him.

She released her hold on him and threw her arms up behind her head. "Wow," she said, breathless.

He said something, too, still in French. And she had a feeling it wasn't a nice word. He pulled away from her, rolled into a sitting position and froze for a moment, before standing and walking into the bathroom.

Well, just great. They'd done it and now he was fleeing the scene.

She didn't know what to do. If she should get her clothes back on and leave, or stay in the bed or…she had no idea what the protocol was really.

Luc returned before she could decide. She was still lying on top of the covers all melted, and pale and naked. She felt like a little snowshoe hare ripped from the safety of its burrow. And that made Luc the fox. Or something.

She was fuzzy on…fuzzy animal analogies.

"Now," he said, his voice cold, "you should have told me that."

"What?"

"Were you a virgin?" he asked, standing nearer to the bathroom than to the bed, as if he was pondering running from the scene of the crime.

"Technically. Yes. I mean…I did stuff with Clint. Sometimes. Not so much for the past…while. But he said he wanted to wait. And I thought...that's so great. Because he loved me enough not to satisfy himself right away. He loved me enough to make it permanent first because he was that sure. Except really, it was just that it was so easy for him because he was that unattracted to me and I... Luc, I needed this. I needed someone to want me."

"Just someone?" he asked, his voice rough.

"No. I don't think it could have been anyone else. I couldn't do that with a stranger, not after I waited so long. Not after it was built up to be such a big thing in my head. I needed it to be with someone I trusted. And I trust you. So please don't look at me like I kicked your puppy because that's messing with my confidence."

"I can't offer you marriage, not like him."

"Well, I don't think I want the kind of marriage he's offering. Actually, no, I know I don't. And I knew with total certainty the moment you kissed me that I didn't want a passionless relationship. The thing is, we'd gone without passion for so long, obviously we never really had it, but we substituted it with this wonderful, warm caring and I was completely taken in by it. I forgot that marriage was supposed to be more than friendship. I was only thinking of it in terms of...family. Of making him my family. Of blending our families. Because it's what everyone wanted."

"You're right," he said. "Marriage is more than friendship. And it's more than a business deal, which during my own engagement I failed to realize, which is just one reason, I'm sure, my fiancée found what she was looking for in the arms of my brother. But marriage is also more than sex. This won't give you more. I can't give you more."

"I know that," she said. "And we would be a terrible couple. Because you would always ask me to bring you coffee and you're grumpy, and you'd have to hear me sing twenty-four hours a day, so I wasn't suggesting that it was the magic marriage component that meant you and I should—" Heat flooded her face and she stuttered over the next words. "It never even crossed my mind, I'm not that naive."

"Funny," he said, leaning against the wall, still completely naked, "because I thought you were that naive. Seeing as how you were a virgin and all."

"Virgin does not equal naive. Granted, not realizing for nine years that the guy you're in a relationship with is really not that into you, because you're not checking the right box on your legal forms, if you know what I mean, is kind of naive. But I had a blind spot because I'd known him for so long."

"My point exactly. I'm not naive."

"No one would ever accuse you of it." She slid off the bed and stood for a moment, then tugged back the covers and climbed back in, covering her body.

"Now what?" he asked.

"I don't know. We're sort of stuck here, aren't we?"

"We are," he said, crossing to the foot of the bed

and standing there, naked still, and much more casual about it than she felt. "So what do you want, Amelia?"

"What do you want, Luc?"

"Me? I'm a man. I would like nothing more than to crawl back into bed with you and spend the entire day inside you, but considering...I feel the choice should be yours."

Her heart was hammering hard, her mouth completely dry. "I want that, too," she said, the words spilling out of her. "I want...I want you and me and this. And you know what? I have for a long time, but I didn't even want to acknowledge it to myself because it seemed so wrong that my boss could get me hotter asking me to fetch him a file than my fiancé could by kissing me, but it's the truth. It's been the truth and I..."

Just like that, he was over her, kissing her, tugging the blankets back, his warm body covering hers. "This," she said, "is my new favorite way to spend a snowstorm."

# CHAPTER SEVEN

IT GOT DARK out early, and Luc didn't care. It didn't matter what time it was. Not when they had a fire going in the living area of their suite, not when he was holding Amelia, naked and bundled in a blanket, against his body.

Not when he felt this good.

Enjoying something, enjoying being with another person, was strange. Or maybe not so strange. He'd always found her to be more enjoyable than most people, so it stood to reason that spending time with her like this would be a good experience.

Though, he hadn't expected to spend naked time with Amelia, for all the reasons they'd already both gone over. And yet, right now, it just didn't seem to matter.

The way that the firelight made her face glow was infinitely more important. More important still was the way her curves felt beneath his hands. The way her breasts fit so perfectly in his palms...

All of that seemed infinitely more essential than an ethical employer/employee relationship and unresolved engagements. Though, some time ago, she'd taken her ring off and stuffed it in the bottom of her gigantic purse. He'd been far too gratified by that.

"Can I ask you a personal question?" Amelia asked, snuggling into him.

"You're naked, I'm naked, I don't think anything is too personal at the moment."

"Fair point," she said. "But you're not going to like this."

"Try me."

"Okay...if you didn't love Marie, why are you still angry with Blaise?"

She was right, he didn't like the question. If only because he didn't readily have an answer for it. He didn't spend a lot of time dwelling on it, he'd just been content to allow his brother to stay at a distance. The rift was fine with him.

"She was mine," he said.

"Obviously she wasn't, Luc," Amelia said. "And I'm sorry if that's harsh, but it's true. Clint wasn't mine. Not really. Or he wouldn't have wanted someone else. And I wouldn't be so...not brokenhearted. And I'm not. So what he did was wrong, and the position he put me in was wrong, but I'm not going to be mad at him for the next eight years. It wouldn't have been a good marriage, and if he wants something else, and I want something else, we shouldn't be together, right?"

"He hates me," Luc said, his voice rough. "He always has. Because I stayed with our father. Because...I'm the oldest. I had to. I had a responsibility to the business. And I think Blaise always felt I betrayed them in some way. That I was part of their banishment back to Africa. But that was our mother's choice. And it was Blaise's choice to go with her. I know he thinks that my life was easy. That I had things I didn't deserve. But he doesn't know. Mansions don't protect you from everything. And our father turned into a drunken, abusive bastard. So I resent the idea that somehow my life was so easy, I didn't deserve what I had."

"I don't know what to say."

"In the end, I think he was the lucky one," Luc said.

"What do you mean?"

"I mean, for all of his flaws, and he has them, he knows how to love people. I don't. That's why Marie couldn't be with me. It's why my father and I found things difficult. But he managed to love my fiancée enough to excuse his behavior. Then she left him spectacularly, just as she did to me, and he went on to love his wife, Ella. I just…can't."

"Why not, Luc?" she asked, pain lacing her voice. And he hated himself for that. For making her sad. That seemed to be his whole life. His reality was just not something people wanted to deal with. Not something they wanted to hear.

"I think you have to see love early. I think you have to learn it. And I never had the chance. I was too busy protecting myself from my father's fists. Sometimes unsuccessfully. But I closed everything down inside myself at a young age, and I don't think I could open it up now if I wanted to."

She wiggled and turned so that she was facing him, her blue eyes glittering with emotion. "If it's still in there, then there's hope," she said.

"You're such an optimist, Amelia. I think that's why I find you so fascinating. You see things with a ring of brightness around them. I envy that. I never did before I met you."

"Nice to know I've made an impact." She kissed him, closing her eyes tight. He kept his open for a moment, so that he could watch her. So that he could see just how much of herself she was putting into the kiss. It humbled him. Fascinated him. Made him envious. Made him conscious of every lock he'd put on his emotions all those years ago.

She climbed onto his lap, pushing his back against the edge of the couch, reaching behind him and picking up a condom—one of the many they'd left handy—holding it up in front of her. "I want you," she said. "Even though you are a grump who doesn't think he can love people."

Something about her words felt hot. Painful. They settled deep and he could *feel* them. Was so very aware of the fact that they'd changed something in him just because he'd heard them.

She dropped the blanket to her waist, baring her breasts, the damp center of her pressing against his hardened arousal. She rocked her hips against him and he put his hand on her lower back, holding her tight.

"You're going to be the death of me," he said.

"I hope not," she said. "I'm not finished with you yet." She smiled, she always smiled, even when she was playing the vixen, and tore the condom packet open, taking out the protection and reaching between them, rolling it over his length.

"Aren't you sore?" he asked, genuinely concerned, but hoping that she wasn't.

"In the best way," she said, putting her hands on his shoulders and flexing her hips so that the slick entrance to her body came into contact with the head of him.

She lowered herself onto him slowly, biting her lip, her eyes never leaving his. So sincere, his Amelia. She felt everything and she held nothing back. It was painful to see. Painful and exquisite. And so much more than he deserved.

She moved over him, taking him in deeper before retreating, then repeating the motion. She clasped her hands behind his neck, holding on to him as she took them both closer to the edge.

He tightened his hold on her hips and pulled her downward, harder, farther. She closed her eyes, a raw, sexual sound escaping her lips as she let her head fall back. If anything was more beautiful than her smile, it was this. Amelia. Lost in pleasure. Lost in him.

He could happily keep her like this forever.

He sucked in a sharp breath, trying to shift the weight that had settled on his chest. Forever wasn't an option. There would never be anything past today. But they had today. They had now.

Fire crackled along his veins, need, desire, building in him until he couldn't think. Couldn't breathe. Until he thought he might be reduced to ash. As though this moment might destroy him forever.

He gritted his teeth, tried to hold his climax back, tried to wait for her. But he was too close. It was too much. His control slipped its leash, and the fire turned into a raging blaze, hotter, more furious than he could have ever imagined.

He came on a roar, and she followed, leaning forward and biting his shoulder, the searing pain adding to the intensity, adding to the impossible surge of sensation that was filling his body.

She melted against him, her skin damp with sweat, her breasts pressed into his chest, her head rested in the curve of his neck, her cheek directly over the place that still burned from her teeth sinking into him.

"Oh, Luc," she said, her breathing hard, fast. "I...I love you."

He stiffened and pushed her away gently so that he could see her face. "You what?"

"I love you. I'm really sorry that I'm saying this now. And I'm sorry that I'm saying it at all. Because you warned me. You told me how things were and you just explained everything to me and

I won't even pretend that I understand what you went through. And I'm not going to tell you that it should be different for you. Because that's not fair. I'm not you and I don't understand what you've been through. But…it doesn't change how I feel. And I would…break the damn locks off your feelings boxes if I could. Or hope that I had a key somewhere, which would be better than breaking things all willy-nilly inside you, but I'm just saying, if I didn't have a key I would."

"Amelia…this is…" He lifted her from him and deposited her on the carpeted floor, her blanket beneath her. "I told you."

"I know. But this is the thing, Luc. I think it's always been you for me."

"What?"

"Clint obviously had his reasons for putting off making love with me, for putting off the wedding, but I obviously wasn't rushing toward the altar, or the bed either. And then…two days with you has taken me from virgin to sexpert. It's not random, Luc. I think when I met you, something in me knew, just knew, that there was never going to be anyone who made me feel quite like you."

"That's now, Amelia. That's not forever. It's not ages with a man who is emotionally nonfunctional. I barely wish *me* on me, I would never wish me on you."

"But that's sort of my decision, isn't it? What if I don't want love and marriage? What if I just want

to be with someone who makes me feel wanted? Is
that so bad? I mean…am I crazy?"

"You're not crazy, Amelia. But you don't know
what you want."

"Hold. On. You do not get to tell me whether or
not I get to sing Christmas carols in my head and
you absolutely do not get to tell me what I feel." Her
blue eyes were glistening with tears and he felt it,
like a knife twisting in his chest. He was hurting
her, breaking her, this beautiful, brilliant woman.
And there was nothing he could do to stop himself.

Because it was what he had to do.

What he wanted was to tell her to stay. To tell
her to never leave him, no matter that he couldn't
give her back what she needed. He wanted to say
to hell with her needs. Her feelings. And hold her
to him, so that he could have a little bit of light.
Just a little bit.

But he knew what happened to a flame that
couldn't breathe. That didn't get what it needed.
He would only extinguish her light. And then not
only would he be in darkness, he'd be responsible
for hers, as well.

"You're noble, Amelia. But you don't always
have to do this," he said, his tone cold.

"What?"

"You don't have to give to people who can't, or
won't, give back to you."

"I don't do that," she said, wrapping the blanket
around her shoulders, covering her body.

"You do. You were considering marrying your fiancé out of a sense of obligation to him and your parents, even though you knew he wanted to be with someone else. And now you're throwing yourself across the altar that is my life, just begging to be burned alive. My own personal virgin sacrifice."

"Luc, what are you doing?" she asked, a tear sliding down her cheek.

He hated himself right now. But not more than he would if he let her do this.

"I'm being honest with you. Clint might be able to ask you to be with him, even though he doesn't really want you or love you, but I won't."

"So you don't love me, or want me," she said, her voice breaking on the last word.

"You already know I don't love you, and as for the wanting, I think it's clear that right now I do. But later…Amelia, I'm not the kind of man who looks for a long-term commitment. I tried it, and honestly, thank God I was liberated from it. I'm not mad at Blaise because he robbed me of marriage, our issues are a lot deeper than that. In the end, I'm happy to have avoided the institution."

"So you're saying you would get tired of me?"

"I've never had a long-term relationship," he bit out, his body rebelling against the idea of ever being tired of her. Of wanting any woman other than her. "I've never wanted one. So even now, you're offering something I'm just not interested in taking someone up on."

"Oh," she said, blinking rapidly. "I see. I see. So…so what? No more sex even? I was offering you free milk, here, Chevalier. No cow-buying."

"Amelia," he said, and he didn't want to go on, because if she made him keep going, he would have to say something worse, or he would break and tell her he would take her for as long as he could keep her. "No."

"Great. Okay," she said. "That's good, actually, because I had not been sufficiently rejected this week. So it's better that we just kind of added emphasis to the whole…my fiancé sleeping with a dude thing. Just to make sure I know my place. Gay men don't want me, straight men don't want me. Just fine."

"Amelia, it's not you."

"Right," she said, her voice dripping with disdain. "It's you. You know what? It is you. And it's Clint. And it's even my parents, as well as they mean. Everyone wants something from me, and I bend over backward to give it. And well, okay, in the end that's me. That's my problem. I'm the one who gives even when I don't want to. But the one thing I do want to give…you won't let me, but you're still trying to tell me what to do, and I hate it. I don't want to do what everyone wants anymore."

"Then don't," he said, forcing the words out. "But I don't want to be with you. And I'm not going to do anything I don't want either."

The side of her mouth twitched, her eyelids flut-

tering. "Well, fine. Great. I can't argue with that."
She stood up, wrapped in the blanket. "I'm going
to go to bed. My bed. Hopefully we get a Christmas miracle and the weather clears up tomorrow."

"Maybe you'll get one, Amelia," he said, his
voice rough.

He certainly wouldn't. He wasn't the kind of person who got Christmas miracles. But she deserved
them.

He watched her walk out of the room and tried
not to dwell on the fact that for her, a Christmas
miracle would involve being relieved of his presence. He had no right to be upset about it, anyway.

He was the one who had pushed her away.

But it was for the best. He wouldn't doubt his
decision.

# CHAPTER EIGHT

FORTUNATELY THE WEATHER had cleared up by morning. But that was the only thing that was fortunate. Everything else was horrible. Amelia felt horrible. Her head hurt, and her heart hurt, and she had no idea what she was supposed to do about either thing.

On the one hand, she now knew for sure that she didn't love Clint, and never really had in that way you should love the man you were going to marry. On the other hand, she was very certain that she *did* love Luc.

And given his spectacular rejection of her that was majorly inconvenient.

They didn't speak in the elevator on their way down to the lobby. They didn't speak when Luc went to check them out.

"Mr. Chevalier!"

They both looked up to see Don Fleischer walking toward them. She stiffened, and said a silent prayer that went unanswered as Luc reached over and took her hand.

It was like being hit with a lightning bolt. One that was heavy with emotion and horribleness.

A reminder of everything that was good between

them, and everything that she wasn't going to have because he didn't want to be with her. And he was still touching her like he did.

All for show. This was her nightmare.

But if she pulled away now, it would seem weird. And if it affected the deal then the whole time here would be utterly pointless. Better to just have her virginity lost rather than the deal, too. Though, if she could go back…

No. She wouldn't change it. Because at least she knew now what she could have. At least she knew she wouldn't settle for less ever again.

Unfortunately, everything would seem like less after stupid Luc.

*He doesn't love you. You deserve more than that.*

Hell, yes, she did.

She gritted her teeth, fought against the tears that were burning her eyes. She wasn't going to let this get to her. And she wasn't going to pine. Not when he didn't deserve it.

Clint had wasted her time. He'd hurt her. But Luc had devastated her.

"Mr. Fleischer," Luc said, smiling. She had no idea how he did that. Maybe he was telling the truth. Maybe he had all his emotions locked up so tight no one could reach them. In which case, she wouldn't ever be able to.

If he could smile now, it meant he could feel nothing, and she really wasn't ever going to be able to break those locks.

"What are your thoughts now that you've stayed here?"

"I think I'll be making an offer," Luc said. "It's definitely the perfect place for a romantic getaway, and I think I have the ability to grow the resort."

"That's wonderful news."

"I'll submit my offer after Christmas," Luc said. "For now, I need to get Amelia back to New York so she can spend time with her family."

After making what felt to Amelia like very awkward goodbyes, they walked out. Their car was waiting for them, and as soon as she thought it was safe Amelia wrenched her hand from his and opened the car door, sat down inside and buckled up, refusing to look at him.

Luc rounded to the passenger side and got in, buckling up as the car pulled away from the hotel.

They rode in silence until the airport, where they exchanged short, necessary words about where the plane was and where the luggage should go.

Amelia managed to keep up the silence a couple of hours into the flight, her brain turning over the past twenty-four hours. Their kiss in the spa, making love with him for the first time, the fifth time. Realizing she loved him. Telling him she loved him.

It had changed her. She was utterly and completely changed and she was supposed to just go back to her life like it had been before.

No. That wasn't happening. She was breaking

up with Clint. And she was going to have to take action with Luc, too.

"I quit," she said, the words leaving her mouth in a rush.

"What?" His response was sharp, shocked and very loud after the prolonged silence.

"I can't work for you anymore."

"You said none of this would be a problem," he bit out. "You said you knew what this was."

"Yes, and it changed. I didn't mean to lie, but I guess I did. I don't want to work for a man who was inside me, then looked at me like I was something stuck to the bottom of his shoe while he rejected my love."

He made a short, incredulous sound.

"Neither do I want to be with a man who does those French…noises you do. It's annoying. You're annoying. I'm not making you coffee ever again. I'm going to eat every peppermint stir stick and scone on your plane and never make you coffee or fetch you a bagel again!"

She was breathing hard, adrenaline pouring through her. She was mad, she was hurt, but at least she was sure of this decision. And she didn't care how it affected him. She didn't care if it was upsetting or disappointing for him, not when it was right for her.

"You won't have a job, and you won't be able to pay your rent. And unless you are marrying Clint—" he said the other man's name like it disgusted him "—then you're going to have a bit of a rough awakening."

"Don't care. I have savings," she said, tugging the peppermint stick from her latte and crunching the end. "I will be fine. Just fine. You on the other hand will have to find another assistant who doesn't care that you're a gigantic pain. So good luck with that." She took another bite of the peppermint and chewed loudly.

"You're being unreasonable. And emotional," he ground out.

"News flash, that's because I'm a human being. And humans are emotional. You, sir, are a robot. A cyborg, actually, because you're part human, but robotic nonetheless!"

"Amelia…"

"Don't talk to me. Unless you want to recant all the horrible crap you've said to me in the past eight hours."

"I can't."

"Then shh. I'm drinking my latte and pondering a career folding leggings at a department store."

She tucked her feet up under her and drank her latte, brooding for the rest of the flight while Luc worked with his head down.

When the plane landed, she stood. "I'm not going to ride with you," she said. "After my bags come out, I'm going to the taxi line like a plebeian. Have yourself a merry little Christmas, jackass." She turned to face the cargo area where the bags were being gathered and started humming.

Luc didn't wait for his bags. He simply got into the waiting car. "Goodbye, Amelia," he said.

"Bye," she said, turning back to the plane, blinking back tears. She heard the car door close, and she folded her arms over her stomach to keep from folding in on herself.

When she got her bags, she started to drag them to the airport door, to the cabs, tears rolling down her cheeks. She drew in a shaky breath and started to sing. "'Oh, tidings of comfort and joy, comfort and joy.'" Her voice broke on the last word and she looked down, wiping a tear off her cheek. She swallowed hard. "'Oh, tidings of comfort and joy.'"

# CHAPTER NINE

HIS OFFICE HAD a disturbing lack of singing happening in it. And he didn't like it at all. All of the things he'd relished prior to having Amelia in his life, and things he'd imagine he would enjoy again if she was ever gone, were just not enjoyable at all anymore.

At the moment, his office was just cold, dark and lacked coffee.

Sure, he could call someone up from another department and demand they make him a drink. And he could make his own. But it wouldn't be the same. He'd taken for granted just how much he counted on her.

And it wasn't just his office that felt empty. It was his chest. There was a gaping hole left behind by that woman and he had no idea what he was going to do to repair it. If he even wanted to.

Because if it could be fixed, it felt as if he would be dishonoring what they'd shared. And why should he care about that? Why should what they shared matter? She was one woman, one in a line of several. While not the legendary playboy his brother was, he'd had his share of lovers, and not one of them had affected him like this. Their breakups had always been amicable. Easy. And he'd felt fine afterward. He'd felt nothing, really.

Marie was the only one to make him feel anything, and that had been nothing like this.

That had been wounded pride. He'd been the laughingstock of society. Being left right before the wedding for his brother.

But it hadn't been this. This had nothing to do with anyone but Amelia and himself.

He gritted his teeth against the onslaught of pain the thought brought on. Amelia and him. The ache was only for her, and yet the reasons he couldn't be with her seemed to involve an army of other people.

He looked down at his desk, staring at the wood grain, one question playing through his mind.

*Why?*

Why did anyone else get a say in what he did? In what he could feel? Why was anything or anyone more important than what he felt than she was?

They shouldn't be. And yet, there was too much in the way. Though part of him couldn't help but wonder if he was just in his own way.

Anger had always protected him. Anger at his father had kept him from caring too much when the old man had struck him, and had stopped it eventually, as he'd become a man and his father realized that Luc wasn't to be trifled with.

Anger had protected him when Blaise had returned to France with a rage matching his own. It had kept him from wanting a reunion, when both of them were so full of resentment.

It had insulated him, driven him, after Marie.

But now it was keeping him from something he wanted. It was keeping him from Amelia. Keeping her from him.

As long as anger was the biggest emotion in him, he really couldn't ever be worthy of her, and every reason he'd pushed her away would hold true.

But if he could change it… If he could change himself rather than just making excuses, then maybe…

She would always be too good for him. Too bright, too lovely and too damn chipper. But he was wallowing in the things of the past, embracing his anger because it was easy, and while his pride rebelled against that reality, it was the truth.

He pounded his fist on the desk, the only sound that had echoed in the room since he'd come in that morning.

He knew what his life would bring if he didn't change. More of the same. Loneliness, a sense of quiet stability, the dull ache of rage and a strange sadness that pushed against his throat when he closed his eyes at night. Whether he was an investor or a real estate developer, if he was ever going to have a different life, changes would have to happen inside him, not just outside.

But if he chose Amelia, there would be no stability in the everyday. It would be too bright, too fuzzy and rarely quiet. It would be full of songs, and when he closed his eyes, she would be next to him. Warm and soft, smelling like peppermint and pine and being more than he'd ever hoped to deserve.

If he was going to hold Amelia, he had to let go of some things he'd been carrying for far too long.

He picked up his phone and scrolled through the numbers. This wasn't one he had memorized, and that said a lot. Though, he had always kept it. And maybe that said a lot, too.

He dialed, not caring that it was ten at night in Paris. That wasn't his problem. He was making amends and he would do it on his time.

"Hello?" A woman answered. American. His brother's wife, Ella.

"Hello," he said, knowing he sounded awkward and stilted. Hating that he cared at all.

"Who is this?"

"This is Luc," he said. "We've never spoken. I'm…"

"Blaise's brother," she said, sounding somewhat shell-shocked.

"Yes."

"Are you calling for….are you calling for him? That's a stupid question. Who else would you be calling for? But then, why are you calling at all? You never have. Well, obviously you have. But never since I've been around."

"I am calling because things have gotten to a point where it's clear I owe him an apology."

"You owe *him* one?"

"Yes," he said, his voice rough.

"Hello?"

It was Blaise. He'd picked up another line.

"It's me," Luc said.

"So it is," Blaise said, not sounding particularly friendly.

"I'll just hang up," Ella said.

"No," Luc said. "Stay on, please. It will be easier. You're a part of this, too, Ella. Because you're family. I'm not good at this kind of thing. At being sincere and saying nice things. I don't have a lot of practice."

"I have more than I used to. I'm sorry," Blaise said. "I want you to know that. I have wanted you to know that. I've wished you would take a call from me for a long time so I could say just that. She wasn't the one for me, no matter how much I believed it. Even if she had been, what I did wouldn't have been right."

"It's immaterial. You've apologized before. And I know…I know I said I forgave you. But that was a lie. I didn't. I know you know that. I know my not talking to you showed how empty that statement of forgiveness was. I was angry. I've been angry. I don't want to be anymore. I can't be. Because I think I understand you now."

"Do you?" Blaise asked.

"Yes. I met a woman. One that…no matter her circumstances I couldn't turn away from. One that

I knew was wrong for me to touch. But I did, anyway. Because sometimes…it's bigger than you are."

"I was just being vindictive at the time, I think, Luc. But I do know what you're saying about love. That's what I have with Ella. The feelings that surpass everything else. Common sense, common decency. Fear."

"Yes," Luc said. "That. But she deserves someone better than me. So I'm trying to be better."

"Don't just try," Blaise said. "Do it. If you've found someone like that…nothing else matters."

"You do. And Ella. I want to be in your lives. I want Amelia and I to be in your lives. First, I have to convince her that she should be with me. After I went to so much trouble to push her away."

Blaise chuckled, a laugh that sounded so like his. Funny how that worked, as they'd spent so little time together. But the bond was stronger than time. And it was a bond he'd spent far too long trying to sever. No more.

"That sounds familiar. Just go admit you were wrong. They like that."

He heard a feminine snort through the phone line. "Well, you are wrong. Most of the time."

"Of course I am," Blaise said, no sincerity in his tone at all. "And, as much as I'm enjoying the reunion, Luc, I think you have some more pressing matters to attend to."

"For once," Ella said, "my husband is not wrong."

"I will call again," Luc said.

"Hopefully with good news."

Luc got off the phone with his brother and sat back in his chair. That was one step. One step in fixing the mess that was himself.

Blaise had talked about love. And Blaise was right. Luc loved Amelia. More than he'd ever loved another person, more than he loved himself.

And that was scary. Really scary. It was, he realized, exactly why he'd fought so hard to convince himself he couldn't love her. Because the thought of being that exposed to her, of needing anyone that badly, was utterly terrifying.

But life without her would be worse than terrifying. It would be empty. Like his office. Like his chest.

He stood up. It was Christmas Eve, and that meant Amelia was at her parents' house upstate. And soon, he would be, too.

AMELIA STIRRED THE POT of gravy quickly before taking it off the burner for a moment, letting the bubbles calm down.

She looked around the room. At the little country village her mother had put on the counter, a roll of batting beneath it, acting as snow. There was tinsel tacked around the perimeter of the room, and the warm smell of boiling potatoes and cranberries filled the air and made it humid.

She and her mother were getting as much precooking done as possible before the big day.

Christmas in her family's historic home certainly didn't have the glamour that flying around the country with Luc did, but it was a lot less painful, too. And less incredible. And less sexy. But then, her family would never let her go either. As days went, it had been an incredibly draining one.

First she'd lost Luc. Then she'd gone to Clint's apartment and broken it off with him. They'd both cried. And it had been awful. And she'd held his hand and told him that neither of them would be happy living that way.

And he'd agreed, his hands trembling in hers.

And then she'd gone to her parents' house and broken the news. Thankfully, her sisters weren't there yet with their husbands and spate of children. They all spent Christmas morning in their own houses and converged on the family home in the afternoon, for more presents and food.

At least this way she'd been alone for the hard talk with her parents. Clint had given her permission to explain, as long as they didn't tell his parents. Which he was going to do after the holidays. Ensuring tomorrow would be extremely awkward, since he and his family were coming for dinner.

Though, they'd both agreed they weren't pretending to be a couple.

"Are you okay, Amelia?" her mother asked.

"I'm fine," Amelia said, lying.

"You don't seem fine."

"It's been a hard day."

"I know. I'm so sorry about Clint. I really had no idea."

"I *should* have," Amelia grumbled.

Her mom threw up her hands. "I don't want to know."

"No, Mom, you probably don't. Or hey, you even might. Since the truth is so very, very tame," she said, rolling her eyes. "Anyway, thank you for understanding. And please, please, no hints to his parents tomorrow about why. That's not exactly the thing you want to give your parents for Christmas."

"No, no," she said. "Though, I think things will be okay for him."

"I hope so."

"You aren't mad at him?"

Amelia shrugged. "I'm upset that he wasted my time, but I sort of understand, too. And if I'm honest with myself, I wasted my time, too. I don't think I ever really loved him, Mom, or I wouldn't have been happy with the relationship we had. He definitely doesn't deserve all the blame."

"You sound too well-adjusted to look so sad."

Amelia sighed. "The sad is another story. And one that probably doesn't belong at Christmas dinner either." She put the gravy back on, keeping her focus on it. The gravy, at least, provided purpose.

"Amelia!" her father shouted from the other room. "Someone at the door for you!"

"Who?" she shouted.

"I don't know. Guy in a suit!" her dad called back.

Amelia frowned. "Stir the gravy," she said, handing the whisk to her mother before walking out into the entryway.

She looked out the door and froze. On the step, in the suit, with snow falling behind him, was Luc.

"Can we talk?" he asked.

"I… Yes." She pulled a coat off the peg—her mother's it turned out, something misshapen and not at all fashionable—and turned to look at her father. "I'll just be a minute." Or a second if all he was here to do was ask for her to come and make coffee again.

Oh, Lord, what if that was why he was here? Not for her at all, not really. But to ask her to take her job back on Christmas Eve because he didn't know how to run his coffeemaker?

She stepped outside and closed the door, crossing her arms under her breasts, her lower lip quivering from the cold and the emotion building in her chest. "Okay, Chevalier, why are you here? I swear if you came all the way down here because you miss my coffee I will—"

"I do miss your coffee," he said.

"Oh." She tightened her hold on herself, the lip quivering intensifying. "Well, then, at the risk of sounding like a grumpy old lady, get off my lawn."

"I miss your coffee. And your singing. And the way you whistle. I miss you talking to yourself. Your loud clothes, your shopping on your phone during business hours."

"If you put that in my letter of recommendation no one would hire me," she said, sniffling, blaming her running nose on the cold.

"Probably not. But I would. All over again."

"Are you kidding me, Luc? This is what you're here for? To beg me to come back and assist you because of my amazing coffee?"

"No. That's not why I'm here. And I'm not finished. I also miss your smile. Your laughter. The way you make me laugh. The way you kiss…" He took a step toward her and wrapped his arm around her waist. "I miss the way it feels to be inside you. How it feels to hold you. I hate myself for never having fallen asleep with you, and even more, I hate myself because when you told me you loved me I pushed you away. I had a chance to say the words back, to hold you to me as you said them, and I didn't. I am a fool, and I will never forgive myself if I ruined my chances with you."

"Oh," she said, a tear rolling down her cheek, the track left by the tear chilling her face in the cold night air.

"I love you, Amelia. And that scares me. So I figured I would protect myself by saying I couldn't love. By believing I couldn't love. Anger is safer," he said, his voice rough. "And I was so walled in my anger I felt very little else. No pain or disappointment. But no joy either. And until you, no love. But what you said before you left…that it was always me, I think I've just realized that for me it was always you. Why else would I enjoy your singing? I hate singing," he said. "I don't like Christmas, or Christmas carols, and somehow you make me enjoy them. You make me like things I never thought I would. You make me like…life. You're right, I'm a grumpy bastard, but you make me less of one."

She laughed, letting her head fall back, before straightening and looking him in the eyes. "Well, that is quite a declaration."

"It's true," he said. "I called Blaise. I made things right with him. Or, I at least started taking steps to make things right with him. Because you've done something to me. Changed me. Made me want more than just a protective coating of anger and a life that's simply livable. You make me want everything. And if you can live with me, put up with me, love me, even though I don't deserve it, I will do everything I can to make you happy."

"You don't have to do much, Luc," she said.

"I don't?"

"Just love me."

"I do. Now and forever, I promise you."

"You're my very own Christmas miracle," she said.

"And you're mine." He bent down and kissed her, and she wrapped her arms around his neck, holding him close, reveling in his touch. In the fact that they'd finally realized what they had, after spending four years in each other's lives.

"You know this means we're having a Christmas wedding next year," she said.

"Did I propose?" he asked.

"Oh! Crap. That's embarrassing," she said, putting her head on his shoulder. "You didn't."

"Well, I will now. Amelia, will you marry me?"

"Yes!" she said. "Christmas wedding?"

"Of course," he said.

"I think we'll have to play a little 'God Rest Ye Merry Gentleman.'"

He smiled and for the first time in her memory, he sang. "'Oh, tidings of comfort and joy.'"

"'Comfort and joy,'" she sang with him. "'Oh, tidings of comfort and joy.'"

"Yes," she said. "That is happening."

"I would never even try to stop you."

"You're marrying this, Chevalier. Think you can handle it?"

"I intend to spend a lifetime trying."

She laced her fingers through his and tugged him up the front step.

"What?" he asked.

"I think it's time you met my family."

"Are they like you?"

She nodded. "They are exactly like me."

"Then it is a very good thing I love you."

"For more than one reason, Mr. Chevalier. For more than one reason."

\* \* \* \* \*

# A Diamond
# for Christmas

## JOSS WOOD

To Tess, my own Christmas angel.
Love you, Belle.

**Joss Wood** wrote her first book at the age of eight and has never really stopped. Fuelled by coffee, her passion for putting letters on a blank screen is matched only by her love of books and travelling—especially to the wild places of Southern Africa—and possibly by her hatred of ironing and making school lunches. Happily and chaotically surrounded by books, Christmas is her favourite time of year, especially when it's crazy with family and friends and ranges from refined to raucous! Joss lives in South Africa with her husband, children and their many pets. Visit her website at www.josswoodbooks. wordpress.com.

# *PROLOGUE*

*July...*

WELL PLAYED, TEQUILA, well played.

It only took three margaritas to get her to drop her guard around James but, because she was Riley Taylor, when she messed up she messed up big. This time by hopping into bed with one of her oldest friends.

Her best friend's brother.

And her boss.

Again.

In her defence, she doubted that few women between the ages of eighteen and eighty would say no when James Moreau crooked his finger at them, kissed them senseless and dragged them off to bed. But she knew better. It was all that witch Tequila's fault, she decided—the cactus juice had definitely lowered her inhibitions and cancelled out a few brain cells.

*One tequila, two tequila, three tequila...yes, James, more!*

As the morning sunlight slipped in from behind the curtains, Riley, still lying on top of James—

morning sex had her on top and her face was now pressed into his very broad shoulder—turned her head and met his fabulous green eyes. Oh, those eyes. They were the rich green of bottle glass and they held a whole lot of panic. A deep frown creased his forehead.

Riley knew that a puckered brow after many bouts of amazing sex spelt trouble. Then again, wasn't that the perfect word to define the relationship she and James had? Trouble worked, she thought, as did difficult and complicated and... messy.

Yeah, messy worked really well.

Time to face the music...

She slid off him, stood up and reached for a nightgown that lay folded across a wingback chair and quickly pulled it on. Riley saw her reflection in the free-standing full-length mirror and winced— mussed hair, stubble rash-covered jaw and languorous, satisfied eyes. Yep, no guesses as to how they'd spent the last ten hours.

After a polite greeting at the beginning of the evening and—admittedly—many, many intense looks from across the crowded wedding tent, he'd taken her hand and led her to his car. She hadn't bothered protesting, hadn't thought about where she was going, what she was about to do. She'd wanted him as much as his eyes had flashed that he wanted her. They didn't need any words; they both knew that they were going back to her room at his childhood home situated on the Western Cape vineyard, Bon Chance, for a night light on conversation and heavy on kisses, pleasuring hands and throaty, breathy cries. Incredible physical pleasure.

After all, this wasn't their first ride on this particular roller coaster.

'Oops, we did it again.'

Okay, it was flippant but at least it was something to break the tense silence between them. James lifted a sandy eyebrow. Without responding, he stood up and walked across the room, picking up his suit trousers from the floor and holding them loosely in his hand.

'Yeah, we...' James swallowed the swear word and ran his hand through his thick blond hair '... *messed* up again.'

Just the words a girl needed to hear after a spectacular orgasm given to her by the only man who'd ever managed to rock her sexual world. Oh, she felt so special.

'So, the post-orgasmic glow doesn't last long for you. Good to know,' Riley retorted.

'I've slept with one of my oldest friends, my employee, my sister's best friend! *Again*!'

'Why can't you think of me as just Riley?' she quietly asked. *Not as the pigtailed girl who pulled your hair, not as Morgan's BFF, not as the window designer for your family's ultra-chic and mega-expensive string of international jewellery stores, Moreau's. Not as your vineyard manager's daughter...*

*Just Riley,* she thought, finding it difficult to keep her eyes on his face. Any woman who had seen James naked would understand... His rugged, hot action-hero face had been known to stop traffic but, dear Lord, his naked body could stop intergalactic spaceships.

His looks, combined with the fact that he was CEO of Moreau International, dealing with every aspect of gemstones from mining to upmarket jewellery stores, made him a whale-size catch and one of the top five most eligible bachelors in the world. Not that she gave a rat's about any of that nonsense—he was just James. Hot, yeah, but he drove her batty.

James ran a hand over his face and she couldn't help but notice the tension in his broad shoulders, his ripped abs, skittering through his muscled arms.

'Why do we keep doing this?' he demanded as he yanked his trousers on and zipped them up.

'Jeez, it's not like this is a habit or anything. Three times in a decade isn't exactly an addiction, Moreau.' Riley watched as he pulled on his dress shirt, idly noticing that it was now missing a couple of buttons.

'It was a mistake,' James muttered, looking around for his shoes.

Riley shoved her hands into her hair and yanked it in frustration. 'So the other times we slept together, when I was nineteen, and when I was twenty-five…were those mistakes too?' Riley said bitterly. 'Then again, you are such a damn playboy that you probably don't even remember me, us…'

'I've never forgotten one minute spent with you.' James snapped his head up, his eyes hot and full of frustration.

Well, what was she supposed to say to that? Wait, she always had something she could say…

'Probably because I'm nothing like the women you usually sleep with. They are all blonde and buxom and long-legged and beautiful and I'm… not.' No, she was still the size of an average four-teen-year-old with grey eyes, copper-red hair and a temper to match. And didn't she sound like a whiny witch. She dropped her eyes and her tone. 'I don't understand you…this…us.'

'There is no us,' James said.

There had been once—for a brief, glorious month there had been a Riley and James. And then she'd let herself be talked out of it…or talked herself out of it…or something.

*There is no us.* Riley twisted her lips. No, there wasn't, not any more. And there was no comfort in the knowledge that James, ever since his failed engagement years ago, hadn't been part of an 'us' with anyone else either. He was the King of the Fling.

Riley jammed her hands into the pockets of her gown and lifted her head, up and up, to his face. At five two, she looked utterly ridiculous standing next to the six-foot-plus James. Without heels, her head barely scraped his collarbone. Riley suspected that if she were any other woman he'd send her a wide smile, flash those sexy dimples, say, *Thanks, babe,* and slip out of the door.

She didn't need his words to tell her she was wasting her time—what he wanted to say was written all over his face. Not wanting to prolong the humiliation, Riley went to the door and yanked it open.

'Ri, this was a—'

'If you say it was a mistake again, I swear I'll stab you with…something,' Riley hissed. 'I think it's time for you to go before you say something else that can't be taken back.'

'Dammit, Riley, you are like my sis—'

Oh, that was a crappy, crazy excuse. Riley slapped her mouth against James's and smacked her hands on his butt. She might not have had many lovers for a woman fast approaching her thirties but she had kissed a lot of men and she knew exactly how to do it. A slide here, a nip there, a quick suck…and James quickly forgot what he was about to say. When she allowed him to come up for air James looked shell-shocked.

Yeah, take that…Mr I-Think-of-You-As-My-Sister.

'You didn't say that when you were moaning my name in the throes of passion last night.'

'Ri— Okay. But—'

'I am *not* your sister or your friend. And I'm done pining away for you. You have ten seconds to decide if you want to explore this heat we have always had or whether you are walking away for good. But you should know that if you walk that's it. You don't get another chance.'

'Riley, I—'

'Ten seconds, nine, eight, seven—'

'It's not that easy.'

It wasn't easy at all, she thought, as she held his eyes as she counted down. Riley, fighting back the tears that she refused to allow to fall, breathed out the last number and shut the door in James's face.

So, that was that. Time to move on, Riley.

It was way, way, *way* past time for her to move on.

# CHAPTER ONE

*The end of November...*

THE WORKERS AT THE diamond mine in South Africa
were threatening to strike again, they had a staff
member at the jewellery store filching merchandise
and he had a board meeting to prepare for.

His plate was full to overflowing and he was
tired and stressed and...horny. Man, he was horny.
He wanted, needed, *craved* sex...and so he should
after a five-month drought. *And whose fault was
that, Einstein?* He could have walked into any function in New York City and had any piece of tail
he wanted—single, engaged, married, even!—
but every time he decided to go for it the image of
storm-grey eyes in a pixie face flicked across his
retina and the moment passed.

He didn't want any woman. James wanted Riley.
That night they'd spent together was the best and
worst time he'd spent with a woman in...hell, *for
ever*. An amazing night because he had shared explosive, passionate sex with a woman he cared about
and that emotional connection added a depth to sex
he'd long forgotten about.

The worst night because he had, a long time ago, deliberately chosen not to combine sex and emotion again.

His body, which apparently did not connect with his, reputedly, very sharp brain, suddenly craved the one person he shouldn't want. *Remind your junk why she is out of bounds, Moreau.* This normally stopped him from storming down to her basement studio in the Moreau International building and taking her on her weird coloured couch.

*Three, two, one...go. Or, failing that, just go back to work.*

Before he could do either his desk phone buzzed, followed by his PA's amused voice. 'James, Riley wants to see… Oh, she's already at the door and on her way in.'

Think of the devil and she appears…

James looked across his spacious office towards the door that was opening and Riley strode inside, dressed in a black skirt, a black cashmere turtleneck and high-heeled black boots. She always wore heels in an effort to look taller, not that they helped… much.

She took his breath away every single time he saw her.

He wished he could run his hand down that fall of bright red hair, feel her silky-smooth skin under that black jumper. She had a perfect body, he thought—all woman, despite her pint-size package. And she'd felt amazing in his arms—fragrant, heated skin, breathy cries. She was still the only woman who had the ability to rocket blood to his groin simply by stepping into the room.

Under his desk, James adjusted the crotch of his suddenly tight trousers and leaned back in his chair, propping his feet up onto the corner of his desk. This was the first time that they had been alone in five months and he wondered what had prompted her to collar him in his office, on his turf.

Colour him intrigued.

Maybe she was as frustrated as he was and she was about to offer some recreational office sex… *Yeah, in your dreams, Moreau.* He knew what Riley looked like when she was turned on and big worried eyes and a tense jaw were not part of her 'do-me-now' look.

No, he immediately clocked that, whatever it was that Riley had to say, it wasn't going to be good news.

James dropped his feet and stood up, unable to help the surge of protectiveness she always generated in him. He didn't like it but he'd known her all his life and it was part of who he was. 'What's wrong? What's the matter? Are your folks okay? Your brothers?'

Riley shook, then nodded her head. Well, that helped…not. She lifted up her hand to halt his progress across the room and James, seeing how she was struggling to get her words out, decided to help her by stopping and waiting.

When she finally found her voice, what she said rocked the foundations of his world. It was nothing that he could ever have anticipated.

'I wanted to personally tell you that I'm leaving Moreau International. I'll have my resignation letter on your desk by the end of the day.'

Without giving him a chance to respond, she turned on her heel and walked straight out of his office.

SHE'D DONE IT, Riley thought, walking past his PA's desk, blindly heading to the elevators at the end of the long passage. She had told James and now she *had* to leave—she couldn't live in limbo any more.

She couldn't live like *this* any more.

Riley blinked back tears, resisting the urge to just stop and place her forehead against the cool wall. This was one of the longest, busiest corridors in the building and she just needed to get to her basement studio, her sanctuary, where she could be alone.

There was nothing left for her in this city any more. She loved her job as chief window designer for Moreau's; it had been the only thing that had carried her through the last nearly half year but it was no longer enough, she thought, as she caught and ruthlessly stopped the sob in her throat.

The past five months had been tough on her, mentally and emotionally. The last whisper of her dreams around James had been shattered that night and since then her life seemed to be spiralling out of control. Not to be dramatic, but she felt as if she'd not only lost her dreams but, to an extent, her way as well. Alienation and loneliness now characterised her life. When her best friend, Morgan, had fallen in love with Noah, it was so natural that he became her priority and she hardly saw Morgan these days. It was so normal and so healthy but Riley acutely felt the absence in her life. Especially since she and James hadn't exchanged more than ten words in far too long. They knew each other too well, shared too many memories, were part of each other's families and their disconnection felt strange, unnatural.

It was better this way, Riley told herself again. She'd finally come to accept that they were simply not meant to be together. She needed to move on and create new dreams, find another way to be fulfilled, happy.

As she went to step into the lift, Riley felt a strong hand on her arm and was pulled to a stop. *Dang, so close...*

'My office, now,' James growled from above her head.

A dark, sculpted eyebrow lifted and her large, expressive grey eyes shot silver lightning in his direction. 'No.'

'We need to talk about the fact that you didn't just blow your budget for the Christmas windows, you blew it with the strength of a Category five hurricane.'

Okay, not what she was expecting. Maybe he

didn't want to announce her resignation in front of the ten-strong crowd of his employees who were waiting for the lifts so Riley decided to play along. 'You'll understand why when you see the windows. They are incredibly special this year.'

'They still need to come in under budget, Riley.' She thought she heard him mutter, 'Damn artists...' under his breath.

'Is that what you came all this way to tell me?' she asked, her expression facetious. 'You could have just sent an e-mail.'

'You could've given me a better explanation as to why,' James replied and they both knew that he wasn't talking about the windows and her lack of budgeting skills.

James clocked the curious glances from his staff, their ping-pong eyes, and his glower immediately wiped their faces into 'not listening' expressions. Hah! Of course they were...

'I'm not arguing with you in front of an audience. My office, now,' James ordered.

Uh...no.

'I'm not going to argue with you at all.' Riley bared her teeth at him in a smile that held all the charm of a snakebite. 'Bye.'

As she stepped towards the open lift, Riley flipped him one last look and abruptly realised that he looked stressed, annoyed and exhausted and that he'd just hit his ceiling of tolerance. He had a slow to burn temper but when it ignited it scorched like a flamethrower. She suspected that she'd put a match to the flammable liquid.

'I said...*my office. Now.*' Then his hands gripped her hips and halted her progress into the lift. Since she weighed less than a feather, he easily spun her around, ignored her annoyed yelp, picked her up and tossed her over his shoulder.

*What the fudge?*

Riley pounded her fists on his back and he tightened his grip as he walked down the passage. 'What the hell do you think you are doing? Put me down, you moron!' she yelled. 'Moreau, let me go!'

'Try to remember that I'm your boss, Taylor.' James spat the words at her knees.

'Try to remember that I can sue you for manhandling me and for sexual harassment and for emotional distress...'

Riley squirmed and James tightened his arms across the back of her thighs and pinned her in place. What was happening here? Who was this person? James Moreau, usually cool and very controlled, must be losing his marbles because carting her around like this was very un-James-like behaviour.

Riley, realising that she had as much chance of surviving a nuclear explosion as she had of fighting James, stopped struggling and sighed when office doors opened and heads popped out to see who was screaming like a banshee. She guessed James had an expression like thunder because those faces disappeared as quickly as they had appeared and the office employees in the passage scuttled to get out of his way. *Oh, yeah, this was going to spread through the building like wildfire.*

James walked into his own office and kicked the door shut with his foot before dumping her onto the leather couch in the corner. Riley instantly sprang to her feet and launched herself at him, drilling her finger into his chest. 'I don't care who you think you are but you can't just issue orders and then, when I don't comply, toss me over your shoulder!'

God, she was still fighting him, James thought as he easily captured her wrists in one hand, twisted her around so that her back was to his front—and Mr Happy in his pants immediately sprang up in excited anticipation. And so it should, since this was the closest he had come to any action in far too many months and no, going solo didn't count.

He really didn't want to think about why the thought of bedding someone else left a sour taste in his mouth...every single time.

Riley stood immobile in his arms and, as he slid his other hand over her stomach and spread his fingers so that the tips rested just above her mound, a fine tremor skittered through her body. She went utterly still and under his fingers he could feel the rapid pulse in her wrists, could hear her uneven breathing.

She was so turned on.... *Let's see how much,* he thought.

James pushed his hand under her shirt and he groaned when it encountered that silky skin of her flat stomach. He couldn't help moving his hand further upwards so that he covered her breast and instantly her nipple bloomed into his palm. She was so responsive, her passion—and temper—was quick to flare. James, thinking that it was safe to release her hands, pulled her hair back and kissed that sensitive spot where her neck and shoulder met. He felt her shudder and she sighed when her small hands moved back to grip his thighs.

'Don't, James,' she whispered. 'Please.'

He nuzzled his face into her hair. 'I can't help it.'

He strained to hear her words and, when he did, they felt like bullets to his soul. 'Why do I only feel like this with you, the man who can't give me anything more than explosive sex? A night here and there. It's not fair…'

Unfortunately, she was right…

James felt the familiar shudder pound through his body and he stepped away, turning to his desk and wishing that it wasn't too early for a belt of that bottle of twelve-year-old whisky in the cabinet next to the door. Riley, and his craving for her, could literally drive him to drink. He jammed his hands in his pockets and looked out of the window, ignoring the magnificent view of Manhattan, the icy drizzle outside echoing the temperature in his soul.

The only time it felt warmer was when he was talking to, holding, arguing with Riley. He'd missed her so damn much these past months. Missed her wide smile, her smart mouth, her pint-size body vibrating with energy. They'd never been friends, precisely—there was too much lust and passion buzzing around them for that—but he used to see a lot of her. At his parents' house, at functions, most often at Morgan's flat.

But not at all for far too long.

And he desperately wanted to make love to her again; his mouth went dry every time he remembered what they'd done to and with each other. It was ironic that the best sex he'd ever had was with a woman he'd known all his life.

Who would have imagined that?

*Getting back to the problem at hand, Moreau. Oh, yeah...*

James scrubbed his hands over his face and turned back to Riley, who was still standing where he'd left her, grey eyes enormous in her cute face. His mind finally left the bedroom and he remembered why he was so angry with her. 'You just walk into my office, drop that bombshell on my head and leave without a friggin' explanation? What the hell, Riley? *You're not going anywhere!*'

Riley immediately pulled on her imaginary boxing gloves, lifting that stubborn chin as if offering him a chance to pop her on it. Why did he find her fighting spirit so attractive and why did she only ever fight with him? As far as he knew, she was perfectly pleasant to everyone else. Unless it was about her work, then she'd take on Genghis Khan and all his warriors to get her own way. And win. No one, including him, messed with her designs.

'*What* did you say?'

'You're not going anywhere,' James stated, his voice now calm but his eyes hot.

He was fairly certain that the red in her hair intensified with temper. 'How dare you, you simple-minded sack of Siberian snot? I'm a contracted employee and I am exercising my right not to renew that contract!'

James blinked at her creative insult. He'd heard a few from her over the past twenty years but that was a new one. And, he had to admit, a good one. 'You're exercising your right to be an irrational, crazy hothead!' he retaliated. 'Why do you want to leave, anyway? You love fiddling with the windows—' He knew that that comment would inflame her even more but what the hell? In for a penny and all that.

'*Fiddling?* That's what you think I do?' Oh, man, was that hurt he heard under the layer of vinegar? James gave himself a mental punch to the head. Why did he always say the wrong thing to her? He was generally quite together with women, except this one. With this one, he never knew what he was doing.

'And maybe that's another reason I should go. You don't respect me or the work I do...you just give me grief about it,' Riley yelled, her eyes now the colour of thunderclouds. Behind the pride he could see the pain, and frustration, in the depths of her soul and his anger receded. It killed him that he'd hurt her. No one should ever be allowed to hurt her, including him.

Time to rein this in, to haul back. The conversation was out of control, like so many other things between them. He ran his hand through his hair. 'Tell me why you are leaving.'

'No.' And there was her stubbornness. She could give lessons to a mule.

'Why not?'

'Because it won't change anything.'

'Tell me why or I'm going to do everything I can to make this as difficult for you as possible,' James warned.

Riley's nose lifted high enough to give her altitude sickness. 'I'm not even going to dignify that stupid threat with a response but I will say that my Christmas windows will be installed next week, they'll run through to the first week of January. The display for January is ready to be installed as soon as they come down—it's simple and classic and my staff can put it up without my help. I intend to leave as soon as the Christmas windows are up. So, basically, at the end of next week.'

'I do believe your contract runs to December thirty-first, Ms Taylor.' Not that he had any intention of letting her leave—she was the most talented window designer in New York; he'd be a fool to let her go. *Yeah, keep telling yourself that's why you want her to stay; maybe you'll begin to believe it... in a hundred years or so.*

'You'd keep me here, twiddling my thumbs for a whole month?' Riley looked horrified. James smiled smugly; he knew that asking Riley to sit still and do nothing was torture. He didn't mind a little torture when she was daring to leave him. Leave the job... *the job.* Not him. Get it straight, moron.

'I'll do whatever I damn well have to. *Tell me why.*'

Riley stalked up to him, stood on tiptoe and put her face as close to his as she could get it. James looked at her mouth and wished that she was about to kiss him but he knew her too well to assume that.

'I am leaving. Deal with it.'

'Over my dead body!' James shouted as she headed out of his office.

At the door Riley stopped and sent him a cold, sharp smile. 'That can be arranged...'

STORMING BACK TOWARDS the lift, Riley punched buttons on her mobile and slapped it to her ear. Ignoring the curious looks of her colleagues, she silently urged Morgan to answer her call.

It didn't matter that Morgan was James's sister; she could speak to her about anything, including what an utter ass her brother could be. As she and Morgan had been friends since their childhood, they'd had a lot of conversations about his ass-like qualities.

Morgan's mobile went to voicemail and Riley left a message. 'Answer your phone, dammit! Your brother is the biggest jerk this side of the Atlantic. You will not believe what he's just said to me—'

*Beeeeeeeeeepppppppp.*

Riley cursed and pushed redial. She'd been eight when she'd first met him; as he was five years older than her she'd had a lifetime of watching women fall at his feet. He'd play with them, get bored and then move on. Pretty girls, smart girls, outgoing girls—he never stuck to any of them. Okay, in fairness, he'd kept Liz around for a while, and no one knew why they'd broken up, but afterwards James had just thrown himself back into his 'bag 'em, tag 'em and toss 'em' routine.

'As I was saying, James drives me freakin' insane. Do you know that he called my art "fiddling"? *Fiddling*, Morgs? I nearly ripped his head off that strong, muscly neck…'

*Beeeeeeeeep.*

Riley considered throwing her mobile against the wall; instead, she stepped into a blessedly empty lift and pushed the green phone icon again and waited as it dialled. James's lack of commitment had always made her wary of him, scared of allowing herself to fall all the way in love with him.

*'This is Morgan. Please leave a message and I'll get back to you.'*

It took Riley a moment to realise why the lift wasn't going up and she furiously jabbed a finger on the button for the top floor. 'He has no respect for what I do, my work or my art,' she continued into the phone. 'And I hate the fact that I just see him and I want to get him naked…. I'm sorry, I know you don't think your brother is sexy, but he is. Gorgeous but such a jerk!'

In hindsight, that had been the main reason why she'd walked away at nineteen. There were other reasons but mainly she'd been terrified to become too involved with him—to run the risk of him becoming bored with her. She'd always known that loving and losing James would be the emotional equivalent of being disembowelled with a butter knife and she doubted she would ever recover. Anyway, that was beside the point, seeing that he no longer had any interest in a relationship with her.

He had once and she'd let him slip away. Right man, but too young and too dumb to realise that you didn't get second chances.

Message finally received, Universe.

*'This is Morgan. Please leave a message…'*
*Aaaarrrrgggghhhh!*

'I am on my way up to see you and you'd better be there! I'm having a meltdown here!'

Riley rested her head against the cool metal of the lift panel and stared at her feet. It would be okay, she told herself. She had years of savings behind her and those dollars allowed her the freedom of options. When she returned to Cape Town she would go back to designing windows, do some graphic design, teach art and pottery, maybe run something similar to the inner city art programme she'd been helping with recently as a way to fill up her time.

She'd do something different to feel a little less lost, not so alone.

When she stepped out of the lift at the top floor, Morgan stood there waiting for her, a cup of coffee and a chocolate bar in her hand.

Riley reached for both with vigour. 'Did you listen to my messages?'

Morgan shook her head. 'Four calls in two minutes signalled a crisis; I knew you were on your way up.' She gestured to her studio. 'Come in and tell me what my idiot brother has done now.'

## CHAPTER TWO

SHE'D DONE IT...

Riley watched her guests step into the lift of her apartment building and smiled in relief at Hannah and Jedd's loving faces. Morgan winked at her as she dropped her head onto Noah's broad shoulder and she blew her a kiss just before the lift doors closed.

With Morgan's encouragement, she'd had the Moreaus over for dinner in her loft apartment, had served them calamari risotto and explained that she was in a rut, that she needed to leave Moreau's and explore her options.

As if she were their child, and she was in so many ways, they'd prodded and poked, interrogated her motivations, discussed her reasoning and then given her their blessing. As Morgan had predicted, they just wanted her to be happy. If leaving meant her being happy then they could live with losing their window designer.

Riley turned to walk down the landing back to her apartment. She was almost at her door when she heard footsteps on the flight of stairs just around the corner from her front door. She peeked around the corner to see James jogging up the stairs—he rarely used a lift—and instantly clocked his furious face, his tense shoulders and the muscle ticking in his jaw.

Riley winced as she noticed his flashing green eyes. He stopped at the top of the stairs and slapped his hand on his hips, lifting his head at her open front door. 'Can I come in?'

'Nope, you're not bringing all that angry energy into my home. We'll stay outside,' she ordered. Not that she really believed in all that stuff, but if he came across her doorway she knew that she would strip him naked and do him on her couch, her yellow wingback chair, on her wooden floor...

She was nuts. Horny and nuts. A dangerous combination.

'Inside, Riley.'

'Not going to happen.' Riley shook her head a couple of times and folded her arms.

James hauled in a breath, looked at the ceiling and sighed. 'Okay, let's do it the hard way then.'

Using his superior strength against her, he looped an arm around her waist and picked her up and walked her into the apartment as easily as if he were carrying a sack of potatoes. Dammit! He was seriously starting to annoy her with this carrying her around kick he was on.

'Stop lugging me around!'

'Stop being a brat.' James dumped Riley on her purple-and-white-checked couch and loomed over her, his hands back on his hips. 'Why did you tell my family that you were resigning when we hadn't finished discussing it?'

Discussing it? Really? That was stretching the truth...

Riley blew her fringe out of her eyes and silently cursed James's mum. Just after she'd told the Moreaus and Noah that she was leaving, Hannah had excused herself to go to the bathroom, AKA rat on Riley. She loved her second mum but right now she could strangle her.

'I don't need to discuss it; you're the one who is harping on about it!' Riley retorted, scuttling past him to head for her kitchen. 'I'm going to make coffee; do you want one?'

'I'll have some of that whisky you keep on hand for Noah,' James replied, following her across the room. Leaning a shoulder into the wall, he took the glass of whisky Riley handed him. She could feel his eyes on her back while she fiddled with the coffee machine.

'What did you tell my parents, Riley?'

'That I needed a change, to do something different.'

'Is that the truth?'

'It's as good as any,' Riley retorted. She hadn't told them that she missed Morgan's companionship now that she was engaged and in love. That without her, and without having any contact with him, her life was duller, lonelier, that she felt distant and separated from this family who she no longer felt a part of.

That she felt compelled to move the heck *on*.

'So, not the full truth. Riley, we've always been honest with each other; you're the one person in my life who has always been unflinchingly truthful.'

'Stop badgering me, James. I'm just trying to… redesign my life.'

'What are you talking about? You don't need a new life!'

Did he actually hear the words that came out of his mouth? Riley wondered. And how dare he say that when all he could give her was a one-night stand three times?

'I won't understand if you don't explain your crazy impulse to me!' James snapped and she heard the frustration in his voice. Riley opened her mouth to speak and abruptly closed it again. What could she say to him? Would he even understand any of what she wanted to say?

*Will you listen, James—really listen? If I say that I have always adored you but I can't be in the same city as you and not talk to you? That I am so damn scared I'll fall in love with you, even though I know that a part of me loves you anyway? That walking away from this half-life is the hardest thing I have ever done in my life? That I am terrified to go but even more scared to stay?*

Riley sighed, pushed the coffee cup away and

took the easy option, swallowing the words she'd been thinking. 'Just let me go, James.'

James shook his stubborn head. 'No. You're staying until the end of the year and I'd keep you longer but you'll probably have me arrested on kidnapping charges.'

'Damn right I will.'

James ignored her. 'I expect you to be at work every day until then.'

'What am I going to do?' Riley wailed. 'My staff are all on holiday and it's a deadly quiet time—'

James tossed back his whisky and smiled his bad-ass CEO smile. 'Oh, don't worry about that. I'll find something to keep you occupied and out of trouble.'

'Yeah, right.' Riley narrowed her eyes at him. 'I suppose that if I don't agree you'll set those sharks in Legal on me for breaching my contract?'

'Damn right I will,' James repeated her earlier phrase.

Riley looked from her kitchen window, where the occasional drop of icy drizzle hit the windowpane, as she tried to ignore the whoosh in her stomach, the thump of her accelerated heartbeat. They were old companions—something she was so accustomed to feeling whenever James was in the same room as her. How could she be so annoyed with him yet still want to rip his clothes off? Her glance flicked over him—dark grey suit trousers, white shirt with the sleeves rolled up past his wrists, red tie pulled down from his open collar. His warm blond hair held furrows that suggested that he had spent the day shoving his fingers through it and there were blue shadows under his eyes, suggesting stress and no sleep.

Situation normal, then.

James returned her stare and Riley watched as his green eyes turned hard and cold. 'Are you leaving because of a man?'

*Yes, you, you jerk-nugget!*

'What?'

'Have you met someone new—are you following him somewhere, acting impulsively again?'

Riley tipped her head and she couldn't help her self-satisfied smile. 'Are you jealous?'

James slowly stood up, walked around the counter and placed his hands on either side of her hips, effectively caging her in. 'Answer the question, Riley.'

To hell with that. 'Maybe.'

James dropped his mouth to hers, his lips brushing hers in a kiss that immediately dissolved her body and sent a wet warmth straight to that pulsing spot between her legs.

'Wrong answer,' he said against her lips before sucking her lower lip between his. He knew she loved it when he did that, the sod! She kept her arms folded across her chest in an effort to keep them from looping around his neck and climbing up and over him. With James she went from irritated to turned-on in ten seconds flat.

'Get rid of him,' James ordered, his lips touching her jaw, moving up to feather kisses along the high arch of her cheekbone, her temple.

*That's what I'm trying to do,* she mentally wailed. *But when you kiss me like this it's impossible!*

'This is crazy, Ri. We can work this out,' James quietly said, resting his chin on top of her head.

No, they couldn't. History had taught them that. She wasn't enough—exciting enough, novel enough, pretty enough—to pull him out of playboy mode and she wasn't prepared to risk handing her heart over, knowing that he could stomp on it. *Like she had on his.*

No, he could continue to play with his bunnies and maybe in time, and halfway across the continent, she could find a man who she could love and who could love her.

'We can renegotiate your contract, talk about your hours, find out how to make this work for both of us—'

And didn't that say it all? He was talking about work and she was thinking about them, their relationship. They weren't on the same page—hell, they weren't even reading the same book!

'I have to go,' she quietly replied. 'It's time.'

James immediately pulled away from her and when his eyes slammed into her grey ones Riley had to fight the urge to take a step back. He had his

don't-mess-with-me CEO look on, his expression
inscrutable, his eyes stony and deliberately veiled.

'If that's the way you want to do this. Tomorrow
is Saturday so I'm working from my apartment. Be
there at eight and I'll give you a rundown of what I
expect from you over the next couple of weeks before and after Christmas.'

And, on that cryptic statement, he headed towards her door, snatching up his jacket as he walked
into her tiny hall. Then her front door slammed and
Riley sank to her haunches and rested her arms on
her bent knees.

Well, okay, then. James was obviously not going
to make this easy for her.

Then again, nothing between them had ever been
easy so why had she thought this would be?

HEADING HOME FROM the gym the next morning,
James jogged up the flights of stairs to his penthouse home. He wished he had time for a swim
in his lap pool, which was in his conservatory on
the top floor of his very exclusive apartment block
overlooking Central Park. The pool had been his pet
project and he loved the idea that it formed the ceiling of his apartment's hallway. He had a recurring
daydream about watching his lover swim naked in
the pool from below, but since he never brought a
woman back to his place it remained only a fantasy.
And since there was only one woman he fantasised
about lately, he could easily imagine Riley, who was

a strong swimmer, naked above him, her shapely body easing through the water, her breasts swaying and her perfectly waxed pubic strip…

James scrubbed a hand over his face as he stepped through the door into the hall of his expansive home. He had to get a grip and, after such a strenuous gym session trying to excise Riley from his mind, a shower.

James stepped into his open-plan living area and abruptly stopped when he saw Riley sitting at the kitchen counter. His heart stuttered. She'd pulled that long fall of deep red hair into a ponytail that hung halfway down her back and her Saturday face held the lightest of make-up, freckles he rarely saw splattering across her nose and cheeks. She was engrossed in the morning paper, a cup of coffee at her elbow.

Seeing her sitting there felt so damned right…

Except that it wasn't. He'd tried the relationship thing. It had led to the engagement thing. That hadn't worked out too well. When he'd found out his fiancée had lied to him and stolen his money, he'd decided never to put himself in the position of being at the mercy of any woman ever again.

Especially one who had kicked him into touch once before. Lesson learnt and all that.

'How did you get in here?' he demanded, conscious that he looked hot, sweaty and, possibly, unhinged.

Riley didn't bother looking up. 'Your lift code is 9562. Morgan told me.'

'Of course she did.' James sighed. She was so pretty. Small, tight, perfect. He only had to look at her and he wanted to nail her, every single time. He'd be meeting with investors and the image of her would pop into his head and he'd stop breathing. And he'd go stone-hard.

'I need to shower—are you going to be here when I get back?'

Riley very deliberately looked at her watch. 'Maybe. It's Saturday morning and I have things to do.'

Why did everything have to be a battle?

'Stay there,' he ordered before walking down the passage, through his bedroom and to the shower.

Slapping his hands against the glass of his huge power shower, he dropped his head and closed his eyes as hot water pummelled his tired muscles. He had a woman in his apartment for the first time in for...well, for ever—liaisons, *okay, one-night stands*, always took place where *he* could leave— and she was already giving him grief.

Situation very normal, then. It didn't escape his notice that the two women he'd let all the way into his life, his heart, his home had both wreaked havoc. Riley—he'd laid his heart at her feet and she'd stomped on it in her haste to go backpacking around south-east Asia—granted, she'd only been nineteen, but still—and Liz, who, after he'd proposed, changed from the sweet girl he'd fallen in love with into a money-grabbing monster.

Not only had Liz burned through his credit cards, she'd also refused to sign a pre-nup and had transferred money out of the credit card he'd given her into her personal bank account. When he'd confronted her, she'd explained that she was not going to leave their marriage with nothing.

They were still months off tying the knot and she was already contemplating divorce? That had been a big *'maybe this won't work out'* moment for James. She went to the press; he went to his lawyers and it had been such a spectacular, messy, humiliating *failure*.

He'd been raised to succeed and failure was never an option. That his failure of an engagement had been so public, a very ugly airing of their dirty laundry, still had the ability to coat his throat with acid.

It still stung that he'd been so comprehensively fooled… And because James had a talent for factual analysis, unbiased by prejudice and emotion—one of the reasons he was the youngest mining magnate in the world and the CEO of Moreau International at the age of thirty-four—he now had issues with that fuzzy concept called love. Since he'd failed so spectacularly at it, once privately, once very publicly, somewhere along the line he'd decided that it was best to be avoided.

He couldn't analyse it, didn't understand it so

he'd rather steer clear of it. But, if he believed that
sex had nothing to do with love, why couldn't he
go out and find some?

Until he had the time and inclination to work
through that dilemma he'd remain horny, dammit.
*Dammit.*

James rushed through the rest of his shower, de-
ciding not to shave. He pulled on a pair of comfortable jeans and the closest T-shirt he could grab from
his walk-in closet, an old grey one with the words
*Instant Human, just add coffee* in faded letters on
the front, and left his bedroom.

'You live in a hospital, Moreau,' Riley said, her
attention still on the paper. She had yet to look at
him and her flat voice and snippy attitude amused
him. So she wasn't happy with his order to be here…
Well, tough. He wasn't happy about her leaving.

He looked around his home and shrugged. 'It's
not so bad.'

It was a penthouse in the most exclusive apartment building in NYC, with superb views, lots of
space and incredible facilities.

'It's very white and hardly has any furniture.
There's minimalistic and then there's ass-cold
empty.'

'Says the woman who lives in an apartment that
looks like a kaleidoscope.' He reached for a mug
and jammed it under the spout of the coffee machine, hit the button and waited for it to dispense
its magic juice.

'I have a degree in art and a diploma in interior design and you have the taste of a polar bear,' Riley retorted after taking a sip of her cup of coffee.

James took a notepad and pen out of the ceramic bowl—white—that held keys and coins and quickly added to a list he had running. And, talking of coffee, where the hell was his? He looked at the screen on the machine where it flashed the only words that, along with *I'm pregnant with your child* and *Moreau stock is falling*, had the ability to freeze his blood.

*Replace coffee beans.*

Especially when he had no damned coffee beans.

Despite his wealth and like the rest of his family, he tried to keep his life as normal as possible and that meant not having people pandering to his every whim. He had a cleaner come in on a regular basis, someone to do his laundry and his housekeeper kept the place stocked with cleaning materials, but he did his own food shopping. He enjoyed cooking and he liked to choose his own produce, liked exploring the food markets of NYC, the delis, the bakeries. Lately he'd been so busy that shopping for food was way down on his list of priorities.

But forgetting to buy coffee? That was unacceptable!

James snatched Riley's cup out of her hands, ignored her protests and swallowed gratefully. Keeping the cup to his lips, he jotted another bullet point on the list before ripping it off and handing it over.

'Give me back my coffee, Moreau.' When he didn't answer or comply, she glared at him before looking at the list in her hand. 'What is this?'

'Read it.'

'Christmas shopping…organise Christmas cocktail party…find Morgan and Noah's wedding present…find your replacement…paint out your office…redesign my apartment…buy more coffee beans… *What is this?*'

'Your to-do list. The reason you are here this morning. You said that you had nothing to do while you were working out your notice,' James said mildly, enjoying the slow burn of anger pinking her cheeks as she read the list again. 'I said that I would find you stuff to do.'

'You have *got* to be kidding me.'

'Nope. That's what you are going to be doing after you get the Christmas windows up.'

Riley looked as if she wanted to bop him on the nose. He glanced down and noticed that her fists were clenched so he took a cautionary step backwards. Not that she would reach him, but why take the chance?

'James, I am a professional artist, not a…a…a whatever who does this is!'

'Then withdraw your resignation and sit on your pretty butt or take a holiday like you normally do.' James emptied her coffee cup and pulled a face. 'Coffee that costs over a hundred dollars a pound should be drunk black, Taylor.'

'I never asked you to drink mine and I am not doing this!' Riley shouted, waving the list in his face.

'Then withdraw your resignation,' James stated patiently. Over the years he'd learned that the way to defuse her temper was to keep his.

*'You can't do this!'*

'Riley, honey, darling, sweetheart...I *am* doing this.'

Temper had her eyes flashing and her small chest heaving. 'I could report you to Hannah, to Jedd. They'd be horrified at you doing this!'

She spat the words out like bullets and pushed every button he had.

He gripped her chin and made her look at him. Keeping a very firm grip on his now bubbling temper, he made certain that his words were very clear and very pointed. 'Ten years ago, I asked you not to go travelling, to see if we had a chance at something and you allowed your father to talk you out of that idea. Now you want to involve my parents in another of our fights? Not happening, honey. This is between you and me. We'll deal with each other like adults this time.'

He saw the embarrassment in her eyes, the humiliation in her wobbling chin and knew that she had been mouthing off in temper.

'The problem is that you have me over a barrel, James. I have no options here.'

'I gave you an option, Riley,' James reminded

her. 'At the beginning of this process I asked you to talk to me, to explain why you were really going, but you won't.'

'We don't talk well, James.'

'Try.'

There was that obstinate shake of her head that he was expecting and he saw her mental retreat and knew that he'd lost the moment, lost her. Her words just confirmed it. 'Look, I've got to go. I'm expecting a delivery of some last-minute goodies for my Christmas windows.'

Her eyes softened as she mentioned her windows and he immediately realised that she still loved her work, the art of creating. So whatever was going on with her wasn't work-related. And it shouldn't be since she had all the creative licence she required... hell, she had all the creative licence of every artist in the city. Riley didn't answer to anyone, not even him. Riley worked the way Riley worked; she was innately in tune with what was hip and happening and her windows were always stunning and ahead of the trends. She might never ask for approval for her designs, which raised his control issues, but she'd yet to let them down so he couldn't complain.

*Wait, hold on...* 'What last-minute goodies?'

'Oh, this and that.'

When Riley was vague that meant she was ducking the question. If she was ducking, then... *Oh, dammit, Taylor.*

'Have they been paid for?' James demanded,

thinking of the skyrocketing costs of her windows. Riley waved his question away, which meant that the bill hadn't come in yet. *Hell.* He thought about trying to explain the concept of a budget to her— again—but he didn't have the energy.

'We are blocking off the windows on Monday morning, we'll work through Monday and Tuesday and reveal them on Wednesday night.'

'Who's the entertainer this year? Have you got permission to block off the street for those hours? Security?'

Riley closed her eyes in frustration. 'James, I've been doing this for years. Lorelei Cranston, the Broadway star, is singing—'

'I know who she is,' James interrupted her.

'The street will be closed off and the small stage will be erected on Wednesday afternoon. I've hired a ballet company to perform as well. There will be waiters circulating to dish out hot chocolate and cookies, your mum will drop the curtain. People will love it and tons of them will go into the store instead of buying online.'

'You're still over budget.'

'But the cost to decorate the store windows is a fraction of what you would spend on a TV advertisement so suck it up. And I guess this will be another year that you won't join the family when they come down to see what I've done.'

James frowned at the hint of hurt he heard in her voice. Was him being there important to her? Riley was so self-sufficient, so supremely confident about her art and designs that he never thought that she needed affirmation, especially from him.

Why would she care if he was there or not?

Damn, but she confused him. And because he didn't like it and because he was a man, he chose to ignore what he didn't understand. So he nodded at the list that she still held in her hand. 'Okay, get the windows sorted then you can get cracking on that.'

Riley balled up the list in her fist and pitched it at him. It bounced off his chest and fell to the floor. 'I'll do it… Mmm, never. Does that work for you?'

## CHAPTER THREE

WHERE MORGAN MOREAU had her jewellery design studio on the top floor of her family's building, Riley's studio was in the basement, where she had ample space to build sets, paint backdrops and assemble mannequins and models. She had an office built into the back corner, as brightly decorated as her apartment in Tribeca. Colourful prints, a cherry-red wall, a lime desk.

She was an artist; colour was what she did. Who she was. She would wither up and die if she had to live in a stark-white apartment like James's.

She loved her office, her basement, her cave, Riley thought, handing Morgan, who was curled up on her raspberry couch, a cup of coffee. How was she going to leave it?

'I don't want you to leave,' Morgan said, echoing her thoughts, as she often did. Her bottom lip wobbled and Riley felt the corresponding tickle of emotion in the back of her throat. 'I know I said that I understood but I don't, not really.'

Riley sat down in her turquoise wingback chair and pursed her lips. 'Sometimes I don't either but

I feel compelled to go, to shake things up a bit, to try something new.'

'Is this about James—about what happened in July?'

'I think it's a culmination of the last decade of what's happened between James and me. I hate that we are so estranged.' She looked at Morgan and knew that she could be honest with her. 'But there's more… I miss you, miss the time you and I spent together. Before you met Noah again and I slept with James again, I had your time and company—'

'Oh, Riley, I'm so sorry—'

Riley held up her hand. 'Don't, Morgs. I'm happy for you—nobody is more happy for you than me. But those nights we spent together, eating out, at home—when James and I were still talking—'

'Bickering,' Morgan interjected.

'Whatever. Your company, his company, the time we spent together, fuelled me. Then you got engaged to Noah and now he's your priority and James and I stopped talking altogether and…and I miss my life. I can't go back so I need to go forward. We are all on different paths and this isn't my place any more. I need to find my place and I think Cape Town might be it.'

'Your place is with James,' Morgan stated firmly. 'It's always been with him but he's too much of a stubborn ass to admit it.'

Riley stared off into the distance. 'It's not all his fault, Morgs. I'm just as much to blame for this mess as he is; possibly more so. He asked me to give him—us a chance, but I went travelling instead.'

Morgan frowned. 'You weren't ready…you were so young…nineteen!'

'I was *scared*! Scared of what I felt for him, scared of what he made me feel! My dad's fear that he could hurt me fuelled my own fears—he was a rich guy and I was just a farm girl; he was older, sophisticated, I was just a passing fad for him, et cetera, et cetera—and I used his arguments as a reason to run. The truth was that I was too much of a coward and the timing has never been right again. I had my chance and I blew it to hell and back.'

'Maybe you could—'

Riley reached over and grabbed Morgan's hand, waiting for their eyes to connect. 'Morgs, stop. I know you want to see James and me together, but if it was going to happen it would've happened by now. After he rejected me—us—in July I've let that idea go and *you* need to let it go too. It's not going to be, honey.'

Morgan let out a long breath. 'It's against all the rules of the universe.'

Riley squeezed her hand, harder this time. '*Let it go.* Concentrate on your wedding and your own happiness; I will find mine in time.'

Morgan frowned in warning. 'It had better be with some man I love and adore. And he'd better be hot!'

Nobody would be as hot as James but she could

try. 'In the meantime, I have to get my stunning windows up and James is insisting that I work until the last day of December.'

'Control freak. Okay, so just clock in every morning and lie here and read or paint. Sneak out of the building and go shopping, skating, look at all the Christmas windows. New York at Christmas-time is stunningly beautiful. Do what you normally do when you have some free time.'

'I would if I could but His Highness wants me to work *work*. He has this list of things he wants me to take care of.'

Morgan cocked her head. 'Like?'

'Decorating his apartment, organising his Christ-mas cocktail party, finding my replacement.' Riley folded her arms. 'Well, I refuse to do it.'

Riley didn't see the mischievous light that came into Morgan's eyes, didn't see the hope that flared within them. She was too busy feeling aggrieved to notice that Morgan had turned contemplative and... sneaky. 'Well, if you do it time will go faster. The days will drag if you do nothing at all and you hate doing nothing.'

'I have an apartment to pack up and I have a ticket to fly home on Christmas morning.'

Morgan looked horrified. 'On Christmas morn-ing? Noooo, Riley...why?'

'What else am I going to be doing? My family is all in Botswana for Christmas this year.'

'I hate the thought of you spending the happiest day of the year in the air.'

Actually, it was the best way to spend Christmas if you were single and your family had left your childhood home to spend the holidays in another country with their oldest son.

That was if she could, somehow, persuade James to let her go so that she could catch her flight.

'You suck,' Morgan said as she stood up. She leaned over and kissed her cheek. 'Do what James asks. It will make the time fly and keep you busy and—'

Riley frowned at Morgan's hesitation. 'What?' she demanded.

'Well, you have given him a lot of grief over the years, Ri...with your overspending and your intransigence when it comes to your designs. No other CEO would've given you so much freedom, leeway. He's been remarkably good, for a control freak, about allowing you to do your own thing. And you get paid well.'

Riley thought of her fat bank account and readily accepted that she could be a bit diva-ish when it came to her art. 'So you think I should do this?'

Morgan shrugged. 'It's up to you but maybe it would be a way for the two of you to find your way back to...friendship.' Morgan held up her hand at Riley's expression. 'Maybe your time *has* passed but you've known him all your life. Maybe you should try to be friends again, reclaim that at least.'

Riley folded her arms and narrowed her eyes. She didn't trust Morgan's earnest expression. 'You're just trying to throw us together in the hope that we end up in bed again.'

Morgan's eyes widened and she placed her hand on her heart in mock outrage. 'You wound me.'

'I wound you, my ass. Get out of my office, Moreau, and go and practice your manipulation skills on Noah.'

'I don't need to manipulate him; I just get naked.' Morgan kissed Riley on the cheek.

Riley returned her hug. 'Lucky you. I miss sex.' She sighed.

Morgan patted her on the back. 'Just get naked in front of James; I promise he'll get the hint.'

Riley pushed Morgan through the door. 'Out! Now!'

What part of *'Let it go'* did Morgan not understand?

ACCORDING TO THE Moreau family, her Christmas windows were her best yet, Riley remembered as she walked through the lobby of the MI building, her feet dragging after the long, long day. The Christmas season, as far as Riley was concerned, had officially started and, instead of feeling the excited anticipation she always did, all she wanted to do was to fall flat down on her bed and sleep for a week.

Riley wound her scarf around her neck, pulled

on a woollen cap and buttoned her coat, preparing to step into the frigid air outside. It was nearly midnight and they'd had a record crowd for the unveiling of her windows earlier. In between rotating her neck looking for James—who hadn't been at the unveiling, again—she'd watched Lorelei sing her heart out. Hannah had been gracious and everyone had oohed and aahed over her displays. But now, at this late hour, the gawkers and guests were gone, the road had reopened and the stage had been removed. Riley, who had supervised the returning of the street and pavement to normal, was running on fresh air and emotion.

Holy smokes, it was cold, she thought as she stepped onto the pavement, hunching her shoulders. She should get home but instead she walked around the corner, heading towards the jewellery store, wanting to see her windows as the customers and tourists would—not as the artist but as the viewer. If she got a visceral punch, that flood of pleasure, then she'd know that she'd adequately translated the vision in her head.

But it wasn't the windows, as spectacular as they were, that momentarily stopped her heart, that had her gasping for breath. It was the blond head in front of the first window, one hand on the glass pane, looking—really looking—at the old-fashioned turn-of-the-century Christmas scene she'd created in the first window. As she quietly approached him she could see his broad smile, his enjoyment of what she'd done.

She'd always thought that she needed James's words of praise for her work but she didn't, she realised; she just needed to see this look on his face. Just once.

'Like it?' she softly asked.

James's head whipped around and his smile broadened when he saw her. 'Like it? *No*. Love it, absolutely. It's fantastic, Ri.'

Ri…something he hadn't called her in far too long. James held out his bare hand and Riley placed hers in it and didn't resist when he tugged her closer and tucked her under his arm. They both turned to look at the first display. 'Why a display of Moreau family Christmases over the years?'

'The interest in Morgan's wedding, the continued interest in your family from the press and people in general.' Riley laid her head on his shoulder, happy to rest there in the strength of his arms. Just for a moment and then she'd be strong again. 'I read an account in Marie Moreau's diary of the first Christmas she spent with Jasper in that tin shack at his first claim, just before he struck it big with that rich diamond pipe. They were dirt poor but it was a happy day. Her next Christmas—' Morgan gestured to the window showing a lusciously dressed nineteenth-century couple and their smart friends sitting by a huge tree drinking champagne '—was very different. Very rich. Marie writes that Jasper

gave her another whacking diamond and impreg-
nated her that Christmas Eve. Apparently they did
it in front of that tree...'

'Hopefully, when all the guests were gone,'
James said, with a rumble of laughter in his voice.
'Did she really write that down? With descriptions
and all?'

Riley rolled her eyes at the hope in his voice.
'There was nothing graphic in her description, you
pervert. Anyway, that sparked the idea of doing a
series of windows depicting how the Moreau family spent Christmas. Hannah gave me permission
and allowed me to trawl through the photo albums.'

'You actually asked permission? Amazing!'
James teased.

Riley gave him a shoulder bump as they moved
to the next window. An animatronic version of a
four-year-old James sitting in front of a tall Christmas tree at Bon Chance, a massive toy train in his
lap. His baby sister, still in a nappy, sat next to him
chewing a teething ring. 'I remember that train.'

'You were a pretty cute kid, Moreau. What happened?' she quipped.

'I'm still cute.' He grinned with smug confidence.

James moved her to the next window—a Christmas spent at their house in Aspen, the snowcapped
mountains an exact representation of the view from
their steel and wood cabin. The scene was straight
from her memory, her first Christmas abroad with

the Moreaus at fifteen, when James had taught her
to ski.

'I owe you for all the hours you spent teaching
me to ski when you could've been chasing those
ski-bunnies.'

James waggled his eyebrows at her. 'Who said I
didn't chase the bunnies?'

The last window depicted the post-Christmas
lunch dining table at Bon Chance, the one on the
veranda where they normally ate their Christmas
meal. It looked like a bomb had hit it—wine bottles
and wrapping paper, a diamond necklace lying next
to a plate, a glass vase full of rings. Place names—
Hannah, Jedd, James, Morgan, Noah—lay on their
sides or upside down and to the side a replica of the
engaged couple, Morgan and Noah, stood in the corner overlooking the vines, his strong arms wrapped
around her slight body, his dark brown head resting
on her bright blonde one. Her delicate hand rested
on his arm and a copy of Morgan's exquisite engagement ring glinted in the artificial sunlight.

There was serenity and peace and happiness in
the window, a sense that another offshoot of the
Moreau clan was coming to fruition. James's arm
tightened around her waist as he stared at the window. 'How did you recreate that old vine, the one
that covers the veranda at Bon Chance?'

'Trade secret,' Riley replied, unable to stop the
shiver that coursed through her at his touch. Neither was she able to stop the question she'd been

dying to ask since she'd first seen him standing in front of the windows. 'Why are you here, James? You've never come down here before, been with me—us—at the unveiling.'

'I'm always here, Riley. Whenever you change the windows and every Christmas, I stand at the back of the crowds and a lot later in the evening, usually past midnight, I come down here and really look at your designs, looking for the tiny details that most people normally miss. The things that make it personal.'

Riley felt a warm glow in her stomach. 'Like?'

James looked over the table and pointed. 'That frame—the one half covered in gold wrapping paper? It's the same frame as the sketch of my folks you gave them for Christmas last year. On the Christmas tree there's always a gold ornament with your name on it...there it is, top right. Um... and somewhere in one of the windows is a mouse in a waistcoat and top hat—he's appeared in every one of your six Christmas windows so far.'

Riley's mouth dropped open. 'I cannot believe that you noticed him. He's tiny and my little secret.'

'I saw him the first year, and the second and now I look for him. There he is—he's peeking out from behind that wine bottle.'

'I never thought that anyone would notice him,' Riley said, still in shock.

'Hell, yeah, I notice your work. I adore your work, even though I wish it didn't cost so much or that you had a vague idea of sticking to a budget.' James blew on his freezing fingers. 'And that's why there is no way I'm letting you walk away without a fight.'

Riley deflated like a popped balloon. Of course this was about her work; it had nothing to do with *her*. Stupid, stupid girl for thinking, if only for a moment, that there was a spark of something more there.

'The temperature has dropped a couple of degrees. Let's get home,' James suggested.

'I need a taxi,' Riley agreed.

James tightened the scarf around her neck and pulled her woollen cap down over her ears before running an icy finger across her cheek. Riley tried to tell herself that it was the cold that made it hard for her to breathe but knew that it was the tenderness, the gentleness in his eyes. 'It's late; you're cold and probably hungry. Come back to my place, get some food in you and crash there. It's a five-minute walk versus a trek across town. And who knows how long it will take to get a cab.'

She shouldn't—she really shouldn't—but she grabbed on to his words as the best excuse she'd ever heard to spend a little time with him. It had been too long since she'd experienced anything but frustration and craziness with James and being with him like this reminded her of the boy she used to know, the friend she'd adored, so she allowed him to take her hand and lead her back to his home.

BACK IN HIS toasty-warm apartment, Riley whipped off her hat and shrugged out of her heavy coat. James took it and hung it on the coat rack. He reached out and ran his thumb across her cheek, wincing at her icy skin. 'Let's get you warm. Something hot to drink?'

'Yes, please. Coffee with a belt of whisky?' Riley looked hopeful as she jammed her hands into the pockets of her jeans and followed James to the massive kitchen.

Riley slid onto a kitchen stool and James tried not to notice how her denim jeans showed off her shapely butt. Or how her long-sleeved jade-green T-shirt made her eyes a deeper, darker grey. Or how the cold made her nipples…

Okay, so maybe inviting her back to his apartment in the dead of the night wasn't the smartest idea he'd had all week. The urge to scoop her up and warm her up in a more basic biological way was shockingly strong.

*Get your mind out of the gutter, Moreau.*

He turned to face the coffee machine, willing his pants to subside. Damn, he was a basket case. 'If you can get the whisky bottle from the drinks cabinet that would be great.'

Riley hopped off the stool, retrieved the bottle, handed it over and took her seat again, chin in her hand. 'Look, about the windows…'

James cocked an eyebrow. 'Another expense?'

'Yeah. The—'

James held up a hand to stop her explaining. 'Ri, it's past midnight and I'm exhausted. The windows are fantastic and, as you pointed out the other night, the cost is a fraction of other media advertising and, right now, I simply don't care. Okay?'

'Sure.'

James took their cups to the counter where she sat and reached for the whisky, cracking the top and slugging in a healthy amount. 'That being said, I do reserve the right to throw my toys when I see the bill.'

'Fair enough.' Riley took the cup he slid over to her, wrapped her hands around it and took an appreciative sip. 'That's fantastic, thanks.'

'Shall we take this to the couch?'

Riley yawned as she took her cup and walked to the lounge area. She placed her cup on the table and took the seat next to the arm. James, inexplicably needing to be close to her, took the middle seat. They sat in companionable silence for a little while, looking out of the massive windows to the night view of Central Park and the bright buildings on either side of it framing the famous park.

'You hungry?' James asked, rolling his head against the back of the couch to look at her. Her eyes were shadowed in blue and she looked played out. 'I've been crazy busy so I sent out a mercy call to Mariah and she sent over some homemade meals that I can reheat.'

Interest sparked in those incredible eyes. 'Any curry?'

And there was another difference between Riley and the women he normally dated. No explanations needed about who was who. She knew that Mariah was his mum's long-time housekeeper and Jackson was the family's driver. She knew them and they knew her…adored her. Just like his parents did.

'Yeah, there's curry.'

Mariah made the best curry in the world and it was his, and Riley's, favourite dish. They were the only ones who could eat it as hot as Mariah liked to make it and it had been a frequent topic of argument about who handled the heat better. Back when they still argued. James missed that. Then again, he missed lots of things about Riley.

'No rice but there's fresh bread in the bread bin—do you want to help yourself?'

Riley hopped to her feet. 'Sure. Do you want some?'

'I ate earlier.'

Ten minutes later, Riley was sitting cross-legged on the couch, food on her lap, dipping her bread into the juice of the curry and making appreciative noises. 'So good, so good.'

He wished she was making those noises while tasting his body but watching her eat wasn't a bad consolation prize.

'For someone so small, you can pack it away,' James commented, watching her lick a drip of sauce from the corner of her mouth with her tongue. It was the sexiest thing ever...*ever*.

'Big metabolism. My mum is the same. So is Morgan, actually.' Riley cleaned her plate with a piece of bread, popped it into her mouth and placed the plate on the coffee table. 'Oh, God, I feel a million times better. Warm and full.'

Riley rested her head against the back of the couch and James could feel her eyes on his face. He turned his head and met her stare straight on. He realised that her eyes held a hundred shades of grey, from silver to lightning to thundercloud. He remembered that her breasts tasted like the sweet grapes grown at Bon Chance, that her ass was world quality. His sex stirred and then jumped to attention, all ready to rock and roll. The sex between them had been off-the-charts stupendous...

But it was much harder to admit that his attraction to her wasn't only about sex; her laugh had the power to turn his day around, her smart-aleck comments and the irreverence she displayed towards him kept him grounded, and she had a super-fast mind behind her artsy exterior. Being with her made him feel like the bigger man, a better man.

'You look exhausted,' Riley said softly. 'No, not just tired. You're stressed and worried...'

He blinked as her words sank in. There were few people who could see past his tough-guy CEO facade and Riley slid right on through. He considered brushing her concern off but instead he told her the truth.

'Yeah…I'm battling to get investors together for a diamond mine we want to open in Angola. There's a strike looming at one of our biggest mines back home. Theft at a store in Hong Kong. I have to fire one of my right-hand people in security because he has a drug problem. Grant has gone home because his father isn't well and I have to deal with someone temporary for the next month or so, which is always a pain. Grant takes care of the small stuff before it becomes big stuff.'

Riley tucked her toes under his thigh and the action was so natural that he wasn't sure if she was even conscious she'd done it. 'How can I help?' she asked.

James frowned at her. 'You want to help? Me?'

Riley yawned and her eyes drooped. 'Despite the fact that you can be a constant nagging pain in my…neck, you still are one of my oldest friends. Despite our craziness, I would do anything I could to make the shadows in your eyes go away.' Her eyes narrowed and he realised that she was very conscious of what she was saying. 'I'll help you, not because you are forcing me to or because you have this stupid idea that I should work my notice; I'll help you because…'

James held his breath, not having a cooking clue what she was about to say. 'Because?'

Riley bit her lip. 'Because you have been incredibly good to me as a boss. I realise that. But also because I don't want to start a new life without us being friends. I don't want to carry that baggage forward with me, James.'

Generous Riley, he thought. As a child she'd always been the one to share a sandwich, would give up her last sweet, anxious to please and happy to give. It was warming to know that she still had that inside her, that generosity, that warmth.

Riley yawned widely and wiggled down so that her head was resting on the arm of the white leather couch. James leaned across and pushed a strand of red hair off her cheek and tucked it behind her ear. 'Why don't you just close your eyes for a sec, Ri?'

'I should go home.'

'Not tonight, honey.'

'I'll close my eyes for a little while and then I'll call a taxi.'

'Yeah, okay,' James replied, knowing that she would be asleep in a minute and wouldn't wake up before sunrise. If he could trust himself he'd pick her up and take her back to the spare bedroom but he knew that as soon as he had her in his arms she'd end up in his bed and then he wouldn't be able to resist waking her up with a couple of strategically placed kisses. No, it was better if he left her exactly where she was. They'd made some progress tonight and if they carried on in this vein then maybe he could get her to talk about why she was leaving so that he could fight fire with fire, so he could *fix* this.

Leave her here, his brain insisted—she would be fine here for the night. The apartment was toasty-warm, but he grabbed a spare blanket and put it over her anyway before turning off the lights.

The thought of waking up to her, even if she wasn't in the same bed, shouldn't make him as happy as it did. But tonight he was too tired to care. He'd worry about it in the morning.

# CHAPTER FOUR

RILEY SNUGGLED INTO the cushions of the couch, smelled coffee and shoved her hand out from under the blanket and wiggled her fingers. 'Gimme.'

She felt James's fingers on hers, positioning her hand to grip the cup and, still lying on her stomach, she pulled the cup to her lips and took a scalding sip. The heat burned her tongue but she didn't care. After a couple more sips, she opened her eyes and saw a pair of muscular thighs covered by expensive material, a fine white pinstripe running through the deep grey fabric. Her eyes wandered up, past a rather pleasing bulge, up and over a hard stomach covered, sadly, in her opinion, by a white dress shirt and a solid black tie lay between those wonderful pecs.

'You shouldn't get dressed. Ever,' she muttered, sipping again.

She heard his snort of laughter and when she opened her eyes again he was on his haunches in front of her, clean-shaven and smelling amazing.

'You awake now, Taylor?'

'Go away,' Riley muttered, conscious that she

probably had canyon-size creases in her face from the throw pillows.

James brushed her hair away from her face. 'It's time to get moving.'

'What part of "go away" is difficult for you?' Riley muttered, yanking the blanket over her head.

James pulled it away again. 'I'm making omelettes. You want one?'

Riley opened one eye. 'Maybe. Mozzarella and bacon?'

'Maybe.' James smiled as he stood up, taking the blanket with him. She was still warm and the couch, though horribly white, was super comfortable…she could just drift off—but James's hand landing on her butt had her eyes flying open again.

'I'm up! I'm up!' she growled at him.

'You never could wake up gracefully,' James said, yanking her to her feet.

'If you want chirpy then go and catch a budgie,' Riley told him, taking her coffee, her bag, and staggering towards the hallway. She needed six more hours of sleep, a shower and a meal and then she would feel human.

She looked up at the transparent ceiling into the clear blue water of the lap pool directly above it. She could easily imagine watching James's perfect body cutting through the water…and if he were swimming naked? She felt the hot rush wet in her panties and swallowed.

Well, *hello*, new fantasy…

Well, that was better than a bucket of cold water for jolting her awake.

SHE HAD A SHOWER and found a toothbrush still in its packaging in the bathroom cupboard. Not having spare underwear meant going commando but she was okay with that because the shower had made her feel on her way to human. She couldn't do anything about the need to sleep some more but food would get her to about sixty per cent human.

She could work with that.

'Morning again,' James said as he slid an omelette and a fresh cup of coffee across the kitchen counter in her direction. He smiled at her and Riley felt that familiar whoosh in her stomach. Ah, she could get used to this…waking up to James, been woken up by him.

It would've happened by now, she reminded herself. *Your time has passed so don't think about what-ifs. Just don't even go there.*

Riley grabbed the cup and went straight to the fridge to dump some milk into it. James groaned when she added a teaspoon of sugar and stirred.

'Dammit, hand-picked beans,' James growled. 'Voted best coffee in the world, picked by a family in Costa Rica. It does not need milk and sugar.'

'You're a coffee snob.'

'You're a coffee peasant,' James retorted, sliding his omelette onto a plate before taking a stool at the counter. He waved his fork at her plate. 'Eat.'

They ate in companionable silence until Riley pushed her empty plate away and placed her chin in the palm of her hand. 'So, about that list…'

'The one you threw at my head?' James lifted his cup of black coffee to his lips and raised his sandy brows.

'Chest. And yes, that list. Make a new one,' she said.

James frowned. 'I'm not following you, Riley.'

'Grant isn't at work and I understand that he makes your life run smoothly so if there's anything I can do to help you that doesn't require typing and spreadsheeting…then I'll give you a hand.' Riley held up her hand when she saw that James was about to speak. 'But then you allow me to leave on Christmas Eve and not at the end of the month—I have a ticket to fly home on the twenty-fifth.'

'You're flying on Christmas Day?' James, like Morgan, was horrified. 'Why?'

'Because, unlike you, I don't have access to a private jet.'

'I'm flying out on Christmas Eve—why didn't you ask me for a lift?'

'Have I ever *asked* for a lift on the MI jet, James? I only *sometimes* accept offers.' Riley waved the topic away. 'Anyway, do we have a deal? You get an extra set of hands and I get out of the city a week early?'

James thought for a moment. 'Yeah, okay.'

Riley slid off the stool, picked up their dirty plates and placed them in the dishwasher. 'So, I remember the bullet point about a wedding present for Morgan and Noah and I can do your Christmas shopping for you. What else was there?'

'The Christmas cocktail party.'

Ah, that Christmas cocktail party. Gorgeous women, slick men… She normally spent the evening dodging fast hands and bitchy women. And she always, always found an excuse to leave early, which had never been a problem since none of the Moreaus ever noticed.

'Do you think you could stay at the party past eight-thirty this time?' James asked her.

Riley wrinkled her nose. So busted. 'It's really not my scene,' she admitted.

'It's not mine either. It's a tradition that I took over from my mother and half the people invited are her cronies, not mine. I'd prefer to have a smaller, more intimate party with the people I actually like.'

Riley sent him a sharp look. 'So do that then.' She waved at the cavernous interior. 'And do it here—it's not like you don't have the space.'

Riley could almost see the wheels turning in his head while he considered the pros and cons. After a minute, he nodded his head decisively. 'Yeah, let's do that. I'll do the invites if you can do everything else, like the catering and the booze. Can you handle that?'

'It's not like it's rocket science.' Riley shrugged. 'I just need to place the order for pizzas and beer and we're set.'

'Funny girl. It'll still have to be black tie, up-market.'

Riley shrugged. 'Okay. That's three items on the list. What else? You said something about me looking for my replacement?'

Annoyance flickered across James's face and Riley realised that, despite their truce, he was still not even remotely accepting her resignation. Then his annoyance disappeared and his lips twitched. 'With regard to your replacement, I do have a couple of criteria of my own.'

Riley pursed her lips and folded her arms. 'Pray tell.'

'Someone who actually has a vague concept of a budget would be nice. Someone who doesn't run their department like a diva, who takes direction and understands that I am the boss. Smoking-hot would be a *real* bonus.'

'Let me guess…tall, stacked, blonde.' Riley snorted her disdain. She rested her arms on the counter and looked at him. 'Keep dreaming, sunshine. Besides, if you were honest you'd admit that you'll be bored without me.'

'I'll be drinking a lot less antacid,' James retorted.

Riley held up her hands at the bite in his voice. 'Okay, let's get off this subject because we'll just end up fighting again. I really don't want to fight with you. I meant what I said about us parting as friends.'

James placed his ankle on his knee and played with the laces on his shoe. When he finally spoke, his voice was low, sexy and very, very deliberate. 'We've been lots of things, Riley, but we've never been proper friends. From the time you were nineteen there's been far too much sexual attraction between us for us to just be *friends*.'

'Well, we can try.' Riley licked her top lip. Looking for inspiration for a subject change, she looked out of the floor-to-ceiling windows and drank in the view of Central Park. The clouds were low over the city today and the occasional drop of icy drizzle hit the windowpane. 'Damn, it looks cold out there.'

'New York at Christmastime. I'm craving some African sun.'

Riley flashed him a relieved smile. 'Me too. Ice cream on the beach.'

'You go pink within the hour.'

'I do but it's a nice fantasy,' Riley agreed as James stood up and stretched. 'Oh, right...there was one other thing on your list that we haven't discussed—this apartment.'

James looked around him and shrugged. 'What's there to discuss?'

'It's white. And you said that you wanted me to decorate it.'

'It's minimalistic and I was just trying to wind

you up.' James grabbed some folders off the dining table and shut down his iPad.

'It looks like you're living in a snowstorm!' Riley protested. 'It's big but so impersonal. And we should do something about it before the Christmas party or else people are going to think you like living in a morgue.'

James shoved his laptop into his briefcase and looked at his watch. Bored with the subject, he shrugged. 'So do something about it then.'

'Okay, but what do you want?'

James looked at her and huffed his frustration. Decorating was not his forte. 'How do I know? As long as I have a bed, an internet connection and the plasma in my bedroom I'm golden. You think I need colour, put colour. Just don't go mad.'

'James, you can't just tell me to redecorate!'

Why were they still discussing this? 'That's what I did with the last decorator.'

'And that's how you ended up living in the Arctic!' Riley tapped her finger against her lips. 'Why don't I do you a couple of mood boards?'

'Yeah, okay.' If she wanted to…

'You don't even know what a mood board is!' Riley accused him on a low laugh. Okay, so busted.

'A mood board is a board, obviously, where I give you an idea of what the room would look like— furniture, colours, art. I can do different colours, different styles and see which one grabs you.'

James nodded. He was a guy and he liked the

'I see, I like' method of decorating. 'That would work…'

'But then you would actually have to look at colour samples and at the mood boards—' Riley picked up an apple from the fruit bowl and took a bite.

James stepped forward, placed his hands on her shoulders and looked down into her fabulous eyes. Her mouth was unpainted and it took all his concentration to stay on the topic at hand because the urge to kiss her was so damn strong. 'Riley, I don't care. Just make it look less morguelike for the party and I'm good with that.'

'Okay. You want to give me a budget on how much to spend?' Riley asked, holding his wrist with one hand.

James burst out laughing. 'You and a budget? You're kidding, right?'

Riley lifted her nose and his laugh deepened. 'That's art—there should be no price on art. I'll have you know that I am very careful about spending other people's money.'

He couldn't argue with that. In the twenty-plus years he'd known her, Riley had never, not once, taken advantage of Morgan, his parents or his wealth. In fact, they frequently had to bully her into accompanying them to their houses in Aspen and the south of France, to flying with them on the corporate jet.

He had a whole bunch of issues around Riley,

most of which he didn't want to analyse too deeply, but her being a gold-digger wasn't one of them. Since he no longer trusted the concept of love, he might not be able to trust her—or any woman, even himself—with his heart, but he did trust her with his cash.

Riley slapped her hands on her hips and tossed her hair. 'I can either pay for stuff and you can refund me, except that I suspect that I don't have as big a credit limit on my card as you do on yours.'

He shook his head. 'That's too much like hard work. Just take one of mine.' He reached for his wallet, yanked out the first card and held it out to Riley. 'The code is eight, nine, double four. I've got to go.'

'You can't give me this card!' Riley protested, her apple half eaten and forgotten in her hand. 'James, this is one of those fancy cards with no limit. I could buy a friggin' country with this card!'

James grinned. 'Since I have mines in most countries, I don't need the country itself so don't bother. But buy my sister a kick-ass wedding present with it.'

'His and hers yachts? His and hers Indian Ocean islands? His and hers super cars?' Riley called after him as he walked towards the door. 'James, please give me an idea of how much I can spend—this is crazy.'

James tossed her a grin over his shoulder. 'I do that every year with the windows…and you've

never managed to stick to it yet. So I'm not going
to waste my breath.'

As he shut the door behind him, James heard the
thud of the apple hitting the door roughly where his
head had been.

He chuckled quietly. Riley had always had one
hell of an arm.

Riley Taylor: I've asked you three times over the past
week to look at the mood boards so that I can get
to work on your apartment.

James Moreau: Too busy and important. ;-)

Riley Taylor: *Snort* Too uninterested is more like
it. I'm running out of time; the Christmas party is
next week. Maybe I should just go ahead and do it
without your input.

James Moreau: Great idea, do that. Going on a two-
day trip to see an operation in Mexico. Don't go
mad with colour.

Riley read the series of instant messages she and
James had exchanged a few days ago and shoved
her mobile in the back pocket of her jeans. If James
didn't like what she'd done with his place then she
had the proof that he'd said that she could go ahead
and do it her way.

He was due home any minute and she bit her

lip, wondering what he'd think of the changes she'd made. The white couches were gone; she'd replaced them with deep brown leather sofas that suited James's long frame and no-fuss personality. She'd scattered rich autumn-coloured Persian rugs on the floor and she'd found a stunningly rendered painting of a herd of African cattle which she knew James would love and she'd placed it above the fireplace.

The throw cushions echoed the coppers and gold in the carpets and the painting; the effect was African-inspired, bold and masculine and changed the whole feel of the room.

She'd gone a bit nuts in his bedroom as well, Riley thought. She'd taken one of her favourite photographs of Bon Chance—a black-and-white image of the vines, the stately house and the towering mountain behind it—and supersized the image, framing it in solid black. His white wingback chair remained but now had an azure-blue throw over it and the solid black bedding was broken up with azure and white cushions.

She'd be mortified if he hated it. Any of it. Riley glanced at her watch and went to stand at the windows, looking out on the faded light. Waiting for him to arrive was worse than waiting to find out whether people liked her window displays or not.

Far, far worse. This was *his* home…

'God, Riley.'

Riley spun around, her heart in her throat. She

hadn't heard him arrive and there he stood, his normally inscrutable face openly surprised.

But was that a good surprised or a bad surprised? She couldn't tell.

Every muscle in her body tensed as he dropped his small suitcase and laptop bag to the floor, pushing back his suit jacket to place his hands on his hips. 'Like it, hate it?' she eventually asked when he just stood there, saying nothing.

'You constantly surprise me,' James said. 'I love it.'

Riley hauled in a much needed breath as pleasure skittered through her system. 'Really?'

'Yeah. I'm not just saying this but it's what I would've chosen for myself, if I knew what to look for. It's…amazing.'

James's smile, open and honest, blew away her last doubts and she held out her hand to him. 'Glad you like it but maybe you should see the bedroom before you say anything more.'

Immediately his warm fingers tangled with hers as she led him down the passageway. 'As long as you have put a mirror on the ceiling and a whip on the wall, I'll love it.'

She snorted. 'Dream on. I did, however, take your plasma off the wall.'

His mouth fell open in shock and disappointment and Riley rolled her eyes. 'You are so easy…' She opened the door and motioned him inside. 'The TV is still on the wall so don't be too scared. You'll get used to the pink in no time at all.'

More shock. So, so easy.

Riley watched his face again and while there was pleasure in his expression—she could see that he liked it—she knew that James didn't care enough about the new bedding and colour scheme for him to wax eloquent about it. For all his wealth, he was a pretty down-to-earth guy.

She knew from Morgan that James never ever brought women back to his apartment, so his bedroom was just a place to sleep, it didn't need to look fantastic. But at least he tried. 'It's nice…not so white. I like the black, those pillow things will just end up on the floor…oh, honey.'

Yeah, that was the reaction she wanted, the reaction she knew she'd get when he saw the photograph. She wasn't the greatest photographer but it was another form of art and she'd explored it and that photograph was one of the best she'd ever taken. 'That is seriously… I'm not sure what to say.'

'It's an early Christmas present…it is nice, isn't it?'

'It's freakin' fantastic.' James finally took his eyes off the photograph and looked at her and the expression in his eyes had the potential to stop her heart. He was looking at her in a way that every woman should be looked at, just once in her life. As if the sun and moon and stars rose with her and only her.

James lifted his hands to cradle her face and
he lowered his head to brush his lips across hers.
'Thank you…for doing this. Thank you for the
thought you put into this. Thank you for my early
Christmas present.'

'Pleasure,' Riley said against his lips. She expected him to step away and then his lips covered
hers in a kiss that shot electricity to her toes. She
opened her mouth to say something, she wasn't
sure what, and he took the opportunity to slide his
tongue inside and she was lost. She was vaguely
aware that his hands left her face so that his arms
could haul her closer to him and then she was
pressed up and against him, his arm easily holding her against his hard, muscular frame. This was
heaven, she thought, and hell. Heaven because there
was nothing better than being kissed by James, hell
because she knew they had to stop before they went
too far.

They couldn't sleep together again, she told herself. She wasn't going to do that again. But she
could just kiss him, just for a little while longer.

His stubble tickled as he touched his lips to her
cheekbone, nibbled her jawbone. His fingers found
her breast and through the material of her shirt he
massaged her nipple and teased it into an excited
peak. She felt her panties dampen and when he
started fumbling with the buttons on her shirt she
knew that she had to stop because if he kissed her

one more time, if he touched her there she would be lost…again.

Riley pushed her hands against his chest. 'James, stop.'

It took a couple more kisses and the zip of her jeans was down before James got the message. He glowered down at her. 'We're really stopping?'

'Yes.'

He dropped an F-bomb into the heavy silence that followed her answer. *'Why?'*

Riley pulled up her zip and straightened her shirt. 'Because we're not doing this again. Because we're not going to have another one-night stand. Because I'm slowly getting my friend back and I don't want to lose him again! Because I'm leaving… Pick a reason, James. Any of them work.'

'They all suck,' James muttered, his eyes tightly closed. 'If I don't get sex soon I swear I am going to die.'

He was James Moreau—surely he got sex all the time? While the thought of him being with anyone else made her feel physically ill, she wasn't stupid. James was a good-looking, rich, charming man who could get all the sex he wanted whenever he wanted it and she couldn't imagine him abstaining for any length of time.

He opened his eyes to glare at her. 'Do you know how long five months actually is when you're not having sex?'

'Um…five months?'

'Far too bloody long.'

Then a bank-load of pennies dropped—five months was when they were last at Bon Chance together. 'You haven't had sex since...me?'

James held her eyes and nodded.

*Well...hell.*

Except that she wasn't idiot enough to believe him. 'According to the entertainment pages, I wouldn't have thought so. Your social life has been as hectic as ever.' Riley grimaced at her waspish tone.

'You know better than to believe anything you read in the press, Riley. I haven't had sex with anyone since you,' he said, emphasising every word.

'Liar,' Riley whispered.

'Truth.'

Not knowing what to think, she waved at his trousers. 'When that subsides, you'll thank me.'

'Trust me, I won't,' James grumbled.

'It's for the best, James.' Riley managed a small smile. 'I'm glad you like what I've done with your place but I think I'm going to go now.'

*As in right now...while my legs are still receiving messages from my brain.*

## CHAPTER FIVE

'THAT WAS SUCH FUN. I haven't skated for years.'

Riley, her face bright pink with exercise and cold, shoved her hand into the crook of James's arm as they walked past the magnificent giant Christmas tree at Rockefeller Center, its two glorious trumpeting angels on either side. Her lips twitched from trying to keep her laugh from bubbling out. 'Your style was…interesting.'

James looked down at her. 'Oh, you like the way that I grip the railing? Jeez, a snail could've passed me.'

'Three-year-olds did,' Riley pointed out. 'It's so nice to know that you suck at something, Moreau. You always do everything so well that it's a relief to know that you aren't perfect.'

'Far from it, Ri.' James knew that her words held merit. And they should since he'd worked hard to perfect the facade he presented to the world—rich, fun, charming, unavailable, and he knew exactly how to project whatever the situation required. Very few people had ever managed to peek behind the mask and he liked it that way. Except that Riley did and always had.

There was little room for failure in his life and it felt odd to feel as relaxed, as comfortable with Riley as he did, the other party in one of his two personal failures. It was all such a long time ago and he'd been young and she'd been even younger and a part of him thought he could almost forgive the stupid kids they'd been. It didn't mean that love was on the cards for him—until he understood the concept, he'd avoid it—but he was happy to be with her, to have her friendship again, even if he did live his life semi-erect these days since sex with Riley was pretty much all he fantasised about.

She was too good a friend and too talented an employee to lose.

'I need to get home, Jay,' Riley said as they stopped at a traffic light, her gloved hand now in his bare one. 'Whistle for a taxi for me?'

James turned to face her. 'Come home with me. I have a surprise for you.'

Riley sent him her patented what-are-you-up-to-now? look. 'A good surprise or a bad surprise?'

'A good surprise, oh, cynical one. And, to sweeten the pot, I'll tell you that I've received a case of Bon Chance's Merlot—'

'My Merlot?' Riley almost danced on the spot. 'The 2004?'

'Yep,' James confirmed. 'But you'll have to come to my place to drink it. And you'll have to do a bit of work.'

'Jeez, I've decorated your apartment, I've bought

your Christmas gifts and I've organised your Christmas party,' she complained good-naturedly. 'What else do you want me to do?'

'You'll see,' James said cryptically. 'You haven't bought Morgan and Noah's wedding present yet; is that why you're hanging onto my credit card?'

She looked at him from under those long, long lashes. 'Mmm. I suppose I should tell you that I used it at a number of Madison Avenue stores today. Thanks for my new winter wardrobe, by the way.'

James shook his head and grinned. 'Liar.'

Riley sucked in her cheeks to keep herself from smiling. 'How can you tell?'

James placed his hand on the back of her neck. 'Firstly, you can't lie worth a damn. Secondly, you're not the type to allow any man to buy your clothes and thirdly, you would consider using my card for your benefit stealing. And you're the most honest person I know. And lastly…'

'What?'

James laughed down at her. 'No banking alerts.'

Riley shrugged and gave him a shoulder bump as they crossed the street. 'So, did you look at those portfolios I gave you?'

He pretended not to know what she was talking about because he hadn't looked at anything to do with the possible candidates to replace her. He had no intention of *ever* looking at anyone to replace her. 'What portfolios?'

'Dammit, Moreau. You told me to look for someone to replace me; I found six people, all of whom would do a stupendous job as window designer.'

'Is your portfolio in there?'

'James…' Riley said in warning.

'Then not interested.' He dropped a kiss on her nose and sent her a grin. 'Stop fighting with me; you're going to spoil your surprise.'

'You are the most annoying human being alive,' Riley muttered.

James shrugged, knowing that she wouldn't feel like that for long.

'A CHRISTMAS TREE? You bought me a Christmas tree?'

'The American tradition is to decorate it on Christmas Eve but I thought that it would be fun to have one up for the Christmas party, and it's your favourite thing to do at Christmastime.'

'That and singing carols.'

'Which you are amazingly bad at.'

Riley pulled a tongue at him and then her eyes went back to the massive bare fir tree that stood in the corner of James's apartment, dropping slivers of green onto his expensive floor. As soon as James took her coat she walked over to the tree and touched its branches.

'As a little girl, your favourite part of Christmas was doing this—decorating the tree. I remember that you'd start sketching designs in mid-November and by the first of December you'd have the one in your house decorated and you'd start nagging us to get ours done.' James shoved his hands into the pockets of his jeans and rocked on his heels. 'When we finally gave in to you, you became a bossyboots, ordering us about and dictating where to place the ornaments and how to place them.'

Riley grinned. 'I did. I love putting up the tree.'

James gestured to it. 'It's all yours; decorate away. Ornaments are in the boxes.'

Riley sank to her haunches and reached for the nearest box and opened the lid. Inside were exquisite hand-blown glass ornaments, crystal angels and perfectly wrapped miniature boxes. 'James, these are beautiful. Where did you get them?'

He shrugged. 'Sorry, no idea. I wish I'd had the time to track them down myself but, you know, mining company to run. I called Mum's personal shopper and told her that I wanted the nicest, artiest, most unusual ornaments she could find.'

'The bill is going to be enormous,' Riley warned him, cradling a golden glass ball with a jewelled angel on it. 'They're exquisite.'

'And they're yours, by the way. For the tree now, for all your Christmas trees in the future. *Your* early Christmas present.'

Riley stared at him, unable to speak past the lump in her throat. What an utterly perfect gift, she thought. The tree, the ornaments, the fact that he knew her so incredibly well. How was she ever going to get on that plane just over a week from now—how would she do that? And how could he let her go when there was so much emotion shimmering between them, so much fun to be had?

*James, say something to make me think that you believe in me, believe in us,* she silently begged him. *Something that will wipe away the confusion and tell me that there is more to the James and Riley story than massive attraction and a blossoming friendship.*

James just rubbed the back of his neck and softly shook his head. 'I'll get you that wine.'

Riley blinked back tears as she started to unpack the boxes filled with the fragile, exquisite works of art. Decorating this tree would take the longest time, she decided, because she couldn't help inspecting each ornament, marvelling at the craftsmanship, the artistry.

'What about some Christmas carols later?' James asked, putting her glass of wine on the floor next to her knee. He ran his hand over her hair. 'I don't have any Christmas songs on my iPod but I thought that, after supper, maybe I could play a couple on my guitar and test how rusty I actually am.'

Riley grinned at him, delighted. 'I haven't heard you play for…jeez…ten, twelve years! That would be amazing. And I could sing…'

'Uh…no; you sing as well as I skate. I'll sing, you decorate the tree. Deal?'

Riley over-exaggerated her pout. 'Can I hum?'

'No. Eat, drink, decorate. That's it.'
'Huh.'

'THANKS FOR COMING with me today,' Riley told
James as they stood in the small meeting room of
the community centre, a plastic cup of warm punch
in her hand. It was the community centre's modest
Christmas party and her art students had begged
her to come. James, dressed in jeans and a leather
bomber jacket, had tagged along. He was looking
around curiously and ignoring the appreciative
looks of her female students. It didn't matter that
they weren't out of school yet—James was hot and
he was worth a second look.

And a third, and a fourth.

'Tell me again what you do here.' James took
a sip of his punch, swallowed manfully and managed not to look horrified. It wasn't twelve-year-
old whisky or Bon Chance wine but James didn't
let that bother him. It seemed that he was only a
coffee snob.

'I teach art to the kids. Mostly at risk teenagers.'
'Okay. How and why and when did this come
about?'

Riley thought about avoiding the question and
then she shrugged her shoulders and quietly answered his question. 'I saw an advert where they
were asking for volunteers…and I started teaching classes a couple of times a week. Pottery, art,

drawing. Lesley, the girl in the black miniskirt and
purple gilet, is hugely talented.'

'I have no idea what a gilet is and I don't care.'
James's voice rumbled in her ear. 'That explains the
how—you left out the why and when.'

Of course he wouldn't leave it alone. 'The why
is because I had a lot of time on my hands; Morgan
and Noah fell in love and they were—are—insepa-
rable. Noah and I get along really well but I always
feel like a third wheel when it's just the three of us.'

'Know that feeling. They exchange these long
looks and I just know that he's thinking about getting her into bed. It freaks the hell out of me, especially since I prefer to think of Morgan as not
having had sex, ever.'

Riley had to laugh at that and couldn't resist the
urge to tease him. 'Well, I have it on very good
authority that she is having lots and lots of lovely,
creative sex…'

'You're a cruel woman, Taylor,' James moaned.
'Why does that turn me on?'

Riley blushed. 'Anyway…'

'Anyway, you were telling me about this place.'

Riley shrugged. 'I was lonely and I've enjoyed
every second of teaching these kids. I was thinking of doing something similar when I get back to
Cape Town.' She felt James stiffen and knew what
was coming next.

'I know that you love your job and I get that you
might be missing Morgan's friendship, her atten-

tion. But how is going back to Cape Town the solution? I just don't understand what's motivating you wanting to move, Ri.'

'Can't you just accept the fact that I know it's the right thing to do?' Riley demanded.

'No. I can't. Because I don't think it is. Because I really believe in the saying that "wherever you go, you take yourself with you". Running doesn't make things go away; sometimes it just exacerbates the problem.'

Maybe. But she was stuck between a rock and a hard place, the devil and the deep blue sea. Either she stayed in New York in a job she loved, in the orbit of a man who seemed to enjoy her company now, but as soon as they slept with each other—because they couldn't hold out for ever—the chase would be over and he'd get bored and break her heart. Or she could leave and not see him for very long periods of time which would—drum-roll, please—break her heart.

*Sucks to be you, Taylor.*

As HE BADE the last of his guests goodbye, James couldn't believe that the party he'd—well, mostly Riley—had prepped and planned for was over, that it was scarcely a week until Christmas and not long before Riley walked out of his life and headed back to Cape Town. How was he going to function in NYC without her?

And why did the thought of needing her feel like

a punch to his heart? He didn't need her, he told himself; he just liked having her around. When she went, he'd be fine. He always was.

Why didn't he feel convinced?

Riley stepped out of her backless shoes and groaned. 'Arrrgh. Gorgeous shoes but they hurt like hell.'

James pulled down his black tie and tugged at the button on the collar of his white dress shirt. 'You looked gorgeous tonight, Ri. Did I tell you that?'

Pleasure sparked in her eyes. 'You did but I don't mind hearing it again.'

'And the musicians were perfect and the food was wonderful.'

'You're full of compliments tonight, Morcau. You feeling all right?'

But he wasn't in the mood for teasing. He placed a hand on her shoulder and stroked her arm from collarbone to wrist. 'Thanks for doing this, for being here tonight. It was fun and you stayed.'

Riley licked her lips. 'I stayed because it was fun.' She stepped back and bit the inside of her lip. 'I should go...or maybe go and make coffee or... something.'

*Or something...like coming to bed with me,* James thought. He knew he shouldn't, but his body was tired of being denied, of listening to his super-cautious brain.

'Or something. Could that something be a kiss?'

Riley's eyes widened. 'We really shouldn't, James.'

He placed his hands on her hips and gently pulled her towards him. His heart soared when she practically fell into his arms in her eagerness to get closer to him. 'So tired of shouldn'ts and couldn'ts and musn'ts,' he murmured. 'I think I should and could and must kiss you…everywhere. Tell me you want to do the same.'

'I want you…I always want you…'

James nibbled her jaw and inhaled her perfume and immediately felt heady. 'That's a good start… keep going.'

Riley groaned and he sighed. 'But I don't think it's a good idea, James.'

'Don't think, not tonight.' Because tonight she was his and he intended to make very sure that she knew that, understood that.

He placed a hand on her heart and her nipple under his hand reacted immediately, instinctively. 'Your heart is pounding and your skin is flushing. You *do* want me. Don't deny yourself—don't deny us. *Don't think.*'

Her eyes drifted over his body, darkened, and he knew that she liked what she saw. Her puckering nipples were a pretty good giveaway as to how turned on she was as well. He stepped closer to her, his fingers dipping down and lifting the hem of her dress to her thighs so that he could slide his thigh between her legs, creating a little friction, a lot of heat. Passion clouded her eyes as her hands came to rest on his chest. He brushed his thumb against her lip, over the throbbing pulse point in her throat, across that pointed nipple.

'Dammit, Jay. That feels so good.'

'You feel so good. You are the sexiest thing I've ever seen. I can feel your heat on my leg and I bet that if I put my hand between your legs, Ri, I'd feel that you're wet.'

Riley let out a breathy whimper.

'You are, aren't you?' he demanded.

'Mmm.'

'Look at me, honey.'

Heavy lids lifted and…those eyes—God, they killed him. Deep, dark, passionate. 'Wet for me?'

'Mmm.'

His erection jumped against the fabric of his black suit trousers. 'Let's go to my room, Riley. Let me love you.'

He thought he heard Riley say, 'One last time,' but then he heard nothing as all his blood headed south as Riley walked over to the bigger of the two couches, dropping her dress as she walked away. She clapped her hands and the overhead lights went off and the fairy lights on the Christmas tree provided the only light in the room. He just stood and looked at her as she stood in front of that tree, naked except the tiniest silver-grey thong. His eyes crossed and he wondered who was seducing whom. As long as he lived he'd never forget what she looked like, perfect skin bathed in the flashing lights of the decorated tree. Almost naked, waiting for him.

Not wanting to get left behind, he yanked his clothes off and went to stand in front of her. When he was close enough, he slipped his hand between her thighs, tested her and sighed at her wet, glorious warmth. Her fingers followed his, burrowing under his to capture her own moisture and then she took her fingers away to draw patterns on his thick, hard-as-steel erection which jumped in response.

'No regrets in the morning, James?'

'No regrets, ever, Ri,' James answered before lowering her to the couch and making her his.

# CHAPTER SIX

WHEN RILEY WOKE up the next morning she quickly realised that she was still naked and lying in James's enormous bed. His empty bed. She patted the space next to her and moved her leg to make sure that he wasn't lying there, out of her reach.

Dammit...how was she going to deal with this? She'd said that she'd never put herself in this position again and yet here she was, about to do the walk of shame again. Except that there was nothing shameful about sleeping with James, not this time. She had been completely sober, totally aware of what she was doing, aware of her actions, prepared to take the consequences.

She had wanted one last night with him, one last experience of loving him, touching him, tasting him. She'd taken every opportunity to do just that and the memories of last night would fuel her fantasies for a long time to come.

'You're going to set the sheets on fire because you're thinking so hard.'

Riley whipped over, shoved the curtain of red hair out of her eyes and saw James sitting on the edge of the chair, his forearms on his knees, looking intently at her.

'How long have you been watching me?' she demanded.

'A while.'

'Why?'

'Because I can.' James sat back and placed his ankle on his knee. 'We need to talk.'

Riley flopped back on her pillow and groaned loudly. 'Oh God, here we go again. Let's just pretend that we've had this conversation already. You only do one-night stands, don't read anything into it, blah, blah, blah.'

'I want you to stay in New York,' James quietly stated.

Oh, *really*?

'Why?' Riley demanded.

James rubbed the back of his neck, a sure sign that he was uncomfortable. 'Riley, you are fabulous at your job; I don't want to lose you!'

Could he possibly have found a more pansy-assed excuse? Riley thought and sent a pillow sailing in his direction. He ducked and it flew past his head and bounced off the wall.

'Try again,' she said between gritted teeth.

'I like being friends again.'

'That's a marginally better excuse but still crap,' Riley stated, shaking her head. 'Neither statement is good enough to get me to stay.'

'Then what the hell do you want?'

'I want more!' Riley shouted. 'Just give me a valid reason not to go!'

James cursed, stood up and paced the room. 'I don't know what you need to hear! We have phenomenal sex together; isn't that enough? Obviously, by that scornful look on your face, it's not!'

*Well read, Sherlock.*

James rubbed his hand across his forehead. 'Okay, well, then, what about going back to what you asked me six months ago? If I have to, I'll do the dating thing...'

'You want to *date* me?' Riley repeated, not sure if she'd heard him right. 'If you *have* to?'

Oh, this was bad. This was so, so bad, Riley thought...and I'm naked. Her heart was being diced and spliced and she was naked.

'Toss me a shirt, will you?' Riley demanded, holding the sheet to her bare chest. She caught the T-shirt James threw and quickly pulled it over her head. When she was adequately covered, she pulled her knees up to her chest and wrapped her arms around them.

'I don't want you to date me because you *have* to—I want you to *want* to be with me.' Riley bit her bottom lip. 'Why is us being together always so damn hard?'

James sent her a hard look. 'It wasn't once and you were the one who walked!'

'And you've never forgiven me for it!' Riley shouted. 'I was nineteen, James, and so scared!'

'Of what?' he demanded.

'I was so young and naive with it. You were so-phisticated and educated—how long would it have taken for you to become bored of me? Six weeks; six months? I would've given up everything, all my dreams for you and been left with nothing!'

'You never gave us—me—a chance!'

'And you never gave me a chance to grow up, to change my mind. You never contacted me once when I was overseas, not by e-mail, social media, not a phone call—nothing! I thought that maybe when I came home—nine months later—we might have a second chance but, when I did, you had al-ready moved on to Liz, moved *in* with Liz! So for-give me for doubting how much you wanted me, how much you've ever wanted me!' Riley told him, her chest heaving. 'God, James, I have loved you since I was eight years old... Why don't you just kick me in the teeth while you're at it?'

'You don't love me...'

'Aaargh!' Riley shouted at full volume. 'James! Really?'

'You walked away from me. You *walked away*, Ri.'

Okay, she'd explain it one last time. 'I was young and scared and I wasn't ready. And you ran from me to that witch and that hurt me. I loved you enough to be happy that you were happy and then you dumped Liz and then you dumped every single woman you dated after her. And boy, there were a lot, James. All gorgeous, all tall, all stacked, all from your snobby social circle. And you never, not once, seriously looked at me again.'

James frowned, utterly confused. 'I have no idea what you're talking about.'

'If they couldn't hold your attention then I didn't stand a chance, being short and a redhead and from a middle-class background.'

'That is such a load of crap! I dated those women because I could never fall in love with them. Because they weren't you! Because there's only been one woman for me since I was twenty-four and you are *it*!'

'Yet all you want to do is date me,' Riley said quietly.

James sat on the side of the bed, his thigh next to her knee. He looked at his hands and Riley watched the emotions play across his face. Confusion, sadness, a lot of despair. 'I don't understand love, Riley. I can't get a handle on it and it has too much power over me to play around with it. I was falling in love with you and you left. I came to love Liz and she lied and cheated on me, stole over a hundred thousand dollars from me,' James stated in a flat voice. 'And, when I found out, I broke it off and she decided to sell the whole sordid story to the press. It was such an ugly letdown, such a public failure. And she didn't have half the power over me that you do.'

Riley hauled in a deep breath, sadness sucking

her lungs against her ribcage because she knew that they were finally over. She couldn't fight this—it was too big. 'I always thought that we couldn't be together because it was the wrong time, but it's not. It's because you're too scared to take a chance. And I understand that—I do. I did the same thing. But I was young and naive and I've regretted it every day since. You want to know why I'm going? I'm leaving because I was lonely and because I wanted a new start, because I couldn't live in the city knowing that you were in it but not in my life. Now I have to leave because I am so in love with you, but you aren't prepared to risk your heart on me.'

'Can't we just take it slow, see where this goes?' James begged.

'That's not going to happen. Essentially, you wanting to "date" me is a flowery way of you saying that you want to keep sleeping with me without risking your heart. Well, stuff that—my heart has always been on the line and if you want me then it's time you put yours on there too!' Riley told him, eyes flashing.

His head jerked back as if her words slapped him in the face. 'You want me? Well, I'm not going to make this easy for you!' Riley twisted her lips. 'You, the big badass diamond CEO, scared of love, scared of what you don't understand! Just happy to have a fling with the one woman who has always understood you just because you're petrified of feeling anything, of life and of living…of loving me! Of failing at love!'

Riley leaned forward and drilled him in the chest with her finger. 'It's so clear now—you only made a move on me after weddings and funerals, when your wall started crumbling thanks to a couple of drinks. Now you want to "date" me because it's the only way you can be with me but allow those walls to stay up around your heart!

'Your offer sucks and, yeah, it's the final insult, James.' Riley dropped her hand and bit her lip. 'I'm done. This time, I *promise* you, I'm walking away for good. I'm going to start a new life in a new town and maybe one day I'll find someone else to love, someone brave enough to love me. Because I won't be too scared to fail and he won't be too scared to trust me with his heart. And that'll be because he'll recognise that I'm loyal and trustworthy and because I'm a damn good bet!'

Riley flung back the covers, scrambled out of the bed and refused to look at the only man who'd ever come close to touching her soul.

'Riley—'

Her heart stuttered as anticipation flooded her system. Maybe, just maybe, she had got through to him, maybe he realised that she was—they were—too good to lose. That—

'I'm sorry. I'm sorry I can't be what you want.'

*Yeah, me too,* Riley thought, feeling her heart snap and then shatter.

JAMES PACED HIS BALCONY, wishing that he was walking the lands at Bon Chance, where the air was pure and he could breathe. In his jersey and jeans, he was vaguely aware that it was another icy afternoon in New York but he'd been perpetually cold since his last conversation with Riley and feeling frozen, on the inside as well as out, had started to feel normal. It had been four days since Riley had walked out of his life and he felt that the sun would never shine again.

Was this what depression actually felt like? He'd never felt anything close to this before, he thought, as he tucked his hands under his armpits. He couldn't think of anything but her, work was a joke and food tasted like cardboard. When he'd dumped Liz, he'd felt angry and hurt—more angry than hurt—for months but he'd never felt this… emptiness. Everything was dim, even the bright colours of the Christmas lights and the decorations of the city were dull and tinged with grey.

'You really are a jerk-nugget, Jay.'

Just what he needed, his baby sister putting a flea in his ear. Oh, joy! James turned around and glared at his slender long-limbed sibling, leaning against the balcony door as if she were a part of the furniture. And she normally was—just not today; probably not tomorrow either. 'I really have to change the code to my lift.'

'Whatever. I just left Riley, who was bawling her eyes out.'

'I told her that I wanted to be with her.'

'You told her that you wanted to date her, you moron! What the hell were you thinking?' Morgan demanded.

He'd forgotten what a good handle Morgan had on sarcasm, James thought, shoving his hand into his hair and tugging. 'I don't have a cooking clue.'

Morgan came onto the balcony and tightened her coat around her slim waist. 'Riley told me about your fight, about Liz, about what happened between you because, you know, Riley and I tell each other everything.'

'Like that's news,' James muttered, leaning his elbows on the railing and looking down on the mostly deserted Central Park.

'You've always had a lot to live up to, James—the family name, the fact that Dad abdicated as CEO and left us to travel the world, appearing now and again to play Dad. You became my hero, the man I relied on…through all my issues, I leaned on you. There was enormous pressure on you to take over as MI CEO, to achieve, to be seen to be achieving. Because of the Moreau name and all of that. You never failed, James, at anything.'

'I failed with Liz.'

'Pfft. She's wasn't a failure; she was a lucky escape.' Morgan looked him in the eye, their identical eyes clashing. 'You never failed…except with Riley.'

Why didn't she take a gun and shoot him between the eyes? 'You failed her, James. You failed her ten years ago when you didn't give her space to breathe; you failed her by running off to Liz; you failed her every time you slept with her and pretended that she was another one-night stand. You failed her six months ago and, boy, you seriously failed her four days ago. But I'm here to tell you that it's grovelling time, bro, because if you don't you're going to regret this every single freakin' second for the rest of your life.'

He was already spending every single freaking second missing her and calling himself a fool.

'And I will also get my ex-SAS fiancé to kick your ass until you do start grovelling.'

She would too.

'It's simple, stupid. You love her; she loves you.'

Could it really be that simple? James thought on a surge of hope.

'She can make you happy, Jay,' Morgan softly said.

'She already does,' he admitted.

When he was with her, every day was Christmas, every day held that same expectancy that something extraordinarily special was about to happen. And then it would, either by her smiling or cracking a comment or sliding her hand into his. Special didn't have to be big, he realised; it just had to be Riley.

'You'd be crazy, and stupid, to let her go. And Christmas won't be Christmas without her,' Morgan said, her tone mournful.

James yanked his baby sister into his arms, hugging her tightly. 'I know. I'll fix it, Morgs.' He had to—he'd always loved her; would always love her. He wouldn't leave New York, wouldn't go back to Bon Chance without Riley…he wouldn't spend another moment without her. Christmas wouldn't be Christmas without her—hell, his life wasn't a life without her. He needed her, craved her…

Morgan sniffed. 'Promise?'

'Promise.'

*So how are you going to get her back, champ?* He had a couple of nights until Christmas Eve. *You didn't leave a hell of a lot of time to figure this out.* James dropped a kiss on Morgan's head before leading her inside and out of the icy wind.

'I'm still changing the code on the lift,' he told her with a small smile.

Morgan's grin was the essence of mischief. 'Okay, you can, but if you manage to get her back Riley will just tell me what it is so you might as well save yourself the hassle.'

'Point taken. Oh, and Morgs? I need to put you to work.'

CHRISTMAS EVE, RILEY THOUGHT, sitting at her desk in her basement office. Six o'clock and she was very, very alone. She'd packed up her office, taken down the colourful prints and had arranged for the maintenance department to have the office repainted back to a boring white in readiness for her replacement.

Whoever that was…

Not her problem, Riley reminded herself, and she had far bigger issues than that.

She'd thought she was so clever, thought that she could handle James and what she felt for him, could deal with being his friend. She'd thought that she could slip quietly into a new life but instead she was tumbling into one with a broken heart and a severely battered and miserable soul.

She was done with love, with men, with James… Oh, dammit, more waterworks! Would they ever stop?

Riley pulled on her coat and gloves and frowned when her desk phone rang. Her staff were long gone, there were no projects in progress at the moment; most of the staff in the building had left many hours ago. She picked up the handset and lifted it to her ear.

'Miss Riley? Security here. I've just had a report that someone has messed with your windows in the jewellery store.'

Oh, no…*hell, no!* She might not be employed by MI any more but those windows were her designs, her baby. No one fiddled with her windows, she thought as temper rose up to close her throat. Ever!

Riley belted up the stairs to the lobby of the MI building and skidded down the hall, frowning as the security officer waved her through the security checks all the Moreau staff endured daily. Not stopping to question why she was receiving a free pass, she belted out of the door, sucking in her breath as a few fat snowflakes hit her face. When had it started to snow? And who cared anyway? What was wrong with her windows?

Ignoring the snow, she pushed her way through the crowds and walked down the wet pavement, thankful that she was wearing her boots and that she wouldn't slip on the wet, sludgy surface. Jeez, the snow was really coming down now... Riley pushed past a tall man in a black overcoat to look at whatever had happened to her windows.

She blinked at the dark window showing the Bon Chance display. It was solidly black. What was going on? Riley put her forehead against the freezing glass, cupped her hands around her face and narrowed her eyes. In the low light of the street lamps it looked as if nothing had changed—there was the messy table and Morgan and Noah in an embrace—and the lights appeared to be the only problem.

Probably just a fuse, she thought—easy enough to fix. She turned around to head back to the jewellery store and James stepped into her line of sight, his blond head collecting snowflakes. Her knees threatened to collapse and she couldn't get air into her lungs.

'Breathe, honey,' James ordered, his eyes focused

on her face. Eyes that were worried but not flat, hesitant but not empty.

'*You* turned the lights off… What have you done to my window?' she muttered, swiping a snowflake off her cheek.

James nodded and the lights in the window flicked back on. Riley turned around slowly and scanned her display, immediately noticing her little mouse, now sitting on a dinner plate, a whopping big diamond ring between his tiny paws. The diamond shot cold fire in her direction and looked like it had more carats than a vegetable garden. She recognised that ring, remembered seeing it on Granny Moreau's bony finger…

'You moved my mouse,' Riley accused, not knowing what else to say.

James had the audacity to grin. 'Only you would bitch about me messing with your windows instead of asking why your mouse is holding a diamond ring.'

Riley glanced at the window. 'I'm scared to ask that,' she admitted, biting her lip.

James moved closer to her and his bare hand came up to cup her face. 'Ask me.'

Riley looked up at him with wide eyes. 'Okay. Why is my mouse holding your grandmother's diamond ring?'

James ran his thumb across an arched eyebrow. 'I'm asking you to stay with me in New York—not as my girlfriend or my lover but as my wife. I'm asking you to marry me. To be mine. Share what's mine. What do you think, Ri? You interested in any or all of that?'

Riley looked from him to the window to the ring and back to his face again. 'Why?' she softly asked, holding her breath. He had one chance to say the right thing here or else she was walking. It would kill her but she would walk…

'I don't have to understand love; I just need to love…to love *you*. I want you, I need you. I want to see your lovely face first thing in the morning, live in a colourful kaleidoscope of a home with you, change the nappies on our kids. I want to make love to you every day for the rest of my life, tell you how much I love you every day for the rest of my life.'

Riley took a deep breath and looked him in the eye. 'And my job?'

'This has nothing to do with your job or where you work. You can do what you want—work, don't work. Design MI's windows, start a new career, don't work another day for the rest of your life. I don't care! I just want you and I just want you happy. I can work around anything else.'

Riley's breath hitched and a smile started to appear on her face. 'You're being serious.'

James huffed a sigh of impatience. 'Do you think I've spent the last two days busting my ass to organise this if I wasn't serious?' He gestured to the window. 'So what can I say—do—to get you to say yes?'

Riley's hand burrowed underneath his coat and she placed it flat against his heart. 'I just want this. I want all of this.'

His big hand covered hers. 'My heart? It's yours. For always. So, about that marriage thing…?'

She flashed him a smile. 'You messed with my windows.'

'I did. Do you want to marry me or not?' James demanded.

'Tell me how much you love me again and I'll think about it,' Riley said, stepping up to him, pushing her hands inside his coat to hold his sides. She rested her forehead on his chest.

James's arm banded around her and she felt his lips in her hair. 'I love you beyond distraction. I've never loved anyone but you.'

She sucked in her breath. 'Okay, thought about it.'

James tipped her head up, his lips quirking. 'And?'

'I love you more than life itself and I'm sick of being miserable without you. I'd love to marry you.' Riley blinked away her tears…more tears, but these were happy ones—she liked those. She stepped back and ripped off the glove on her left hand and waggled her fingers. 'So, hotshot, how are you going to get your grandmother's ring in the window onto my finger?'

James tipped his head. 'Do you like that ring?'

*No, not really.* 'What's not to like? It's about a

million carats and is traditionally passed down to
the eldest son's bride.' Riley bit her lip when James
just kept looking at her. 'Okay, I don't really like
it but I'll wear it if you want me to. I just always
hoped for something warmer, something like an
emerald or a Maw-Sit-Sit—something the colour
of your eyes.'

James dug in his pocket and pulled out another
ring and held it between his thumb and forefinger.
'Maybe something like this?'

It was a square-cut emerald, bordered by green
diamonds—bold, unusual and arty. 'Oh, my God.'
Riley's jaw dropped open. 'This is it… This is my
ring! This…God, James…I love it. How? How did
you know?'

'It might have something to do with the fact that
your best friend is a jewellery designer,' James said
wryly, sliding the ring onto her finger.

'That would be why. So that's why she wasn't
taking my calls!'

'That's why,' James agreed. 'She's pulled two
all-nighters to get it finished.'

'Love her. *Love. Her.* And you for getting her to
design it, make it.'

'I knew that you would want her to.'

'Thank you so much for my ring and for not asking me to wear that monstrosity,' Riley whispered
against his mouth. 'And for asking me to marry
you.'

Riley pulled his head down so that she could kiss

him. As his mouth explored hers, her heart picked up its scattered pieces and started to patch itself back together again. It would be stronger, she realised. Happier, but never hers again, she realised. And she was super-okay with that.

She knew that James would take excellent care of it.

A long while later, James pulled his mouth from hers and placed his cheek on her head. 'Let's go home, Ri.'

'Sure…race you there!' Riley said, turning in the direction of his apartment. James's hand on her arm halted her progress and she turned back to see him pointing at the SUV idling at the corner.

'No, darling, we're going home to Bon Chance. Our family is there, waiting for us.'

Riley's heart jumped. His family that had always been hers. How right it felt that they were going home together.

'We'll head to your place, pick up your luggage; my bags and presents are in the car…' James slapped a hand against his forehead. 'It's Christmas Eve…presents. Oh, damn. Damndamndamn.'

'What's the matter?' Riley asked.

James pulled a face. 'I don't have a Christmas present for you…sorry. I've been a bit busy.'

Her laughter rang out in the freezing night. 'James, I think a stunning engagement ring more than qualifies as a kick-ass Christmas present.'

Riley gave him a smacking kiss and her eyes sparkled with love and laughter.

'And I also gave you my heart…' James said on
a broad smile, thinking on his feet.

Riley placed her hand on his cheek. 'Which will
always rate as the biggest, best, most treasured gift
ever. Merry Christmas, Jay. Love you.'

'Merry rest of our lives, Ri. Love you back,
honey.'

* * * * *

# MILLS & BOON®

**Power, passion and irresistible temptation!**

The Modern™ series lets you step into a world of sophistication and glamour, where sinfully seductive heroes await you in luxurious international locations. Visit the Mills & Boon website today and type **Mod15** in at the checkout to receive

## 15% OFF

your next Modern purchase.

Visit **www.millsandboon.co.uk/mod15**

1014_PROMO

*Snow, sleigh bells and a hint of seduction*

Find your perfect Christmas reads at
**millsandboon.co.uk/Christmas**

014/MB506

# MILLS & BOON®

## Why shop at millsandboon.co.uk?

Each year, thousands of romance readers find their perfect read at millsandboon.co.uk. That's because we're passionate about bringing you the very best romantic fiction. Here are some of the advantages of shopping at www.millsandboon.co.uk:

* **Get new books first**—you'll be able to buy your favourite books one month before they hit the shops

* **Get exclusive discounts**—you'll also be able to buy our specially created monthly collections, with up to 50% off the RRP

* **Find your favourite authors**—latest news, interviews and new releases for all your favourite authors and series on our website, plus ideas for what to try next

* **Join in**—once you've bought your favourite books, don't forget to register with us to rate, review and join in the discussions

Visit **www.millsandboon.co.uk**
for all this and more today!

MILLS_WEB

*It's an unforgettable, luxurious Christmas with an irresistible alpha male when you spend*

# Christmas
## with a
# Billionaire

# Christmas
## with a
# Billionaire

CAROLE      MAISEY      JOSS
MORTIMER    YATES       WOOD

MILLS
BOON

All rights reserved including the right of reproduction in whole or in part in any form. This edition is published by arrangement with Harlequin Books S.A.

This is a work of fiction. Names, characters, places, locations and incidents are purely fictional and bear no relationship to any real life individuals, living or dead, or to any actual places, business establishments, locations, events or incidents. Any resemblance is entirely coincidental.

This book is sold subject to the condition that it shall not, by way of trade or otherwise, be lent, resold, hired out or otherwise circulated without the prior consent of the publisher in any form of binding or cover other than that in which it is published and without a similar condition including this condition being imposed on the subsequent purchaser.

® and ™ are trademarks owned and used by the trademark owner and/or its licensee. Trademarks marked with ® are registered with the United Kingdom Patent Office and/or the Office for Harmonisation in the Internal Market and in other countries.

Published in Great Britain 2014
by Mills & Boon, an imprint of Harlequin (UK) Limited,
Eton House, 18-24 Paradise Road, Richmond, Surrey, TW9 1SR

CHRISTMAS WITH A BILLIONAIRE © 2014 Harlequin Books S.A.

*Billionaire under the Mistletoe* © 2014 Carole Mortimer
*Snowed in with Her Boss* © 2014 Maisey Yates
*A Diamond for Christmas* © 2014 Joss Wood

ISBN: 978-0-263-24676-6

025-1014

Harlequin (UK) Limited's policy is to use papers that are natural, renewable and recyclable products and made from wood grown in sustainable forests.The logging and manufacturing processes conform to the legalenvironmental regulations of the country of origin.

Printed and bound in Spain
by Blackprint CPI, Barcelona